KB147129

Shakespeare · The Tempest

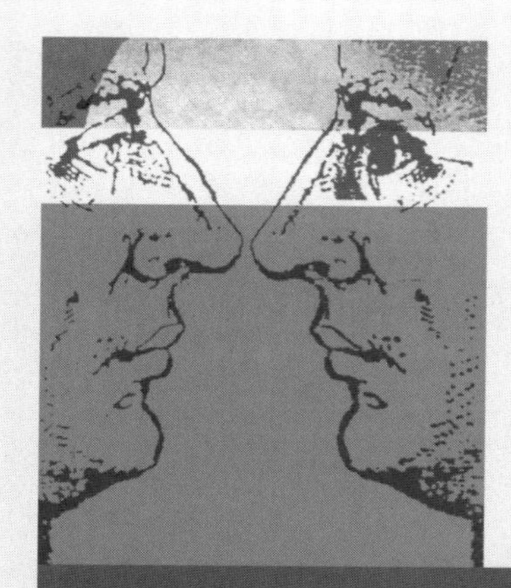

『템페스트』의 미학적 읽기

하 해 성

푸른사상

『템페스트』의 미학적 읽기

하 해 성 지음

머리말

필자가 셰익스피어 『템페스트』에 관심을 갖기 시작한 것은 은사 김주현 교수님의 추천을 받아 읽은 A. C. Bradley의 *Shakespearean Tragedy* 와 R. A. Foakes의 *The Shakespeare: the Dark Comedies to the Last Plays*라는 비평서들 때문이다. 뿐만 아니라 필자의 은사 현역 극작가이며, 극평론가 이근삼 교수님의 아도르노의 미학 이론의 소개와 격려에 힘입어 미학 연구에 더욱 박차를 가하게 되었다. 필자는 이들 평서들을 반복하여 읽으면서 셰익스피어 극들을 이해하는데 미학적 접근의 중요성을 깨닫기 시작하였다.

그 후 대학 강단에서 셰익스피어 극들을 강의하면서 점점 미학적 읽기에 심취하기 시작하였다. 특히 『템페스트』는 셰익스피어의 후기 극으로서 미학적 분석이 없이는 그것을 이해한다는 것은 올바른 연구 태도가 아니라고 생각되었다.

따라서 필자는 이 극의 본문 주석의 연구가 포함되어야 한다는 생각에서 주석본을 수록하기로 하였다. 이 조그마한 필자의 노력의 소산 '『템페스트』의 미학적 읽기'가 셰익스피어에 접근하려는 학생들에게 조금이라도 도움이 되기를 기대한다.

이 책이 나오기까지 원고 타이핑과 교정에 수고한 사랑하는 아들 영회 군과 편집을 맡아 수고해준 제자 안종훈 교수, 김종환 님과 그리고 출판을 할 수 있도록 배려해주신 도서출판 푸른사상의 한봉숙 사장님께 깊은 감사를 드린다.

2001년 7월 25일

진주 선학 동산에서 저자 씀

차 례

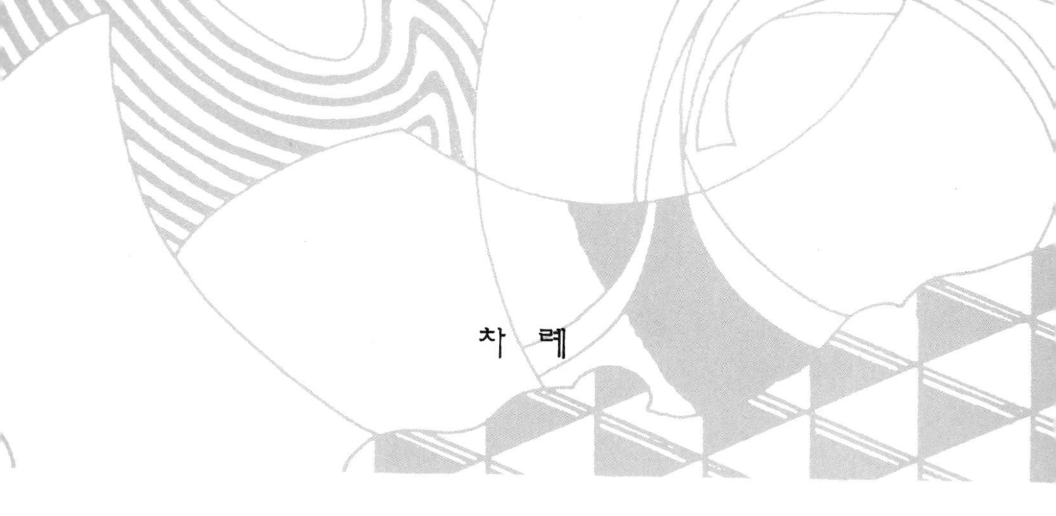

차 례

제 2 부

제 1 부

제 1 장 서 론

전통적 문학 이론과 비평에 의존하는 많은 셰익스피어 비평가들이 특히 셰익스피어 후기 극들을 해석하는 데 있어서 많은 오류를 남긴 사실은 미학에 관심 있는 학자라면 인지할 수 있는 사실이라 할 수 있을 것이다.

필자가 『템페스트』를 분석하는 과정에서 발견한 것은 셰익스피어는 극 액션에 의해 체계적 극 환경을 창안하였다는 것이다. 몇 가지 예외적 사례가 있지만 지배적 비평 체계는 극의 시·공간에 있어서 극의 액션보다는 인쇄된 대사에 국한하는 문학 규칙들에 의해 평가되었기 때문에 이러한 비평 경향은 극 구조에 대한 우리 셰익스피어 독자의 이해를 왜곡시켰으며, 그러한 비평적 편향은 이 극의 실질적 실연의 호응과 비평적 시각들간의 괴리라 생각된다. 그것은 마치 우리 독자들이 극(劇)의 플롯구조의 분석에 의해 무도의 미학적 특성들을 시험했던 것과 유사하다 할 수 있겠다. 필자는 셰익스피어 후기 극들이 드라마의 속성이 무시된 해석에서 오류가 발생한다고 생각한다.

전통적 비평에서는 셰익스피어 후기 극들에 미학적 분석 이론을 적용하는 것이 금기시되었었다. 따라서 필자는 분석의 기조를 미학 요소인 비언어적 요소 무도와 그것들에 수반된 예술, 음악으로 논제를 전환하고자 한다. 셰익스피어 학자들은 이 두 가지 요소들이 후기 극들을 비평하는 데 있어서 핵심요소들임을 주지한 바 있다. 따라서 필자는 르네상스 사회에서의 무도와 음악의 철학적 개념 연구와 전통 문학적 비평에서의 비평적 오류를 지적하고 그것을 무대 미학적 시각에서 시어(詩語)와 액션의 융합에서 표출되는 상징적 의미를 발견하고자 한다.

필자는 후기극본들의 각 장면들의 극 구조의 총체적 이해를 위해 바로크 시대의 특수 미학환경을 시험하고자 한다.

셰익스피어 후기 극들에 내재한 그 세계의 비전이 엘리자베스적 시각과 상이했다. 제임스 왕궁의 미학원리들은 이상의 표방으로 신플라톤 철학 형식에 근간을 두었다. 시간과 공간의 사실적 과정이라는 특성 때문에 드라마는 이 철학의 가장 완전한 예술적 표현으로 시각된다. 본고에서 필자는 극의 총체성의 중요한 부분으로서 극 액션을 논하고자 한다.

제임스 궁에서 발달된 극 형식의 미학은 유럽 극의 영향력이 반영되었다. 특히 이탈리아인들은 극 액션이 완전한 사실 세계를 만드는 매체인 극의 사건의 총체성을 창안하였다. 비록 여기에 인용된 유럽의 극적 실험들은 본고의 참고적 자료적 근간이 되지만 필자는 영국의 미학 극작가 벤 존슨과 이니고 존스가 공저한 극에 국한하였다. 그들은 제임스 궁의 계관시인과 궁중 건축가로서, 셰익스피어가 집필했던 창의적 극 환경, 즉 미학적 극 환경에 기여하였다. 벤 존슨과 이니고 존스는 제임스 왕을 위하여 극 액션과 대사의 의미가 점진적 융합된 일련의 가면극을 공동집필하였다. 따라서 그들의 가면극 『오베런 왕자』는 셰익스피어 후기 극들을 해석할 수 있는 하나의 극의 모형을 제공할 것이다. 따라서 필자는 특히 『템페스트』를 미학적으로 분석하였는데, 그들이 제시한 미학적 모형을 통하여 이 극에 산재한 미학적 요소들을 분석함으로써 셰익스피어 후기 극에 대한 이해를 돕고자 한다.

제 2 장 『템페스트』의 이원구조(二元構造)

I

James 왕조(王朝) 초기는 영국예술(英國藝術)의 대륙화의 시기다. 따라서 새로운 불란서풍과 이태리풍의 예술양식이 유입됨으로써 스튜어트 왕가의 사치와 낭비를 가져 왔으며, 또한 James 왕조의 풍요한 국고는 왕으로 하여금 많은 작위를 궁신(宮臣)들에게 하사하게 함으로써 그들의 경제적 안정을 도모하였다. 궁중 예술은 이 후대로 인하여 반사적 이익을 얻게 되었다. 그래서 스튜어트 왕가의 궁신들은 영국의 최초의 대궁중 건축가에 의해 설계된 궁중 대연회장에서 공연되는 축소적 궁중예술형식(가면극)을 관람하기 위하여 운집하게 되었다.

또 셰익스피어 역시 궁중연회행사에 참석함으로써 그의 극작 환경(후기 극들)에 영향을 미쳤을 것으로 생각된다. 따라서 필자는 *The Tempest* 극에 나오는 무용과 음악 장면들은 궁중의 미학적 환경이 반영되었으므로 비언어적 액션이 의미를 전달하는 데 기여할 것으로 생각한다. 그럼으로 필자는 무대미학(舞臺美學)을 통하여 이 극의 주제적 해석을 하고자 한다.

Ⅱ

이 극에 나타나는 자연의 개념과 자연 자체의 모호성(模湖性)은 혼란을 야기시킨다. 자연에 대한 통찰력에 따라 모호한 다양성이 존재하며, 극 구조에 반영된 대위적 모호성은 1막 1장에서는 자연 질서를 파괴하고 인간에게 너무 혹독한 자연(1막 1장)으로 시사되지만 그것을 대행하는 자에게 동정적이며 자신의 능력을 통제할 수 있다는 Foakes의 주장에서 보듯이,[1] 이러한 모호한 대위성이 1막 1장에서 섭리(攝理)의 세계와 모호한 관계지만, 1막 2장에서는 구체적으로 섭리의 작용을 언급하고 있다:

> "By accident most strange, beautiful Fortune.
> Now my dear lady, hath mine enemies

---

[1] R. A. Foakes points out that "…Prospero's art is so powerful that with his 'prevision' or foresight, he can destroy and save simultaneously" in the *Shakespeare : the dark comedies to the last plays*(London: Routledge & Kegan Paul, 1971), p. 146.

> Brought to this shore; and by my prescience
> I find my zenith doth depend upon
> A most auspicious star, whose influence
> If now I court not, but omit, my fortunes
> Will ever after droop." (I. ii. 178-185)

> … Prospero tells Miranda, 'By Providence divine'(I. ii. 159); now a strange chance has brought his enemies to the island:
>
> ………………………………………………………………………………
>
> …
>
> Fortune, once hostile to him, brought about his fall, but is now his 'dear lady,' and he must seize the opportunity she offers. So Prospero's powers are circumscribed, dependent geographically on the island, and operating in relation to providence on the one hand, and fortune on the other.[2]

Foakes의 주장처럼 자연에 대한 개념은 이 극에 공존하는 근본적으로 상이한 두 개의 자연 개념(하나는 지상에 건설된 우주의 질서이며 또 하나는 야성(野性)의 자연적 원시(原始)의 비문명사회)이다. 이 극에서 자연 대 인간과 자연의 관계에 관한 대위는 미학의 특성으로 부각되며, 질서의 구조와 신과 자연의 법칙이 파괴될 때 이 극의 개막 때부터 발생하였던 무질서는 극 구조에 반영된 미학적 기능을 돋보이게 한다.

1막 1장의 폭풍과 파선 장면은 자연 세계의 무질서이며 동시에 사회 질서의 파괴다. 또다른 측면에서 고찰하여 보면 주인공 Prospero의 극렬한 감정의 재현과 기존 과거 사회의 무질서(Milan 國

[2] Foakes, *op. cit.*, pp. 146-7.

에서의 Prospero의 유배)의 표출로 미학적 기능이기도 하다.

셰익스피어가 그리는 자연 세계는 거칠고 원시적인 비문명 사회로서 존립하며 문명 사회와는 대위적인 자연 원시 세계를 Caliban을 통하여 조명해 보는 것은 시각적 미학의 의의성이 내포되어 있다. 독자들이 1막 1장에서 목격한 변화적 모순 형태의 자연의 이원적 병치(倂置)는 분명히 문명의 질서와 야만성의 대위(對位)로써 미학의 특성을 부각하고 있다. 여기에 등장하는 인물들(Caliban : Antonio : Gonzalo)의 자연 이상(理想) 국가관을 조정할 수 있다. 우리 독자들이 조망하는 자연에 관한 모든 시각은 주인공 Prospero의 성격과 그의 체험의 미학이다.

Gonzalo가 이 황량(荒粱)한 섬에 그의 일행과 처음 상륙할 때 자신의 이상(理想) 국가를 설계한 그의 이상국(理想國) 묘사에서 나타난 낭만적(浪漫的), 목가적(牧歌的) 이미지는 가상적 왕권과 이상 국가에서 정치권 부재의 모순의 정립이기는 하지만 그의 이상 국가관은 Antonio와 Sebastian의 논평에서 가상적 침울한 분위기로 전도하게 된다. 그것은 Gonzalo의 이상국가에 거주할 결백한 남녀를 게으른 건달과 창녀로 논평하기 때문이다. 따라서 대위적 이상국가관의 정립은 태자(Ferdinand)를 실종한 Alonso 왕(王)을 즐겁게 하기 위한 극적 분위기 전환에 있지만, 어려운 환경에 처할 때도 매사에 최선을 다해 보고자 하는 Gonzalo의 인간적 소양을 셰익스피어는 미학적으로 표출하고 있다.

Gonzalo가 이 섬에 상륙한 후 이 황량한 자연의 원시섬에 인간이 살 수 있는 낙원을 구상한다. 그것은 이 섬의 사회를 계발(啓發)할 가능성을 시사했던 것은 이들 일행보다 12년 전에 먼저 이 섬에 상륙한 Prospero의 이상국가관과 유사(類似)한 시각이다. Gonzalo는 자신이 이 섬을 식민지화하고 왕이 되면 자신은 무엇을 할 것인가를 명상한다. Gonzalo의 말이 주인공 Prospero의 과거와 현재의 위상을 청중에게 묵시적으로 시사하듯이 자연 환경의 수난을 통하여 자신이 귀속된 문명사회(Milan 國)로부터 황량한 이 고도 Setebos에 상륙했던 Prospero가 이 섬을 관리할 수 있는 기회를 12년 전에 얻어, 그는 이 섬의 지배권을 취득했을 뿐만 아니라, 이 자연 원시 섬에서 사실적 이상국가(理想國家)를 건설했다.

Prospero는 이 극의 사실 세계에서 아직도 그 섬의 주권을 행사하고 있다. Foakes가 Prospero의 Setebos 섬의 주권 행사를 찬탈 행위로 보듯이 찬탈자의 모습의 일면도 그에게 있지만, Prospero가 처음 이 섬에 상륙하였을 때 그의 진의(眞意)는 그 곳에 살고 있는 자연원시인 Caliban을 문명사회의 구성원으로 교화(敎化)시키고자 하는 것이 그의 의도였음이 본문을 통하여 시사되었다.

따라서 Gonzalo의 낙천적(樂天的) 이상주의(理想主義)와 Prospero의 순수한 이상주의의 유사성(학문과 비밀 연구로 명망 높은 Prospero의 자기 자신의 친제(親弟) Antonio에 대한 무한한 신뢰와, "인간은 근본적으로 선하다"는 이상적, 질서적, 자연의 교훈을 주장하는 Gonzalo의 Utopia적 이상과 유사점)이 있다. Milan에서 정치적 질서와 도덕의 파괴로 인하여 이곳에 유배된 Prospero는 그의 순수한 이상주의를 실현코자 이 문명사회에 오염되지 아니한 Setobos의 순수한 자연원시인 Caliban을 교화하여 사회의 구성원으로 인간 개조를 시도하였던 그의 이상은 Gonzalo의 그것과 유사하다. Prospero는 원시인의 순결성을 덕과 동일시함으로써 Gonzalo의 순결한 이상관(理想觀)과

일맥상통하다 할 수 있겠다.

물론 정부, 노예 제도, 부(富)의 부재는 Alonso 왕과 Sebastian과 같은 고도로 세련된 인간들에게는 부패를 유발할 수 있으며, 그 사회의 질서를 위축(萎縮)시킬 수 있다. 술이 없으면 과음이 없듯이 학문이 없으면 예술적 자만심도 없을 것이다. 또한 악의 목적 수단의 악행도 부재할 것이다. 그리고 Antonio나 Sebastian과 같은 인물들의 인간 경시와 염세는 인간의 사악한 일면을 보여 주었지만, 교육에 의해 미덕을 갖춘 젊은 사람들(Miranda와 Ferdinand)의 실존으로 인하여 Gonzalo의 낙천적(樂天的) 인본주의(人本主義)의 순결미는 타당시된다.

그러나 이 극이 표출하는 현실 세계에 직면될 때 Gonzalo의 이상국가(理想國家)는 산산이 부서져 현실 세계에서 이탈된다. Prospero의 말처럼 자연의 신이 인간에게 때로는 동정적이며, 또한 이 황량한 섬에서 생존 수단도 제공하지만, 이 섬의 인간들은 순박한 생을 영위하지 못할 뿐 아니라, 낙원의 상실을 경험하고 있다. 즉, Caliban과 Ferdinand가 각각 땔감 나무를 운반하며 등장할 때, Alonso 왕의 일행이 실종된 왕자(王子)를 수색하다 피로에 지쳐 실의에 차 있을 때, 또한 Prospero가 자유 의지의 달성을 위해 계속 노력을 경주할 때, Ariel이 Prospero의 명령 수행을 위해 노력할 때, 우리 독자들은 이 극의 현실 세계에 실존하는 노동의 세계를 목격한다.

또 다음 장면에서 술은 순수한 원시인 Caliban을 술 취한 수성적(獸性的) 존재로 격하(格下)시키며, 낙원에서는 부재해야 하는 무기의 열거(Alonso 왕 일행이 Prospero에게 대항하여 휘두르는 단검과 Prospero를 살해하기 위한 Caliban의 언급("… With a long batter his skull, or paunch him with a stake, or cut out his wezand with thy knife" Ⅲ. ii. 87-90)는 Gonzalo의 이상적 낙원국가 건설과 현저히 대위됨을 시사하고 있다. 물론 Caliban이 열거하는 무기가 문명사회의 그것과 비교하면 정교하지 못하지만 이 무기들이 침략의 도구로 사용될 때는 치명적이라 할 수 있다. 그러므로 Gonzalo의 낙천적 이상국가는 극 구조에 실재하는 물질적 사실 세계에 직면하면서부터 정치적으로, 도덕적으로 인간의 위상은 음영(陰影)에 가려진다.

역설적으로 자연 세계의 순결성과 결백성을 신뢰하고 있는 일행들이 그들을 살해하고자 음모하는 자들(Sebastian과 Antonio)의 보호하에 수면을 취하는 것은 마치 선과 악이 시간 세계 속에 병존하는 아이러니 현상이다. 이것은 Prospero가 섭리에 대하여 가지는 자세와 Antonio의 그것과는 괴리적이다. 왜냐하면 Antonio는 신의 섭리를 우연히 제공되는 자기 발전을 위한 기회로 생각하기 때문이다. 아래 Traversi의 설명(It is no accident that Antonio at this point echoes, in his own way, some of leading principles of Prospero's thought. He too has his own view, perfectly logical and consistent, of what is implied by the conception of 'destiny.' 'Destiny' indeed, is so far as it has meeting for him, lies in the performance of his own will.[3])처럼, Antonio는 신의 섭리를 왕위 찬탈(簒奪)을 위한 호기회(好機會)의 매체(媒體)로 생각함으로써 Gonzalo가 Setebos 섬에 설정한 이상 국가관을 야만과 타락으로 경멸하며, Antonio는 Alonso 왕의 태자를 실종시키고 그의 공주 Claribel과 Naples 국(國) 간의 격리시킨 이 대해(大海), 이상스러운 졸

---

[3] Derek Traversi, *Shakespeare: The Last Phase*(London: Hollis & Carter, 1954), p. 218

음을 유발시키는 이 섬의 기후 풍토의 특질을 자신의 이득을 추구할 수 있는 호기회의 환경으로 생각하는 데서, 그들간의 이상관의 병치적 대위가 반영됨으로써 미학의 이원성을 명시적(明示的)으로 보이게 한다. 그는 Prespero나 Gonzalo가 생각하고 있는 자연에 대한 도덕적, 정신적 신앙을 소유하고 있지 못하기 때문에 Prospero와 Gonzalo가 공유하고 있는 시각과 Antonio의 그것과는 상호 대위적이며 미학적 시각이라 할 수 있겠다. 그러나 다음 장면에서 대위적 주제가 구조[4]상에 순환 병치(倂置)됨으로써 미학적 주제의 혼란은 Caliban이 Prospero를 혹독하게 불평하는 데서 발생한다. 이러한 문제점은 Gonzalo가 조망하는 이 자연 원시 세계에 설정한 이상 국가관은 이 자연섬에 거주하고 있는 원주민 Caliban에 의해 수정이 불가피한 데 있다. Caliban은 이 황량한 자연과 야만인을 대표하는 인물로 생각되지만, 그가 혈통이 순수한 자연의 소산인지, 인간의 소산인지 Text에 의하면 약간 혼란스럽다:

> Caliban is described in the Folio edtion of the *Tempest* as 'a salvage and deformed slave.' The word 'savage' is an earlier form of modern 'savage' but is Shakespeare's day it meant 'wild and uncivilised' rather than 'cruel or bestials.' Most people in England believed men were below their civilized counter-partners in the hierarchy which had God at its apes and inanimate nature at its base.

---

[4] Cf. "As I told thee before, I am subject to a tyrant, a sorcerer, that by his cunning has cheated me of the island"(Ⅲ. ii. 46-).

위의 Todd의 설명처럼, 셰익스피어는 Caliban을 퇴행된 노예 내지는 야만인으로 간주하고 있다. Hazelton Spencer는 Caliban을 다음과 같이 설명한다.

> It passes, indeed, from conception broad and inclusive in their humanity to explorations and experiments beyond the limitations of our species—to Caliban, only half human but sufficiently a man to be capable of thought and of development— …[5]

그는 Caliban을 야만인으로 간주할 뿐만 아니라 개화 가능한 인간으로 시사함으로써 셰익스피어가 창안한 원시인은 명시적 모호성을 내포하고 있음을 알 수 있다. 셰익스피어가 이 극에서 모호하게 기술하는 퇴행된 자연 원시인(原始人)은 자연 상태의 순결을 주장하는 Gonzalo의 이상적 '이미지'에 부합되지 않고, 또한 새로운 정치적 이상 국가론자(國家論者)와 대위적 언행(言行)을 하게 함으로써 노예(奴隸)나 노동자로 시각(視角)하게 하는 모호성을 표출한다. 비록 그에게서는 문명인처럼 세련된 언행을 찾아볼 수 없지만, 그렇다고 도덕적으로 순결하다고 볼 수 없다. Foakes는 그의 도덕적 부패성(腐敗性)[6]을 언급하고, Edward Dowden도 그의 노예 근성[7]을 언급하고 있

---

[5] Hazelton Spencer, *The Art and Life of William Shakespeare*(New York: Barnes & Noble, Inc., 1970), pp. 373-4.

[6] Foakes, *The Shakespeare*, pp. 147-148: "Miranda tried to educate him, and taught him language as Prospero had taught her, but the purpose of his brutish nature could only seem vile to her, as he would not take any print of goodness…"

[7] Edward Dowden points out that "To Caliban, a land-fish, with the duller elements of earth and water in his composition, but no portion of the higher elements, air and fire, though he receives dim intimation of a higher

듯이, 의 천진난만(토라짐)은 자기 도치의 무례성일 뿐만 아니라 셰익스피어가 그린 원시인 Caliban은 Miranda가 지니고 있는 미덕(美德)과 Ferdinand가 소유하고 있는 고매성(高邁性)을 결여(缺如)하고 있다. 따라서 천부적 재능과 교육 수준에서 보면 이들은 Caliban을 훨씬 능가하고 있다. Frank Kermode는 Miranda와 Caliban을 대비 설명하고 있다:

> It(*The Tempest*) conscientiously elaborates the parallel between Miranda and Caliban in respect of their 'nature' or education. Hers is the good seed which benefits by nature; he is the 'born devil on whose Nurture will never stick'. That they were at first brought up together and educated a like by Prospero merely emphasized this difference. She is astonished by the beauty of the brave new world; he comes to terms at once with cruelty and foolishness. She is the cultivated plant, he is the wild which rejects cultivation.[8]

위의 설명처럼 Miranda는 교화된 식물로, Caliban은 교화를 배격한 야생 식물로 비유하는 것은 근본적으로 이 두 인물들은 동시에 교육을 받았지만 혈통(血統) 근원부터 차이가 있다는 것으로 선과 악, 미와 박색으로 대위(對位) 병치됨으로써 미학적 주제들을 돋보이게

---

world, —a musical humming, or a twingling, or a voice heard in sleep—to Caliban, services is slavery. He hates to bear his logs, and he fears the incomprehensible power of Prospero, and obeys, and curses" in *the Shakespeare: A Critical Study of His Mind and Art*(London: Kegan Paul Trench, Trubner & Co., Ltd., 1982), pp. 419-20.

[8] Frank Kermode, *Shakespeare, Spencer, Donne: Renaissance Essays*(London: Routledge & Kegan Paul, 1971). p. 251.

한다.

결국 Caliban이 Stephano에 대한 우상적 숭배심이나, 또 성적 충동에 의한 이성간의 사랑에 대한 경험은 3막 1장에서 Miranda와 Ferdinand가 표현하는 사랑에 대한 심오한 감정과 이들간의 비이기적 사랑에 비하면 조잡한 성격의 발로에 불과한 것이다. Caliban의 야만적 무뢰성은 그를 비인간적 수성인으로 폄하(貶下)시키는 Prospero의 도덕관에 국한되는 것이다. 2막 2장에서 Caliban의 시무룩하고 교활(狡猾)한 행위와 술 주정은 그의 결점을 노출하며, 정서적 욕구와 비천한 충동심에 대한 그의 본래적 노예 근성 속에서뿐만 아니라 흙과 물의 구성 요소보다 저차원의 요소와 또한 풍부한 시적 감정과 더불어 그의 풍성한 인격 구성이 시사된다. 그러나 Caliban은 Prospero에 반목(反目)함으로써 징벌을 받고 저항하는 것은 그 자신의 체험에서 오는 조건 반사적 충동[9]처럼 생각된다.

그리고 Caliban의 1막 2장 321행과 2막 2장 1행의 대사들[10]은 상호 미묘한 유사성을 발견할 수 있다. 이때 Caliban은 그의 주인 Prospero를 저주하면서 등장하는데 Prospero는 몸에 경련이 발생케 하는 혹독한 징벌을 가하려고 결심한다. 그러나 Caliban은 "I must eat my

---

[9] *Cf.* "All the inflections that the sun sucks up
From bogs. fens, flats, on Prospero fall, and make him.
By inch-meal a disease: his spirits hear me,
And yet I needs must curse(Ⅱ. iii. 1-)."

[10] *cf.* "As wicked dew as e'er my mother brush'd
With raven's feather from unwholesome fen
Drop on you both: A south-west blow on ye,
And blister you all o'er: (Ⅰ. ii. 321)," and
And the inflections that the sun sucks up
From bogs, ...··· a disease: (Ⅱ. ii. 1)

dinner. This island's mine, by Sycorax my mother, which thou tak'st from me."라고 완강하게 저항한다. 위의 대사가 시사하듯 이 원시인 Caliban은 이성을 통하여 자신의 언행을 통제할 수 없는 자로 시사되지만, 또 한편 여기 Caliban의 행위를 통해서 Prospero의 이중적 성격을 살펴볼 수 있다. Prospero는 인간의 지능과 무한한 잠재력(I. ii. 201-6)을 소유한(I. ii. 190) 전지전능자로서뿐만 아니라 화를 내는 인간으로서의 양면성을 보여준다.[11]

그러나 이 충동적 악의는 Prospero의 감정의 발로(I. ii)와 가면극이 종료될 때 Prospero의 분노의 재발과 유사점을 발견할 수 있는데, 자신의 능력으로 통제할 수 없는 Caliban의 무능력과는 대위적으로 경외(敬畏)적 통제 능력을 소유한 Prospero가 자제 능력을 결여하고 있는 것은 우리 청중에게는 분명 아이러니하다. 또 3막 3장의 풍요한 연회석 장면에서 Alonso 일행을 초대하는 괴물스런 가면극의 인물들의 환대를 주시하며 관찰하는 Gonzalo의 논평 속에서 Caliban과 Prospero의 태도를 재평가할 수 있도록 계기를 마련해 준다. 즉 가면극에 등장하는 괴물스런 모습의 극중인물들에 대한 환대는 문명 사회로부터 이 원시의 Setebos 섬에 상륙한 이민자들에 대한 원시인들의 환영행사로 생각할 때, 그것은 상징적인 유사한 기능을 나타내고 있지만, 이들 등장 인물들에 대한 Gonzalo의 응답은 문명 사회를 표상한 자들에 비유되며 이 자연 원시 세계의 피조물들의 친절한 환대를 표상한 교육적 시각이다. 즉, Shakespeare는 문명 사회의 덕과 부덕을 대비하기 위하여 하나의 척도로서 가면극을 연출시켰을 것으로 생각되는 바, 셰익스피어는 이 자연원시인을 Miranda나 Ferdinand와 같은 고매한 인물

---

[11] *Cf.* G. B. Wilson Knight, *The Crown of Life*(London: Methuen Co., 1982), pp. 233～34.

과 비교의 척도로 사용하지 않았지만 기존 문명 사회의 타 인물들(여기서는 Antonio, Trinculo, Stephano, Sebastian 등등을 언급함)에 비하면, Caliban이 월등히 도덕적 위상이 상위에 있음을 시사하고 있다. 그런 이유로 셰익스피어는 Caliban 대 Stephano : Trinculo와 대위시키고, 또 Antonio와 Sebastian과 이들(가면극에 등장한 원시인들과 Caliban)과 대위시킴으로써 자연 세계의 피조물들과 문명 사회인들과를 대비할 수 있는 미학적 시각을 청중들에게 표출하고 있다. 그런고로 이 부분은 자연과 자연 원시인에 대한 청중의 조망을 어떻게 부각시킬 것인가 하는 문제가 발생한다.

Caliban이 저속한 관능적 욕정에 대한 선천적 성향을 가지고 있는 반면, 그가 접근한 Naples인(人)들은 방종적 인습에 훨씬 더 익숙하다. 그들은 Caliban을 조롱하기 위해서 그가 소유하고 있는 선천적 비굴성(Stephano와 Trinculo는 Caliban에게 스스로의 판단을 흐리게 하고 존경심으로 그들을 고무하고 복수심에 불붙이는 술을 제공한다)을 이용한다. 우리 청중들은 2막 2장에서 순박한 Caliban이 Naples에서 온 이들에 의해 착취당하고 타락하는 것을 목격한다.

또 3막 2장에서는 바다 건너 Naples 왕국에서 유입된 술은 도덕사회를 타락시킬 뿐만 아니라, 철저히 부조리한 토양을 이 섬에 조성한다. 여기에서 우리가 주의 깊게 관찰할 수 있는 것은 문명사회가 방탕한 탕아나 어리석은 인간으로 시각될 때 이 원시의 섬 Setebos에 거주하는 Caliban은 대위적으로 절제력이 있으며 매혹적인 사람으로 시각(視角)되는 것도 아이러니하다. 특히 원시인 Caliban과 고매한, 부패한 Naples 왕국의 궁인들간의 대위는 더욱 더 명시적(明示)적 미학적 시각이다. Antonio와 Sebastian은 셰익스피어가 창안한 이 자연 원시섬의 Caliban보다 훨씬 부도덕하고 죄악시되기 때문이다.[12]

즉, Caliban이 도덕 교육 혹은 자유 의지와 충동적인 부덕의 음모 성향의 한계성을 나타내는 데 비하여, 이 문명 사회에서 온 세련된 인간들은 합리적 부패와 범죄 행위를 속행하는 데서 청중들은 Caliban을 기존 사회의 인습 속에 있을 수 있는 개구쟁이로 주시할 뿐 아니라, 그러한 자연 환경(즉, 문명의 기준이나 그 문명 사회의 행동 규범밖에 존재하는 것으로 보는)에 처해 있는 도덕과는 무관한 존재로 생각할 수 있을 것이다.

그러나 문명 사회에서 Setebos에 상륙한 사람들은 저속할 정도로 부도덕하고 자신들이 설정한 질서를 스스로 파괴하며 자신들의 이기적 목적에 필요할 때만 질서를 내세운다. 따라서 이 극에 등장하는 그들은 이기적 목적을 위하여 질서를 내세운다. 그러므로 이 극에 등장하는 Antonio는 죄, 혼돈, 무법의 장본인이라 할 수 있을 것이다. 어떤 의미에 있어서 타락, 잔인성, 야만성의 선택은 이러한 자연 원시섬에서 적합할 수도 있을 것이다.

또 Harpy로 분장한 Ariel이 세 사람의 죄지은 자들을 비난하고 난 직후 Alonso는 자기 자신의 과거의 대죄를 인정하고 고통 속에 급히 무대를 퇴장한다:

> O, it is monstrous:
> Methought the billows spoke, and told me of it;
> The winds did sing it to me; and the thunder,

---

[12] Gary Schmigall point out that "…These(ignorance and ambition) are reflected in the plots of Caliban and Antonio, resectively. Caliban's conspirary is one of the 'ignorant mutitude,' while Antonio is of the 'ambitious and malicious'" in *the Shakespeare and The Courtly Aesthetic*(Los Angeles: University of California Press, 1981), p. 193

That deep and dreadful organ pipe, pronounce'd
The name of Prospero: it did bass my trespass.…
(Ⅲ. iii. 95-9)

이 장면은 *Tempest*에 내재한 자연에 대한 근본적으로 대위되는 미학적 시각의 표방일 것이다. Ariel의 고발과 Alonso의 고통스러운 시각을 통해서 현실 세계의 자연 요소들은 사회적, 정치적 영역과 우주의 영역과 결합한다고 볼 수 있다. 왜냐하면 기상학적인 매체(billow… The wind…, thunder… 3막 3장 95-9)를 통해서 스스로의 죄를 고백, 참회한다. 3막에서 나타난 자연은 보다 고차원의 섭리 질서와 화합하여 도덕적 힘으로 Alonso에게 나타난다고 생각된다. 그들의 비전은 교훈적인 비전이므로 우리 청중들은 Alonso 왕이 알지 못하고 있는 사실(Ferdinand의 생존뿐만 아니라, Prospero가 이 연극의 연출자라는 사실)을 알고 있기 때문에 Alonso의 계시적 조망(眺望)을 어느 정도까지는 공감할 수 있을 것이다. 4막 1장 183-93에서의 Prospero의 자연관은 복잡함을 알 수 있다:

A devil, a born devil, on whose nature
Nurture can never stick; on whom my pains,
Humanly takes, are all lost, quite lost;
And as with age his body uglier grows,
So his mind cankers. I will plague them all,
Even to roaring. (I. i. 188-93)

이것을 Traversi는 다음과 같이 설명한다:

> The lines are pregnant with the rotting, cankering effect of evil on man's being, driven home by the contrast between 'nature' and 'nurture,' between savegery and the civilizing sense implied in 'humanly.'[13]

Prospero의 삶의 시각(선천적 노예 근성과 교양적 소양과 대위, 자연과 교육과의 대위에서 발생하는 인간의 죄악에 대한 부패를 함축하고 시사하는)은 Gonzalo의 자연관을 통해서 관찰해 볼 때 Prospero의 자연 질서의 조화가 그의 능동적 감시와 권위 없이도 가능했을 것으로 생각된다. Gonzalo가 설정한 이상국가관은 안일한 자연 생활보다도 철학과 예술에 대한 연구를 촉진하는 한 Prospero는 이 사회 질서 속에 적절한 위상을 인정받을 수 있는 자격을 상실한 것으로 생각된다. 철학과 예술을 연구하는 것은 Gonzalo의 이상국가관의 개념을 벗어나기 때문이다. 그러므로 만약 자연과 자연의 법칙을 Prospero가 믿는 것처럼 섭리가 존재한다면 이 태만한 공작은 찬탈의 공작으로써 계율을 파괴했다고 볼 수 있다. 즉, 연구와 명상을 통해서 자연의 비밀을 발견하고자 하는 Prospero의 시도는 과학적 지식을 알게 되었으며, 또한 묵시를 통하여 죄를 발견하게 되었으며, 죄에 대한 그의 반응은 분노, 고통뿐만 아니라 딸 Miranda가 실의에 찬 자신을 구원했다고 하는 말('O, a Cherubin thou waste, that did preserve me! Thou didst Smile, Infused with a fortitude from Heaven, …(I. ii. 154-5))을 통하여 그의 르네상스적 환멸과 사실 세계에 의해 직면된 인본주의자(人本主義者)의 일면을 엿볼 수 있다. 이 극 속에

---

[13] Traversi, *Shakespeare,* pp. 263～4.

서 Prospero의 비통한 환멸의 체험은 냉소, 폭력적 성격의 특성을 유발시키는 요소였음을 알 수 있다. Milan의 국사(國事)에서 자진하여 퇴진함으로써 자신이 귀속(歸屬)했던 기존 사회로부터 유배와 고립을 자초하지만, 이 극에서 우리는 Prospero의 분노의 대사를 통하여, 또는 그의 과묵(寡默)한 성격에서 현재와 과거와의 맥락적 연관성을 알 수 있다. 그러나 섭리적 의지와 도덕적 질서에 대한 그의 자연의 신봉은 자연에 내재한 원시적 자유 방종적 정신의 일면을 불신하며, 그 자연을 능가하려고 노력한다.

결론적으로 이 극을 통해서 우리들은 Caliban과 Alonso 일행 및 Ariel, 기후, 바다, 사람이 졸음이 들게 하고 잠을 깨우게 하는 그러한 섬의 특성, Miranda에 대한 이해, Ferdinand에 대한 육체적 노동, Alonso의 비탄, 궁중 일행의 사고와 지각 등에 대한 초자연적 통제를 그가 행사하는 것을 목격한다. Milan 국(國)의 실권의 포기에서부터 자연 원시섬에 강력한 의지를 심기 위해 Prospero는 자신의 마력을 엄격히 제어한다.

다른 시각에서 보면 Caliban과 Prospero의 관계에서 마력 행사가 필요하며 이 자연 원시섬의 Caliban은 교육의 강요와 감시의 통제를 받아야 된다고 사료되지만, 4막 1장 188행에서 Caliban에 대한 Prospero의 과장된 혹평은 극단적인 면과 동시에 신빙성(信憑性)의 결여가 있다. Caliban은 어떤 제한된 범주 속에서 교화가 가능할 수 있다고 본다. 그것은 Caliban이 Prospero에게 자신의 저주가 Prospero로부터 보복이 있을 것을 예견[14]하는 데서 교육을 통하여 교화할 수

---

[14] *cf.* "His spirits hear me And yet I needs must cure... (II. ii. 4-)."

있는 가능성이 있기 때문이다. 즉, 자신이 주인으로부터 징계를 예상하는 것은 그의 양심 속에 도덕적 흔적이 내재한다는 증거가 된다. 그러므로 이런 사실을 통해서 우리는 더 현실적으로 더 이해력 있는 인간의 정이 넘치는 사실이 존재한다는 것을 알 수 있다. 문명 사회에 귀속된 문명인은 자연 원시인을 수용하는 포용력을 배워야 할 것이다. 그리고 Prospero 자신도 원시적 충동과 절충할 수 있는 포용력을 배워야 할 것이다. 그것은 주인공 자신이 달성하고자 하는 자연 질서의 조화를 위한 자유 의지 달성의 목적이다. 즉, 자연의 주제를 발전시키는 대위적(對位的) 미학 극 구조의 고안을 통하여 Shakespeare는 복잡한 문명 사회에 귀속된 청중의 교화 계발(啓發)을 위해 이원적 주제들을 병치시킴으로써 구조에 반영된 미학을 돋보이게 표출하였다.

제 3 장 Shakespeare 후기 극의 미학적 해석

Shakespeare의 로만스 극들은 이 시인의 노년기의 원숙(圓熟)한 삶의 반영으로 회개(悔改)·화해(和解)·평화(平和)의 무드를 취급하였을 뿐만 아니라 이들 극본의 문체들 역시 전환되었으며, 또한 셰익스피어가 극 청중들의 무드와 취미에 민감한 극작가가 되었을 때에 그의 후기 극본들은 The Beaumont와 Fletcher Romances와 연계되어, Blackfriars 극장을 드나드는 궁중의 세련된 청중들의 취미에 부합하는 극본의 형식으로 구성되었다. 최근에 연극계의 영향력 있는 비평에 의하면 이 후기 극본들은 우화·상징·신화의 매체들을 소재로 사용한 '상실'·'부활'·'재난'·'발견'·'죽음' 및 '재생'의 주제들을 취급하였다고 한다. 따라서 최근의 극비평가들이 인정하듯이 셰익스피어의 초기와 중기의 극본들 속에 있어서도 로만스 전통의 여러 가지 주제들이 내재하고 있음을 인지할 수 있다. *The Comedy of Errors*의 Aegeon Aemilia적 플롯, *Much Ado about Nothing, Twelfth Night*과 *As You Like It*의 로만스적 요소들이 그것들의 사례라 할 수 있겠다.

또 이 비평가들은 로만스의 구조는 필연적으로 황금 시대의 세계(Eden, The Forest of Arden, The Literary Arcadia)로 향하여 시련과 흥망성쇠(興亡盛衰)를 거치는 극의 진전과정을 구조한 것임을 인정하고 있다. 그러므로 중요한 것은, 셰익스피어의 후기 극들은 신화적(神話的)・우화적(寓話的) 차원에서 존재할 뿐만 아니라, 미와 평화 및 기만적(欺瞞的) 양상 이면의 사실로 우리를 인지(認知)케 하는 삶의 신비를 설명해 준다. 또한 이 로만스 극들은 종결의 비극, 노출(露出)된 과오(過誤), 부활과 신생(新生)의 목적 달성의 매체로, 스펙터클을 통한 환희의 수단으로서의 가치들이 인정된다. 이러한 주제들은 인간의 욕망과 경험의 보편성이라고 할 수 있다. 그럼으로 셰익스피어의 로만스 극들은 확실히 희랍 로만스 전통에 귀속되어 있으므로 이 극본들은 Elizabeth 조(朝)와는 전혀 상이한 James 왕조 시대에 저작되었기 때문에 James 왕궁의 미학적 이론에 근간(根幹)을 두고 있음을 알 수 있다. 셰익스피어가 그의 후기 극본들을 만들 때 극의 액션에 의한 전체적인 극 환경을 구성하였음에도 불구하고 대부분의 극비평가들은 이 극들의 시공(時空) 속에 존재하는 극의 액션보다는 오히려 극본의 대사에 무게를 두고 비평함으로써 우리 독자들이 셰익스피어 후기 극본들의 구조를 이해하는 데 있어서 왜곡된 이해의 길잡이가 되어, 극의 실연에서 발생하는 극의 양면성을 무시하는 오류를 범하게 되었다.

필자는 셰익스피어의 후기 극본들의 구조들을 분석할 때 극에 실재한 액션의 기여도를 설명하고자 한다. 따라서 이러한 시각에서 우선 셰익스피어가 그의 후기 극본들에 사용한 미학 요소인 무도(舞蹈)와 음악의 극적 효과와 그것들의 기능이 극본들의 해석에 있어서 의의성을 설명하고자 한다.

본 글은 로만스 극본들 속에 내재해 있는 비언어적 요소들의 잘못 해석된 하나 하나의 장면들의 의미를 바로잡고자 한다. 왜냐하면 James 왕조 때 발전된 궁중미학(宮中美學) 형식은 셰익스피어 후기 극본들 속에 반영되어 있으므로 필자는 셰익스피어의 후기 극본들(특히 *The Winter's Tale*과 *The Tempest*)의 분석을 위해 Ben Jonson과 Inigo Jones의 합작 극본 *Oberon the Fairy Prince*에 접근방법으로 셰익스피어 후기 극본을 설명하는 데 일조를 하고자 한다. Jonson과 Jones는 극의 액션과 대사의 의미가 점진적으로 융합되어 있는 가면극을 James 왕을 위해 공동으로 합작한 이러한 가면극 형식은 셰익스피어 로만스 극본들의 미학적 해석에 도움이 될 뿐만 아니라, 그들의 극 속에 내재한 무도와 음악이 상호 관련성을 가지고 있기 때문이라 할 수 있다.

I. 은유로서의 액션: 무도(舞蹈)와 음악의 르네상스적 개념

셰익스피어 로만스에 대한 비평의 전통은 극 구조를 체계적으로 이해하는 데 있어서 독자의 생각을 왜곡시킨 문제점은, 극 속에 나타난 주제의 내용을 극 액션과 분리하여 논평하는 데 있었다. 이러한 극본들에 대한 비평상의 오류가 자주 발생하는 이유는, 극의 형식이 문학의 여러 가지 장르 속에 국한되어 논평되었기 때문이며, 이러한 문학적 비평의 인습은 극 의미의 중요한 전달의 매체로 언어에 의한 편견(偏見)을 야기하였다. 비록 언어가 극 구조의 구성에 중요한 위상을 차지하고 있지만 비언어 형식의 극 의미 전달 역시 극 구성에 중요한 것은 셰익스피어 로만스 속에는 극 언어뿐만 아니라, 비언어적 요소들 역시 극 맥락의 한 부분이기 때문이다. 극 액션과 관계없이 극본 속에 나오는 극 언어의 창의적 의도와 주제적 내용을 해석하고자 하는 비평적 체계는 극본을 전체의 맥락 속에서 유기적으로 이해하고자 하는 우리의 생각을 왜곡시켜 왔다. 이러한 사실을 설명하기 위하여 19세기 후반의 대표적인 극비평가 Edward Dowden의 비평을 고찰하여 보고자 한다. Dowden은 셰익스피어의 로만스들을 세속적인 사실들을 초월하고자 추구했던 한가한 천재의 작품으로 설명하였다:[1]

> There are moments when was not wholly absorbed in his work as artist at this period; it is as if he was thinking of his own life, or of the fields and streams of Stratford, and still wrote on; it is as if the ties which bound him to his art where not serving with thrills of strong emotion, but were quietly growing slack.[2]

> Shakespeare still thought of the graver trials and tests which life applies to human character, of the wrongs which man inflicts on man; but his present temper demanded not a tragic issue—it

---

[1] Dowden, *Shakespeare: A Critical Study of His Mind and Art*(London: Kegan Paul, Trench, Trubner & Co., Ltd., 1892) pp. 378-430.

[2] Dowden, p. 359.

rather demanded an issue into joy or peace. The dissonance must be resolved into a harmony, clear and rapturous, or solemn and profound…, The resolution of the discords in these latest plays is not a mere stage necessity, or a necessity of composition, resorted to by the dramatist to effect an ending of his play, and little interesting his imagination or his heart. Its significance here is ethical and spiritual; it is moral necessity.[3]

그는 창의적 의도와 주제 내용에 대한 비평에서 액션과 분리하여 논함으로써 극 해석의 오류를 범하였다고 생각된다. 고매한 환상과 난폭(亂暴)한 언어의 병치를 표출하는 극이 어떻게 예술에 실증을 느낀 작가의 작품이 될 수 있는가를 이해하기는 어려운 일이라 생각된다. 부조화의 명료(明瞭)한 극이 만약 도덕적 필연성에 의해 강요받는다면 그러한 극 구조가 부진해진 옛 천재의 작품이 될 수 있다는 것은 과연 가능할 수 있을까? Dowden의 비평의 오류는 창의적 의도와 주제적 내용을 설명하는 선입관적(先入觀的)인 시각에서 야기된 것이라고 볼 수 있다. 대부분의 셰익스피어 비평가들이 그러하듯이 Dowden 역시 극 구조를 극 언어와 극 행동을 상호 관련시키지 않고 창의적 내용과 주제적 개념을 분리 비평한 데서 이러한 편견을 야기하지 않았나 생각된다.

특별히 필자는 G. E. Bently와 Una Ellis-Fermor과 J. F. Danby의 연구(Blackfriars의 전통과 Jacobean 시대의 시형의 전통 속에 셰익스피어 로만스를 분류하는 연구)뿐만 아니라,[4] 셰익스피어의 로만스 극

---

[3] Dowden, p. 361.

[4] Bently, Shakespeare and the Blackfriars Theatre, *Shakespeare Survey I* (1948), pp. 38-50; Ellis-Fermer, *The Jacobean Drama* (London: Methuen & Co. Ltd., 1936);

들에 대한 Sidney의 *Arcadia*의 영향을 논증한 Danby의 도움을 받았다. J. M. Nosworthy와 Frank Kermode, 또 Howard Felperin과 Carol Gesner 등은 셰익스피어가 희랍 로만스의 영향을 받은 확고한 증거들을 제시하였다.[5] 또 Frank Kermode의 *Shakespeare : The Final Plays*에서,

> Not that *Cymbeline* is lucid play; its language prevents it being that. The Romance plot is not matched by any assumed simplicity of diction, but set off against tough late Shakespearean verse; and this produces an effect almost of irony, so that several critics, among them professor Dandy, have tried to convey their sense that the dramatist is somehow playing with the play. I think that is true. For example, *Cymbeline* is the only play in the canon which has characters given to such tensely obscure ways of expressing themselves that not only the audience but the other characters find it hard to make out what they mean…, But it is a superb nevertheless, and in some ways perhaps it shows more of the difficulty, tortuous, ironical mind that made the sonnets, than other greater works in which the main effort goes into the making explicit of some more public theme.
>
> The opening scene is a good example of the obliquity that will prevail throughout. The annoymous gentlemen constitute a simple device for telling the audience what it needs to know about the

---

Poets on Fortune's Hill: Studies in Sidney, Shakespeare, Beaumont and Fletcher. (London: Faber and faber, 1953)

5 Nosworthy, Introduction to *Cymbeline the Arden Shakespeare* (London Methuen & Co. Ltd., 1980), Kermode, Shakespeare: *The Final Plays*, Editors and Their Work, No. 155, gen. ed., Bonamy Dobree(London: Longmans Greens & Co., 1963): Carol Gesner, *Shakespeare and The Greek Romance*(Lexington: The University Press of Kenturky, 1970)

situation. The explanation of the first Gentleman to his guest do indeed cover a lot of ground in only 70 lines, but there is nothing simple about the way he goes about it. Everybody looks angry because the King is become:

You do not meet a man but frowns; our bloods
No more obey the heavens that our courtiers
Still seem as does the King's.[6] (I. i. 1-3)

Kermode는 당연히 언어의 복잡성을 인지(認知)했을 뿐만 아니라, 그 언어가 만드는 아이러니한 효과를 주지시켰다. 그는 이 아이러니는 셰익스피어 후기 극본들의 시 형식의 복잡성과 로만스 플롯의 단순성과 병치의 결과라고 생각함으로써 그의 비평은 언어와 액션을 구조적으로 관련시켜 취급하였다. 그러나 그의 결점은 극 액션 속에 내재한 극의 맥락과 관계없이 언어의 복잡성에 초점을 맞춤으로써, 그는 극중 인물들이 모호(模糊)하게 말하기 때문에 이 극의 상황이 완곡한 것으로 생각하였는데, 이 시행(詩行)들은 극의 맥락 속에서 고찰하면 그리 단순한 의미는 결코 아니다. Kermode가 열거한 "Everybody looks angry because the King is."의 의미는 왜곡된 것이다. 이 시행들이 의미하는 것은 왕의 비탄(悲嘆)이 궁중의 조화적(調和的) 질서를 무질서로 만들게 되었기 때문이다. 이를 다시 해석해 보면 모든 것이 불일치하다는 것을 알게 될 것이다:

not a courtier,
Although they wear their faces to the bent

6 Kermode, p. 22.

> Of the King's looks, hath a heart that is not
> Glad at the thing they scowl at.[7] (Ⅰ. i. 12-5)

극도로 복잡한 극 시추에이션의 흐름에서 보듯, 어둡고 고통스러운 아이러니한 마음을 반영시켜 주는 것은 셰익스피어가 아니고 궁신(宮臣)들이다. 그러므로 Kermode의 비평은 극 구조가 모순되었다는 가정(假定)에서부터 시작했었기 때문에 극의 해석에 오류를 야기시켰다. 그러나 셰익스피어의 로만스 극 구조들이 통일되어 있다고 믿는 다른 비평가들의 비평에서도 이와 유사한 편견들을 발견하는 것은 놀라운 일이다. 예를 들면, *Cymbeline*의 'Arden Shakespeare' 서문에서 J. M. Nosworthy의 논평을 보자:

> At the time when he set to work on *Cymbeline*, then, tragedy was Shakespeare's current medium; comedy, however congenial it may have been to him, a somewhat rusty one. The danger of tragic thought and feeling, overwhelming the comic in this untried romance form was a considerable one, especially with the wager throw in··· At times *Cymbeline* does come a little nearer to the tragedy than it should be, notably in its portrayal of the mental tortures of Imogen and, to a lesser extent, Posthumus and Pisanio, of Cymbeline's wrath and Iachimo's villainy.[8]

Nosworthy는 구조의 복잡성과 문체의 다양성을 설명하는 통일 이

---

[7] Hardin, Craig, ed., *The Complete Works of Shakespeare*, (Glenview, Illinoise: Scott and Company, 1973).

[8] Nosworthy, *Cymbeline*, p. xxxiii.

론을 강요하지만, 그 이론에 부적합한 요소들을 무시해 버림으로써 Nosworthy의 로만스 극에 대한 정의는 극 구조의 실재를 무시한 비평적 오류를 범하게 되었다. 따라서 비평의 편견적인 방법은 극 비평의 중요한 위험이며, 때로는 우리 모두에게 비평의 오류를 발생하게 하는 원인을 제공하였다. 셰익스피어의 로만스 극들을 이해하는데 우리에게 많은 통찰력(洞察力)을 기여해 준 Nosworthy가 이러한 편견을 반영시키는 것은 비평가로서의 실패라기보다는 비평적 체계로 인한 실패의 표상이다.

극의 시공 속에서 엄연히 존재하지 않는 규칙들을 적용하는 것은 극의 이해를 제한하고 왜곡시키는 것이다. 극적 시각에서 보면 대사들은 극 구조상에 존재하는 일부분의 요소에 불과한 것이다.

따라서 셰익스피어 후기 극들은 대부분이 비평적 접근 방법의 오류 때문에 부조리하고 모순된 것으로 비평되어 온 것은 문학의 이론들을 극 구조에 무리하게 적용함으로써 편협된 비평의 결과를 초래하였다. 따라서 극본의 체계적 원리는 '액션'이기 때문에, 이것은 곧 청중에 의해 경험되는 총괄적인 극의 환경을 형성하는 액션을 의미하는 것이다. 극 구조상에서 고찰해 볼 때 극의 요소, 특별히 대사는 액션의 맥락 속에서 보아야 한다. 예를 들면 F. D. Hoeniger는 *Pericles*의 *Arden*판 서문에서 이 극 속에 '진정한 극 장면'들을 발견하였으며, 나머지는 '극적이라기보다는 그밖의 어떤 효과를 겨냥한 spectacle이다'라고 언급하였다.[9] 위와 같이 Hoeniger의 비평적 접근 방법은 현대의 극비평가들 중에서 가장 전형적인 비평이라 할 수 있다.

---

[9] Introduction to *Pericles*, *The Arden Shakespeare* (London: Metuen & Co. Ltd., 1979), pp. Ⅰxxⅶ-ⅠxxⅷⅠ.

극 액션에 대한 소홀은 셰익스피어의 극본 속에 실재하는 무용과 음악의 사용을 전통적 극 비평에서 취급하지 않는 결과를 초래하였으며, 과거의 전통적 비평은 Jacobean 시대의 청중의 취미를 충족시켜 주기 위해서 무용과 음악이 삽입된 것으로 시각하게 된 이러한 편견은 오늘날의 극 연구에서도 상존하고 있지만, 셰익스피어는 한 장면의 매우 중요한 극적 의미를 전달하기 위하여 무용과 음악을 종종 사용하였다. J. M. Nosworthy는 셰익스피어의 로만스 극에 등장하는 '음악과, 음악의 기능'에 관한 그의 논문에서 르네상스 사회에 있어서의 음악과 무용은 기분 전환으로뿐만 아니라 신앙의 행위로서 그리고 신분의 개념, 정치, 해학(諧謔) 등등에 못지 않게 총괄적(總括的) 형식의 필수적인 것으로 시각된다고 주장하였다.[10] 이 개념은 Elizabeth 조(朝) 시인 Sir John Davies의 시(詩) "Orchestra"(1599)에서 예증(例證)된 바 있는데, Davies는 무용과 불가분의 동반자인 음악을 우주의 질서와 우주의 조화의 반영으로 보았으며, 더욱이 그는 원시의 혼돈을 능가하는 질서의 승리로 보았다:

Dancing, bright lady, then began to be
When the first seeds where of the world did spring
The fire air earth and water, did agree
By Love's persuation, nature's might king,
To leave their first disorder's combating
And in a dance such measure to observe
As all the world their motion should preserve.[11]

---

[10] Nosworthy, *Shakespeare Survey* 11 (1958), p. 60.

[11] "Orchestra," ed., E. M. Tillyard (London: Chatto and Windus, 1947), p. 19 and cf. R. A. Foakes points out that "In making Daedalus interpret the dance here

모든 자연은 신의 사랑, 질서, 힘의 표상으로써 대우주의 무도(舞蹈)에 참가한다고 하였으며, R. A. Faokes 역시 무도를 다음과 같이 설명한다:

> The dance exhibits through the 'wisdom' of the dancers' feet a pattern in what appears to a maze, and the beholder who can understand this may be made wise, as he sees an image of order in the intricacies of movement, suggesting that all human actions, though inexplicable and bewildering to us, make pattern in a larger scheme of order, the cosmic dance, the order of providence.[12]

무도의 동반자 음악은 우주가 무도할 때 만들어진다:

> And thou, sweet music, dancing's only life,
> The ear's sole happiness, the air's best speech,
> The soft mind's paradise, the sick mind's leech
> With thine own tongue thou trees and stones canst teach,
> That when the air doth dance her finest measure…[13]

우주 조화의 체현(體現)으로 음악은 마음을 진정시키고, 치료하고, 심지어 나무들과 돌들까지도 교육하는 능력을 소유하고 있으며, 수용적인 청취자들의 생의 질서를 가져다주는 능력을 가지고 있다고

in this way, Jonson was exploiting in sophisticated and complex way a familiar Renaissance analogy, as exemplified in *Orchestra* (? 1969), addressed by Sir John Davies to Queen Elizabeth" in *Shakespeare* (London: Routledge & Kegan Paul, 1971), pp. 158~9.

[12] Foakes, p. 158.

[13] Davies, p. 26.

주장하였다. *The Merchant of Venice*에 등장하는 Lorenzo도 이러한 생각을 명료하게 표현한다:

> The man that hath no music in himself,
> Nor is not mov'd concord of sweet sounds,
> Is fit for treasons, strategems and spoils;
> The motion of his spirit are dull as night
> And his affections dark as Erebus. (V. i. 83-7)

'음악의 질서적 힘을 인간들의 생명 속에 들어가는 것을 불허하거나 청취할 수 없는 사람들은 밤처럼 어둡고 혼돈의 영역(領域) 속에 살기 때문에 신뢰할 수 없다'라고 언급하는데, 우주 질서의 반영으로 무용과 음악의 개념은 단순하고 유사한 조화를 암시하는 우주 질서의 체현(體現)이다. 그러므로 연기자가 우주의 조화를 이해하고 그것에 의해 융합될 수 있는 것은 무용과 음악의 공연, 즉 특수한 액션의 수단에 의한 것이라고 생각한다.

G. Wilson Knight는 혼돈과 무질서의 반정립으로써 음악적 조화의 심상이 셰익스피어 작품의 본질 속에 어떻게 침투되었는지를 논증함으로써,[14] 셰익스피어는 우주 질서를 반영하여 무용과 음악의 르네상스의 신앙을 전수받았음을 예증하였다. 또 이 무용과 음악의 우주의 개념은 유사한 조화 이상의 의미를 시사(示唆)하고 있음이 강조되어야 한다. 셰익스피어의 극본들 속에 실재하는 무용과 음악은 한 장면의 극적 의미를 전달하는 중요한 극적 기능을 하고 있다.

*The Winter's Tale*에서 극중에 무도를 사용하는 실례를 볼 수 있다.

---

[14] *The Shakespeare Tempest* (London: Oxford University Press, 1932)

4막 4장에서 극 언어는 극 내용의 단지 일부분적인 표현에 불과하지만, 이 전모제(剪毛祭)의 장면이 개막될 때 자신의 실체가 공주의 신분임을 알지 못하는 Perdita는 자신이 입고 있는 우아한 의상이 목양녀(牧羊女)로서 자기의 실질적 지위를 감추고, 왕자인 Florizel이 목자의 의상을 입음으로써 신분을 격하시키는 기능을 나타낸다:

Your high self,
The gracious mark o' the land, you have obscure'd
With a swain's wearing, and me, poor lowly maid,
Most goddess—like prank'd up: but that our feasts
In every mess have folly and the feeders
Digest it with a custom, I should blush
To see you so attir'd, sword, I think
To show myself a glass. (Ⅳ. iv. 7-14)

거기다가 Perdita는 자기의 천한 신분 때문에 왕이 그들의 사랑을 반대할 것이라는 두려움을 표현하지만, Florizel은 그들의 결합은 불가피한 것이라는 확고한 신념을 표명함으로써 Perdita를 고무시키고자 한다:

Lift up you countenance, as it were the day
Of celebration of that nuptial which
We two have sworn shall come. (Ⅳ. iv. 49-51)

변장을 한 Polixenes 왕이 등장하여 당장 Perdita의 미와 순결성(純潔性)에 매료되어 그들이 나누는 다음 대화들은 결합의 주제를 반영

하고 있음을 알 수 있다 :

Per. For I have heard it said
There is an art which in their piedness shares
With great creating nature
Pol. Say there be;
Yet nature is made better by no mean
But nature makes that mean: so, over that art
Which you say adds to nature, is an art
That nature makes. You see, sweet maid, we marry
A gentler scion to the wildest stock,
And make conceive a bark of baser kind
By bud of nobler race: this is an art
Which does mend nature, change it rather, but
The art itself is nature.
Per. So it is.
Pol. Then make your garden rich in gillyvors.
And do not call them bastards. (Ⅳ. iv. 86-99)

위 인용문의 야생화와 교양화의 접목에 관한 대화는 결합을 위한 그들의 욕망은 말할 것도 없고 그들 상호 신분의 불균등에 처한 Florizel과 Perdita의 상황을 반영시키고 있다. 외양(外樣)과 상반된 신분의 Polixens는 Perdita를 목양자들이 표출할 수 있는 마술과 외모가 청초한 인물을 폄하(貶下)하며, 결국 그녀를 탄핵(彈劾)하였다(423~24). Florizel의 결혼 배우자로서의 결합과 Perdita의 가치성의 표출은 무도 장면에서 정점에 달한다. 만약 어떤 비평가가 극본의 대사에만 초점을 두게되면 Folio판 무대 지시("Here a Dance of Shepherd and shepherddess")에 의해 극의 시각이 빛나가게 될 것이다. 노목양자(老牧羊者)의 아들 Mopsa와 Dorcas의 광대 놀이를 이미 독파한 비평가는 수명의 참석자들 중에서 Perdita와 Florizel, 단 두 사람과 함께 군무(群舞)를 한다고 쉽사리 가정할는지도 모른다. 그러나 무대 전후에 Florizel이 Perdita에게 한 말과 르네상스 무도의 규칙에 의하면 셰익스피어는 우리 청중의 시각적 초점을 이 Perdita와 Florizel의 한 쌍을 주목하고 있는 것은 명백한 사실이다. 즉 목양자들의 군무와 더불어 축제가 시작되지만 Perdita와 Florizel이 극의 중심적 인물임을 언급하였다. 또 Elyot의 주장(The significance is diligently to be noted that the associating of man and woman in dancing, they both obseruuinge one nombre and tyme in their meuynges, was nat begonne without a special cosideration, as well for the necassarye cionunction of those be by them represented. And for as moche as by the association of a man and a woman in dauncing may be signified matirimonie, I coulde in declarynge the dignitie and commoditie communely knowen to all men…)[15]은 무도는 결혼의 상징인 남녀의 결합으로 보았다. 무용을 함으로써 남녀 개개의 특성들이 융합된다고 믿었다.

무도에서 이성간의 상반된 특성은 조화로 결합되며, 무도는 결합의 상징성을 의미함으로써, 무도는 결합의 발생 과정을 제공할 뿐만 아니라 극 구조상으로 Perdita가 자기의 실체를 정립할 수 있는 매체를 제공한다. 즉, Florizel에게 무도는 Perdita와 사랑의 결속을 하는 과정임을 설명하였다. 또 Florizel은 Perdita의 무도의 재능을 다음 대사에서 설명한다:

---

[15] Thomas Elyot, *The Boke Named the Gouernour*, ed. by Henry Herbert Stephan Croft,
2 vols(London: K Paul, Trech & Co., 18883), vol I, p. 233.

> When you do dance, I wish you
> A wave o' th' sea, that you might ever do
> Nothing but that; move still, still so,
> And own no other function: each your doing
> So singular in each particular,
> Crowns what you are doing in the present deeds,
> That all you acts are queens. (Ⅳ. iv. 140-6)

Perdita의 무도는 그녀의 본성을 표출하였으며, 그녀의 행위들은 여왕의 행위로 시사됨으로써 이 무도의 시적 심상을 결합과 결혼의 상징적 표출의 극적 극점이 되었다. 무도의 중요성이 외형적 극 구조에서 소홀시 되면, 또 Perdita와 Florizel이 무도의 합창 속에 빠져 버린다면 이 장면(4막 3장)의 의미는 왜곡될 것이다.

> In Hamlet the oboes are still functional, since music was required for the play within the play as much as for ballroom dancing and banqueting. But in the Scottish and Roman tragedies it is the supernational and fantastic points towards the wonderous world of *The Winter's Tales* and *The Tempest*....[16]

Sternfeld의 언급처럼 셰익스피어 로만스 극에 나오는 음악의 기능은 *The Tempest*에서 ① 길 잃은 Ferdinand를 Prospero의 의지 달성을 위한 'magic cycle'로 인도하고, ② 죄지은 3인을 회개시키는 기능 역할, ③ Setebos 섬을 장중한 음악으로 가득 차게 함으로써 초자연적 경

---

[16] F. W. Sternfeld, *Music in Shakespeare Tragedy* (London: Routledge and Kegan Paul, 1967), p. 245.

이의 세계로 만드는 중요한 극의 기능을 한다. 또 John P. Cutts도 "Music and the Supernatural in *The Tempest*" 에서 특별히 Ariel의 노래에 대해서 상술하고 있듯이[17] *The Tempest*에서 중요한 극 액션이 발생하는 것은 음악이다. Ariel은 그의 노래를 듣는 사람의 마음을 전환시키는 능력을 가지고 있다. H. W. Auden은 Ariel의 노래의 특성을 언급했었다. "Come into these yello sands"(1막 2장 76행)라는 Ariel의 첫 노래는 Ferdinand에게 놀라운 사건으로 수용되었다. 노래는 그의 슬픔을 체념(諦念)시키거나 앉아서 통곡하게 한 것이 아니고 그의 마음을 진정시켜 주는 데 있었다. 그래서 그는 일어나 이 음악 소리를 따라 나선다.[18] Ariel의 두 번째 노래("Full fathom five thy father lies" =1막 2장 394행)는 Ferdinand의 슬픈 마음을 변화시켜 비통한 마음에서 경외와 경건한 수용의 마음 자세로 변화하게 하였다.[19] Ferdinand의 심리 변화는 음악에 의해 발생하였음을 알 수 있다:

> Fer. The ditty does remember my drown'd father.
> This is no mortal business, nor sound
> That the earth owes:—I hear it now above me.
> (I. ii. 402-03)

---

[17] John P. Cutts, Of some 30 publications which have appeared between 1952～1962, cf. the following: ______ed., jointly with F. Kermode, Seventeenth Century Songs, Reading 1956. Other articles have appeared in *Journal of the American Musicological Society*, Music and Letters, ...*Shakespeare Quartly, Shakespeare Survey*. cf. *Music and Letters*, (1955), pp. 347～58.

[18] "Music in Shakespeare", *Encounter*, 9, No. 6 (December 1957), p. 43.

[19] Auden, p. 43.

이와 같이 Ferdinand의 심리 변화는 음악의 구조에서 체현(體現)된다고 볼 수 있다.

*The Winter's Tale*에서도 우리들은 청취자에게 그러한 효과를 만들어내기 위하여 악기가 사용되는 장면을 발견한다. Paulina는 외형적 사망을 상징하는 석상(石像)으로 변장한 Hermione를 소생시키기 위하여 음악을 사용한다. 음악은 돌에 생명을 불어넣고 그것에 생명을 부여하는 극 기능을 한다:

Paul. Music, awake her; strike! (Music)
'Tis time; descend; be stone no more; approach;
Strike all that look upon with marvel. Come,
I'll fill your grave up: stir, nay, come away,
Bequeath to death your numbness, for from him
Dear life redeems you. You perceive she stirs:
(Hermione comes down.)
Start not; her actions shall be holy as
You hear my spell is lawful: do not shun her
Until you see her die again; for then
You kill her double. Nay, present your hand:
When she was young you woo'd her; now in age
Is she become the suittor?
Leon. O, she's warm!
If this be magic, let it be an art
Lawful as eating
Pol. She embraces him.
Cam. She hangs about his neck··· (V. iii. 98-112)

Paulina는 Hermione를 소생시키고 이 극에서 발생한 사건들의 조화적 결론을 성취하기 위하여 표면적으로 음악에 호소한다. Paulina의 명령에 Hermione가 깨어나고 청중들이 Hermione가 걸어 내려오는 것을 보는 동안 청중들의 반응을 보일 휴지부(pause)[20]를 제공한다. Paulina의 말이 끝나자 왕비는 Leontes에게 손을 내밀고 왕을 포옹한다. 이 장면의 대단원(Hermione와 Leontes의 사랑의 재결합)은 음악에 의결한 것은 '음악'의 기능에 의해 해결된다.

만약 성악과 기악이 이 장면의 중요한 극적 장면을 해결하기 위하여 사용될 수 있다는 개념이 수용될 수 있다면 문학의 장르 속에 포함될 수 있을 것이다. 그러나 많은 비평가들이 이러한 연구와 발견을 해 왔으나 그들의 발견은 셰익스피어 비평의 주류에 통합되지 못했었다. 르네상스의 음악과 무도의 지식은, 셰익스피어 로만스 극들의 이해에 필수적인 것이 명백하다고 해도, 이러한 지식들은 비평의 영역 밖의 특수한 것으로 취급되었다.

지금까지 본 글의 목적은 극 장면의 주요한 극 의미를 전달하기 위해서는 때때로 셰익스피어가 로만스 극에 음악과 무도를 사용하였다는 사실을 논증하는 데 있다.

따라서 Traversi는 시어(詩語)와 극 액션은 너무 완벽하게 융합되어 있기 때문에 극 전체의 개념을 왜곡하지 않고는 시어와 액션을 분리하여 평하는 것은 불가능하다고 하였으며, '확대(擴大)된 심상(心象)'에 대한 그의 정의는 언어를 초월하여 극 액션, 그 자체에까지 확대라고 보아왔다.

---

[20] Charles Frey points out that "they mean 'awaiting the climax of kinesthetic tension' in *Shakespeare's Vast Romance : A Study of The Winter's Tale*" (London & Columbia: University of Missouri Press, 1980), p. 163.

> It is simply to say that the characters and situations of Shakespeare's final comedies are more exclusively conditions than ever before by the poetic emotion, that the plays themselves are to be regarded accordingly as expanded images, and that these images in turn attain their full expression by moulding to their purpose the conventions of the stage. A study of such plays as *The Winter's Tale* and *The Tempest* reveals the full meaning of the commonplace assertion that poetry and drama are in Shakespeare intimately fused into the unity of 'poetic drama.' (Traversi, p. 18)

Ⅱ. 의미(意味)로서의 구조(構造) : 자코비안 궁중미학(宮中美學)

Jacobean 시대의 미학적 이론은 개념의 표상으로써 형식과 액션은 신플라톤 철학에 근간을 두고 있다. 무도와 음악과 스펙터클이 통일된 요소를 가지고 있는 가면극은 미학의 가장 예술적 표상이다. 결국 Jacobean 시대의 James 왕궁에서 발달된 미학적 형식은 Ben Jonson과 Inigo Jones의 가면극 속에 특별히 반영되어 있다. 궁중 시인으로서 Jonson과, 왕실의 건축가로서의 Jones는 James 왕궁의 신플라톤 철학의 예술적 표현의 극을 만드는 데 공동 참여하였다. Jonson의 시 극본은 신권(神權)(물질적 우주의 중심으로서의 왕)의 체현이었다.[21] Jonson의 가면극의 시적 심상은 그 원형이 희랍 신

---

[21] Strong, *Splendor at Court: Renaissance Spectacle and The Theatre of Power* (Boston: Houghton Mifflin Company, 1973)

화에서 유래하였든지, 혹은 Welsh의 전설에서, 또는 저자 자신의 고안이든 간에 그것은 James 궁의 왕 중심 체제의 계급 구조로 형성되어 있다. Jones는 Jonson이 쓴 이 시의 심상을 무대와 의상 설계에 의해 극의 형식으로 옮겼다. 그들의 합작품으로 1611년 Henry 왕자를 위해 쓴 *Oberon The Fairy Prince*라는 가면극을 발표하였다.

Jones에게 있어서는 Jonson의 시적 심상을 극의 형식으로 체현하는 과정은 그 시어의 심상에 대한 Jonson의 창의력보다 더 월등했었다. 결국 그는 가면극에 대한 평판에서 Jonson의 명성을 능가했었다.[22] 이에 대해 Jonson은 도장공과 목공이 가면극의 넋이 된 mechanic 시대를 개탄(慨歎)하는 "Expostulation with Inigo Jones"(1631)라는 시적 독설(毒舌)로 공개적으로 Jones를 공격하였다.

Jonson은 Jones와 합작할 때부터 가면극의 의미를 전달할 수 있는 언어의 불가능을 인식하였으며, 그는 *The Masque of Blackness*(1605)의 서문에서 다음과 같이 언급했다:

> The honor and splendor of these spectacles was such in the performance as, could those hours lasted, this of mine now had been a most unprofitable work.[23]

가면극은 이러한 특성 때문에 최종 공연에 기여하는 많은 동참자들의 종합 예술 — 배우, 무용수, 궁신, 무대 구성자, 발레 연출가,

---

[22] Enid Welsford, *The Court Masque* (1927; rpt. New York: Russel Inc., 1962), p. 220.

[23] *The Masque of Blackness*, in *Ben Jonson: The Complete Masques*, p. 47.

디자이너, 시인 — 이다.

그러나 가면극 형식은 신플라톤 철학의 James 왕궁의 미학적 환경의 소산이다. 따라서 시어와 극 액션의 통일로 향한 셰익스피어의 로만스 극들은 미학적 환경에 놓일 때 가장 성공적으로 이해될 수 있다고 시각되는데, 이것은 셰익스피어의 로만스가 가면극이라는 것을 주장하는 것이 아니고, 가면극 형식의 극이 전적으로 구조적 복잡성을 설명한다고 주장하는 것도 아니다. 필자가 주장하는 것은 이 궁중의 미학적 시험과 그 미학 사상의 표출로서 극 액션의 시험이 셰익스피어의 로만스를 유기적인 전체로서 고찰할 수 있는 맥락을 제공한다는 데 의미의 무게를 두고 있다.

France Yates는 *The Theatre of The World*에서 이 개념을 상세하게 시험하였다.[24] 그녀가 주장하는 중요한 문제들 중의 하나는 셰익스피어 극 구조 자체도 우주의 질서와 우주 조화의 원리들을 의식한 정교한 상징적 표현들이라는 것이다. 실제로 극장은 소우주인 배우가 공연하는 대우주라는 것을 믿고 있는 Yates는 우주와 조화적 균형의 플라톤적 개념들이 Vitruvius의 건축 논문에 의해 영국의 르네상스에 어떻게 전파되었는지를 논증하였다. Yates는 이러한 개념들이 Globe 극장의 원형을 만든 James Burbage에게 영향을 주었을는지도 모른다고 믿고 있다. 그녀는 그것을 다음과 같이 추론하고 있다:

> A theatre with a name such as the Globe, and which was recognized as representing the world(See the world's ruins— exclaimed Ben Jonson when surveying the charred remained of the

---

[24] (Chicago: The University of Chicago Press, 1969)

> first Globe after the fire) must··· have aimed at expressing in terms of sumbolic geometry attitudes to man, to the cosmos, to God, which lay behind Renaissance architecture.[25]

Yates의 추론은 어느 정도 가정적(假定的)이지만, 그럼에도 불구하고 Elizabeth 시대의 극장과 Jacobean 시대의 극장이 상징적 표상으로서 건립된 것을 증명하는 데 성공하였다. 이 개념은 피타고라스의 수식과 플라톤 수식에 영향을 받은 그 시대의 건축 원리에서 나온 것이라 생각된다.

James 궁의 극장은 '생을 위한 상징' 혹은 '은유(隱喩)' 이상의 것이었다. 극의 액션에서 체현되는 의미가 신은 물질적 우주에서 체현되고, 왕의 실재는 극의 액션들 속에서 체현된다는 신의 과정과 직접적으로 일치되는 것으로 관찰되어 있었다. 그러므로 극의 형식과 무도와 음악의 통일된 요소들을 가진 가면극은 신권의 표상으로써 왕에 대한 James 왕의 개념들 중에 가장 완전한 표현으로 사료되었다.[26]

그럼으로 가면극의 형식은 그것이 셰익스피어의 로만스 극들의 구조에 기여함으로써 극 액션의 분석을 위한 유형을 제공하였다. Jones과 Jonson의 합작품 *Oberon The Fairy Prince*는 셰익스피어의 로만스 극들이 발표된 시기에 쓰여졌다. 이 가면극은 시어와 극 액션 통일의 좋은 사례가 된다고 생각한다.

---

[25] Yates, p. 134.

[26] 극장의 폐관이 혁명 기간 중에 중요한 문제들 중의 하나가 된 것은 Stuart 왕조의 통치에 극장의 중요성의 표시이다.

Orgel과 D. A. Traversi의 연구에서 보듯이 Jacobean 시대의 극 형식의 발달은 시적 상징과 극 액션의 결합을 내포하고 있다. 가면극 *Oberon*의 극의 과정은 시적 상징의 확대된 심상으로서 관찰될 수 있다. 구조적으로 무질서에서 질서의 운동은 가면극의 중심적 의미를 체현하는 것이며 무용, 음악, 스펙터클의 액션(즉 비언어[27] 요소들)에서 성취된다.[28]

Jonson의 가면극 *Oberon*의 분석은 세 개의 상호 관계되는 개념들을 보여주는데, 이 세 개의 개념들은 셰익스피어 로만스 극들의 해석을 위해 매우 중요한 것이다. 첫째, 비언어 요소들은 중요한 극 의미들을 전달할 수 있다. 둘째, 극 액션은 시적 상징의 확대된 심상으로서 가끔 사용될 수 있다. 셋째, 전체의 극 구조는 극의 시공(時空) 속에서 시적 의도의 물질적 체현으로서 해석될 수 있다.

Jacobean 왕궁의 극이 신플라톤 철학의 가장 완전한 예술의 표현으로써 관찰된 것은 이러한 이유들 때문이다. 극 형식이 시의 상징의 창의적 과정으로 물질적 형식이 실재를 체현한 'divine process'의 직접 모방으로 관찰되었다. Jacobean 궁중에 의해 수용되어 정교하게 만들어진 이 형식의 인지는 극 형식에 대한 Jacobean 시대의 개념과 그 시대 이전의 극 개념을 구별하는 요소로서 고찰될 수 있다.

셰익스피어의 로만스 극들은 비록 가면극들은 아니지만 Jacobean

---

27 Benedeto Croce(1866～1952)는 그의 *Aesthetic*(1902)에서 표현이라는 용어를 언어 표현에 국한시키고 있는데, 그는 이 용어를 선, 색채와 음향의 비언어적 표현을 나타내는 데도 쓰고 있다. 본 논문에 있어서 비언어적 요소들(non-verbal elements)—음악, 무용, 가면극—도 미학에서 비언어적 요소라고 칭하기 때문에 사용하였음.

28 제2장, 주 17) 참조 Foakes, *op. cit.*,

궁중극이 가지고 있는 것과 동일한 미학 원리를 공유하고 있으며, 또 그와 동일한 시어와 극 액션의 통일성을 가지고 있다. 사실상 극 구조는 극 과정이 상호 관련된 불가분의 요소들에 의하여 취급된다면, 셰익스피어의 로만스 극들이 가지고 있는 중요한 해석적인 많은 문제들이 해결될 수 있을 것으로 시사된다. Northrop Frye는 극 구조에 대한 셰익스피어의 기교적 관심사를 점차적 발전 단계의 종말로 로만스 극들에 집중시켰다. 로만스 극들이 셰익스피어와 상호 관계되는 것은 *The Art of Fuge*가 Bach와 상호 관계하는 것과 같다고 말했으며 그것은 현학적(衒學的)인 후퇴(後退)가 아니고 기교의 최종적 명료성(明瞭性)이라고 말했다.[29]

Bach의 위대한 작품 속에서 형식과 내용은 불가분의 관계이므로, 음악 구조의 연구는 그것의 의미를 한층 더 명시적으로 밝히는 데 도움을 주었다.

셰익스피어의 로만스 극작 시기를 특징짓는 극의 상징적 개념은 이 극 *The Winter's Tale*에 이르러 그 최초의 성공을 이룬 것으로 시사되었다. 그리고 이 상징[30]이란 말은 시와 극에 부여한 추상적인 말

---

[29] *A Natural Perspective* (New York and London: Columbia University Press, 1964), p. 8.

[30] Cf. Derek Traversi, *Shakespeare : The Last Phase* (London: Hollis & Charter, 1954), p. 3: "Shakespeare's power of uniting poetry and drama is now such that the plot has become simply an extension, an extra-vehicle of the poetry. His experience has come to require not only verbal richness and complexity not even simply deep insight into human motives and the sources of moral impulse, but this type of 'symbolic' incidents as part of his purpose; and his elaboration of the poetry of each play has become so complete so homogeneous, that such 'symbolic' fit naturally into it …"

이 아니다. 이 극 *The Winter's Tale*에 있어서 명료한 시적 표상과 광범위한 심상, 리듬의 통제는 찾아내야 할 것이다. 극의 인물과 동기를 명료하게 규명하기 위하여 일관성 있게 사용될 뿐만 아니라, 시와 인물 역시 그 여러 개의 부류 속에 완전히 균형화한 극이 액션 속에서 차례로 통일된다는 사실도 중요하다. 또 개연성(蓋然性)이 있는 일반 법칙에 속하지 않는 '이야기'와 '우화(寓話)'에 대하여 반복해서 강조되는 그 이면에 내재하는 액션과 우화를 인간 경험의 조화적 이해를 위한 도구로 만들고자 한 일관된 욕망이 있는 것이다. 이 극의 비현실성은 환상의 세계로 향한 단순한 현실 도피가 아니며, 이 우화의 여러 가지 단계들은 비극의 부조화나 조화적 의미가 배제되지 않는 다양한 감성의 통일 속에 내재하는 단계들과 엄격하게 부합된다. 인물과 사건 결과의 상호 작용은 이 극에 의해 전달되는 총체적 인상은 매우 중요하다. 그들의 완전한 의미는 인물과 사건 속에 잠재되어 있는 심상의 발전에서 그 완전한 의미가 나온다고 말할 수 있을 것이다.

이 극의 통일된 구조를 이해하기 위하여 *The Winter's Tale*의 극본 분류는 전통적 분류 방법을 피하는 것이 중요하다. 이 극은 다섯 개의 극의 진전과정으로 형성되어 있는데, 제1의 극의 진전과정은 한 인간의 격노한 어리석은 행위로 인하여 이 극에 등장하는 중심적 인물들 간에 내재하는 비극적 파탄을 취급하였으며, 그의 어릴 적부터의 친구를 규탄하고 그의 신생아를 비와 바람이 부는 황야에 버리도록 명령한다. 제2의 극의 진전과정은 배경의 이면에는 Leontes의 신생아에 대한 목양자의 발견이 하나의 에피소드 속에서 출생과 사망의 개념을 통일하고 최후의 화해와 예견 속에서 행복한 미래와 비극적 과거를 연결한다. 이 화해가 성립되기 전에 제3의 극의 진전과정은 대 목가의 장면에서 신생을 확신할 뿐만 아니라, 이 신생아를 역경들 중 가장 성숙한 영향력 속에 노출시키는 봄의 환희를 만든다. Perdita와 Florizel은 서로 사랑을 맹세하지만 이 장면에서 Polixenes의 분노의 폭발은 서로 공통적인 결점을 소유하고 있는 두 아버지를 구조적으로 융합할 뿐더러, 최후의 화해(아직 시기 상조지만)가 Leontes 궁에서 발생하는 것을 확증한다. 제4의 극의 진전과정과 제5의 극의 진전과정은 부활의 서곡(序曲)으로 회개의 개념을 충분히 소개하고, 두 아들의 결혼을 성사시킴으로써, 이 두 아이들을 통해 양가 부모의 화해를 달성하며, 은총의 충만 속에서 Hermione의 부활을 성취시킨다. 이와 같은 연속적인 극의 과정을 통하여 계절의 리듬에 조화된 인간 경험의 조화가 포괄적인 조화 속에서 해결된다.

이와 같이 세신(歲神)의 도래와 결합과 재생의 심상으로 충만한 봄의 세계(제3의 극의 진전과정)는 Leontes가 파괴와 우주의 무질서를 야기시키는 겨울의 세계(제1의 극의 진전과정)와 직접적으로 병치되며 봄의 세계의 조화적 우주의 심상은 음악과 무도를 통해서 체현된다. 즉 여섯 곡의 노래, 두 개의 무도, 단편으로 된 두 개의 노래는 조화의 시적 상징과 융합이 잘 되어 있기 때문에 목가 장면의 구조는 실제로 조화적이라고 할 수 있겠다.

구조상으로 제3의 극의 진전과정(목가적 장면)의 서정과 해학이 제1의 극의 진전과정(Sicilia의 비극의 세계)과 직접적인 대위 상태에서 극적 액션을 통해서 확대된 심상이 체현될 수 있을 것이다. 제1의 극의 진전과정(Leontes의 궁중)에는 음악이 없다. 오히려 이 궁중의 세계는 우주의 불균형 상태로 극의 진행을 시키는 Leontes의 시적 분노로 충만하다. 그러므로 셰익스피어는 구조상으로 제1의 극의 진전과정과 제3의 극의 진전과정이 대립되는 두 개의 극 환경을 대위 병치시킴으로써 시적 상징의 확대된 심상을 만들어낸다. 즉, 두 개의 대위되는 극적 환경의 병치는 극 구조의 강도를 높여 준다. 특히 제3의 극의 진전과정에서도 Perdita와 Florizel 간의 결합을 파괴하려고 시도하는 Polixenes의 분노의 상징적 효과를 봄의 꽃을 말라 죽게 하는 겨울의 난폭한 침략으로 규정했었다. 이 시적 침략도 극의 액션에서 체현된 확대된 심상이다.[31]

또한 Polixenes는 이 제3의 극의 진전과정 속에서 무도를 통해서 체현된 Perdita에 대한 Florizel의 사랑의 심도를 이해하지 못한다. Polixenes가 변장을 함으로써 극 액션으로부터 고립된 상태에 처하므로 극 액션에 포함하지 않았다. 그러므로 그의 아들과의 대좌(對坐)는 결국 이 목가 장면의 침략일 것이다. Ewbank가 주장한 것처럼 변장된 모습으로 Polixenes의 참석은 겨울 환경의 침략으로 본다.[32]

Polixenes가 그의 변장(變裝)을 벗어 던질 때, 그는 연인들의 결별을 강요하고자 시도한다:

> I'll have thy beauty scrach'd with briers, and made
> More homely than thy state. For thee, fond boy

31 "The structural Pattern of *The Winter's Tale,*" *A Review of English Literature*, 5 (1964), pp. 76~7.

32 "The Triumph of Time in *The Winter's Tale*," *A Review of English Literature*, 5 (1964), p. 95.

> If I may ever know thou dost but sigh
> That thou know more shalt see this knack, as never
> I mean thou shalt, we'll bar three from succession;
> Not hold thee in our blood, no, not our kin,
> Far than Deucalion off: mark thou my words:
> Follow us to the court. Tou churl, for this time,
> Though full of our displeasure, yet we free thee …
> (Ⅳ. iv. 435-45)

이와 같이 Polixenes의 말 속에 내재한 잔인성(殘忍性), 호색(好色) 그리고 성적(性的) 히스테리는 구조상 제1의 극의 진전과정 속에서 Leonter의 그것들이 메아리친다. 제3의 극의 진전과정 속에 있는 Polixenes의 분노는 목가 장면의 상징적 침략일 뿐만 아니라, 실질적인 침략에 해당된다고 보는 것이다.

결국 이 극 *The Winter's Tale*의 구조는 다섯 단계의 극의 진전과정들로 구성되어 있다. 제1의 극의 진전과정(비극부)과 제3의 극의 진전과정(목가장면)으로 전이할 때 제2의 극의 진전과정(Perdita가 황야에 버려지고 동시에 목양자에 의해 발견되는 장면)은 극의 전환점이다. 제3의 극의 진전과정에서 무도를 통하여 무질서에서 질서로의 시어와 극 언어가 확대된 심상으로 체현된다. 제4의 극의 진전과정과 제2의 극의 진전과정은 이 극의 조화적 해결의 서곡의 기능으로 Hermione의 부활을 은총의 완성으로 성취시킨다. 그리고 극 구조상 제1의 극의 진전과정과 제3의 극의 진전과정은 상호 대위적으로 병치되어 있으므로 다음과 같은 대위적 병치(對位的 併置)가 성립된다: 겨울의 세계/봄의 세계, 옥내의 세계/옥외의 세계, 궁중의 세계/전원의 세계, 인간이 만든 문명의 세계/자연이 만든 자연의 세계,

동계/춘계, 청년세대/노세대의 기능을 가지며, 플롯의 리듬도 소우주의 내면적 인간/외면적 인간을 통제한다. 또 이 극의 플롯 역시 대우주의 차원에서 인간을 먼 곳에서, 큰 우주의 조망(眺望)으로, 오랜 기간의 '세월' 속에서, 인간이 관조(觀照)하는 반면에, 소우주의 차원에서는 한 개인의 인물 속에서 강력하게 초점이 겨냥된 비극적 조망에서 인간을 관조하기 때문에, 직접적인 경험의 순간에 대한 생각만이 오직 현실적이다. 비극적 영역과 목가적 영역의 구성이 너무 완벽하기 때문에 셰익스피어의 로만스 극들 중에서 가장 특징 있는 대위적 병치(즉 현실적/비현실적, 일시적/영원적, 특수적/우주적, 객관적/상징적)의 극에 의하여 짜여진 것으로 사료된다.

이것을 극 무대에 올려놓고 대위적 병치로서의 무대 장치를 하면 제1의 극의 진전과정과 제3의 극의 진전과정의 대위적 효과가 잘 나타날 것이며, 이 두 개의 극 진전과정의 상이한 극적 환경은 시적 상징의 확대된 심상들로서 강도 높은 극적 기능을 표출할 것이다.

Ⅲ. 『템페스트』의 구조 분석에 있어서 가면극과 음악의 기능

E. M. Tillyard는 이 극에서 Prospero의 액션을 과거 과정의 재현이라고 하였으며, Prospero의 계획을 심각하게 생각하는 것은 잘못된 견해라고 주장한다.[33] 반면에 J. D. Wilson은 Prospero를 계획된 복수

[33] Tillyard, p. 52.

(復讐)를 추진하는 비극적 인물로 평가하여 서로 상반된 견해를 표명한다.[34] 이 극 구조 해석의 핵심은 Prospero의 액션에 두는 것이 비평가들의 견해지만, 이 견해에서 climax 문제는 해석상(解釋上)의 이견(異見)을 야기하고 있다. 이 극의 climax를 3막 3장 53-82행 ("You are three men of sin.")에 설정하는 비평가와 5막 1장 1-32행 ("the rarer action is in virtue than in vengeance")에 설정하는 비평가들이 있다. D. Traversi는 Ariel의 대사(3막 3장 53-82행)에 극 구조의 climax를 설정하는 비평가들 중의 한 사람이며, R. A. Foakes는 복수보다는 덕을 취하겠다는 Prospero의 말(5막 1장 1-32행)에 극의 climax를 설정한다.

전자의 주장은 다음과 같다:

> Ariel's great speech addressed to Alonso and his companions before he derives them of the enchanted banquet is, in fact, nothing less than the keystone upon which the structure of the play rest:
>
> You are three men of sin, whom Destiny,
> That hath to instrument this lower world,
> And what is in't, the never-surfeited sea
> Hath caused to belch up you; and…[35]

이 극은 혼돈 속에서 시작한다. 제일 첫 무대 지시는 폭풍의 특성을 암시하다. "A TEMPESTUOUS NOISE OF THUNDER AND

---

[34] *The Essential Shakespeare* (Cambridge University Press), p. 143.

[35] Traversi, *The Last Phase*, p. 248.

LIGHTNING HEARD." 천둥과 번개의 소음은 폭풍의 소리에 응답할 때, 승무원들, 승객들의 소리에 의해 확대된다. 그 배의 호각 소리는 큰 소리로 반향된다 :

> Take in the topsail: Tend to the master's whistle.
> Blow, till thou thy wind, if room enough! (I. i. 6-8)

선실의 아우성 소리는 수부장(水夫長)의 으르렁대는 소리에 의해 설명된다.

> A plague upon this howling! they are louder than the weather or our office. (I. i. 33-40)

Sebastian과 Antonio도 무질서에 기여하는 인물이며 그들의 난폭한 고함 소리는 폭풍의 강도를 강조하고 소리를 혼란시킨다:

> Seb. A pox o' your throat, you bawling, blasphemous, incharitable dog! Boats. Work you then.
> Ant. Hang, cur! hang, you wholeson, insolent noisemaker! We are less afraid to be drowned than you art.
> (I. i. 43-8)

이 배의 승객과 승무원들이 그 배를 포기할 때 부서지는 소리가 들린다 :

> *A confused noise within*: 'Mercy on us?'—

> 'We split, we split!'—'Farewell my wife and children!'—
> 'Farewell, brother'—'We split, we split, we split!'
> (I. i. 57-9)

이 승객들의 광적인 대화와 아우성과 배가 난파되는 환상을 만들어내는 청각적 효과는 이 극의 액션에서 직접적으로 압도적인 어조에 의한 분위기 조성일 것이다. 이러한 어조의 환경은 폭풍의 상징에 대한 극적 체현이다.

폭풍은 Prospero의 정신적 불안의 확대적 심상이다. 그의 마술(1막 2장 28행)의 산물로써 폭풍의 환상적 특징은 청중에게 극적 효과의 강도를 경감시키지 않고 오히려 강화시킨다. Traversi는 다음과 같이 첫 장면을 설명한다:

> In *The Tempest*, the storm has become a point of departure, present indeed throughout the later action in the minds of those initially exposed to it, but present rather as memory, a prelude to further development, than as an incident related both to the past and the future unfolding of events.[36]

청각의 혼돈은 Alonso가 폭풍우의 힘에 굴할 때 우주 조화의 붕괴를 병행한다: "What cares these roarers for the name of King?"(1막 1장 15-16행). Prospero는 우주 질서를 붕괴시킴으로써 혼돈의 대행자로 고찰된다.

이상의 바다 폭풍의 혼돈의 배경과는 정반대의 냉철한 자세로

---

[36] Traversi, p. 195.

Prospero가 등장하며, 바다 폭풍의 희생자들에 대한 그의 딸 Miranda의 고민을 위로하는 양면성을 보인다.

> I have done nothing but in care of thee,
> Of thee, my dear one, thee, my daughter, who
> Art ignorant of what thou art… (I. ii. 16-8)

여기에서 청중들은 Prospero의 인격의 양면성을 감지하게 된다. 즉 그의 이 부드러운 말들을 Miranda에게 언급할 때 동정도 할 수 있지만, 동시에 파괴도 할 수 있는 인격의 양면성을 보여준다.

Prospero는 그를 유배시켰던 사건들을 설명할 때, 그로 하여금 폭풍을 발생하게 했던 정신적 불안을 나타낸다. Prospero가 그의 동생 Antonio를 언급하는 순간부터 그의 말이 율동적 강도로 흔들거린다. 그는 반역자의 동생 생각에 사로잡혀 있으며, 43행의 여백 중에 24번을 명사 내지 대명사로 그의 동생을 언급한다. 그리고 Prospero는 Miranda에게 이 부분을 설명할 때 5번의 'interjection'을 사용한다 : "Dost thou attend me?"(I. ii. 78) / "Thou attend'st not."(I. ii. 87) / "I pray thee, Mark me."(I. ii. 98) / "Dost thou hear?"(I. ii. 105) / "Mark his condition and the event; then tell me." (I. ii. 118)이 interjection들은 하나하나 강도를 유지하고 있다. 이에 대해 Miranda의 유명한 대답("Sir, most heedfully"(I. ii. 78) / "O, good sir,! I do."(I. ii. 87) / "Your tale, sir, would cure deafness."(I. ii. 106))들은 Prospero의 분노의 극단의 표출의 시사이며, 그녀가 후에 Ferdinand에게 하는 말("Never till this day / Saw I him touch'd with anger to distemper'd" (IV. ii. 144-5))들을 확

증하는 시사라 할 수 있다.

이러한 난폭한 말과는 대위적으로 Prospero는 극중 가장 뼈에 사무치는 말로써 Miranda를 달랜다.

Mir. Alack, what trouble
Was I then to you!
Pros. O, a cherubin
Thou wast that did preserve me. Thou didst smile,
Infused with a firtitude from heaven,
When I have decked the sea with drops full salt,
Under my burthen groan'd; which rais'd in me
An understanding stomach, to bear up
Against what should ensue. (I. ii. 152-8)

Prospero가 비교적 짧은 시간 속에서 심리적 환경을 전환할 수 있는 것은 그의 정신 상태의 극단적 표현이다. Miranda는 아버지의 분노와 감정의 여러 단계를 체험한다.

그런데 1막 2장의 Prospero와 Miranda의 대화를 Traversi는 다음과 같이 설명한다:

… Although this understanding comes to us, in the nature of things, gradually, the tone and phrasing of Prospero's first speech is itself significant:

There's no harm done…
No harm.
I have done nothing but in care of thee, …[37]

Prospero의 설명은 논리 정연하며, 이 설명에 대응하는 Miranda의 재치있는 응답은 위의 설명과 대위되며, Prospero의 설명 목적은, 그녀의 망각된 과거를 회상시킴으로써 이 섬에 유배되어 온 후, 인간으로서 도덕적 성장과 그녀의 현 위상을 주지하는 데 있다. 이것에 대한 관객들의 필연적 이해의 전진과 이러한 이해의 발전은 극 속에 있는 에피소드가 목적하는 필수적 이해의 진보라 할 수 있다. 왜냐하면, 그러한 운동은 극의 climax로 향한 의도적인 변화의 율동성을 정적인 이 대화에 부여함으로 이러한 개념의 이해가 이 극본을 이해하는 중요한 단계임이 시사된다.

그러나 Prospero의 첫 대사의 어조와 표현 자체는 율동성의 동요가 나타남을 알 수 있다.

또 Prospero의 질서에서 무질서에로의 운동은 1막 2장 187행에서 그의 정령 Ariel과의 첫 상면(相面)에서도 나타나는데, 이 장면은 그들 상호 관계의 정감을 반영한다:

Ariel. All hail, great master! grave sir, hail! I come
To answer thy best pleasure; be't to fly,
To swim, to dive into the fire, to ride
On the curl'd clouds, to thy strong bidding task.
Ariel and all his quality.

(Ⅱ. ii. 189-93)

파선을 설명할 때의 Ariel의 말은 자발적이고, 환상적이며, 우아하고, 원숙하다. 그의 말이 청중에게 주는 기쁨은 Prospero 역시 공감

---

37 Traversi, pp. 195~6.

함으로써 자만심과 흥분 상태에서 Ariel을 "My brave spirit"(206)라고 찬사와 격려를 한다. 그러나 Ariel의 업무 수행에 만족한 Prospero는 "There's more work."라고 언급하면서 명령을 부과한다.

> … but there's more work:
> What is the time o'th' day?
> Ari. Past the mid season.
> Pro. At least two glasses. The time 'twixt six and now
> Must by us both be spent most preciously.
> (I. ii. 239-43)

Prospero의 명령에 이의를 제기하며 1년이 끝나면 자기를 석방시켜 줄 것이라고 했던 Prospero의 약속을 상기시킨다:

> I prithee,
> Remember I have done thee worthy service,
> Told thee no lies, made thee no mistaking, serv'd
> Without or grudge or grumblings: thou didst promise
> To bate me a full year.
> (I. ii. 246-50)

Prospero는 Ariel의 항변(抗辯)에 대하여 잔인하게 독설을 퍼붓는다. 그는 Ariel을 '사악한 것'(257), '노예'(270)로 호칭하며, 마녀 Sycorax가 Ariel에게 준 고통을 상기시킴으로써 거의 40행의 대사를 통해 그를 위협한다. 여기에서 그의 성격의 양면성은 물론 그의 마술이 'white magic'이냐 'black magic'이냐는 의문의 논쟁을 발생시켰다.

결국 Prospero의 마술이 'white magic'이냐 혹은 'black magic'이냐의 차이는 마술을 사용하는 방법에 있을 것이다. 왜냐하면 Prospero의 마력은 Sycorax의 마력보다 고차원적이기 때문에 Prospero가 그의 종들에게 행사하는 마력은 타당성이 있는 바, white magic이라고 생각된다. 그러나 선과 악은 양면적인 데 사용할 수 있다. 왜냐하면 그것은 사용자에게 의존하기 때문이다. Prospero는 그의 '마술'에 의해 Ariel(It was mine art, 'When I arrived and heard thee, that made gape' The pine and let thee out (I. ii. 291-))을 구했지만 이제는 역설적으로 마술로써 Ariel에게 고통을 가하려고 위협(If thou more murmur'st, I will rend an oak / And peg thee in his knotty entrails till / Thou hast howl'd away twelve winters(I. ii. 294-5)하는 것은 아이러니하다.

또 Prospero가 원시인 Caliban을 취급하는 데도 성격의 양면성을 Caliban의 대사를 통해서 알 수 있다. Caliban도 한때는 그의 주인 Prospero에 의해 동정의 보살핌을 받았음을 알 수 있다:

> When thou can′st first,
> Thou strok′st me and made much of me
> Water with berries in ′t, and teach me how
> To name the bigger light, and how the loss,
> That burn by day and night: and then I lov′d thee
> And show′d thee all the qualities o′th′isle,
> The fresh springs, bring-pits, barren place and fertile:
> Curs′d be I that did so! (I. ii. 332-9)

Prospero는 Caliban이 배은 망덕하게 자기 딸의 정조를 유린하려고 시도한 것을 비난하면서 그의 분노를 다음과 같이 표현한다.

Abhorred slave,
Which any print of goodness wilt not take,
Being capable of all ill! I pitied thee,
Took pains to make thee speak, taught thee each hour
One thing, or other: When thou didst not, savage,
Know thine own meaning, but wouldst gabble like
A thing most brutish, I endow'd thy purposes
With words that made them known…
therefore wast thou
Deservedly confin'd into this rock,
Who hadst deserv'd more than prison. (I. ii. 351-62)

Prospero가 Caliban을 그의 동굴로 데려가서 그의 친자식처럼 양육하고 그에게 언어 교육과, 사고의 능력을 길러 주었다. 그러나 이런 동정의 행위들은 Prospero가 훗날 Caliban을 잔인하게 취급하는 역설적인 계기가 된다. 그리고 정령(精靈)들에 의해 괴로움을 당한 Caliban은 그가 당한 고통을 상세히 열거한다:

For every trifle are they set upon me:
Sometime like apes that mow and chatter at me
And after bite me, then like hedgehogs which
Lie tumbling in my bardfoot way and mount
Their pricks at my football; sometime am I
All wound with adders who with cloven tongues
Do hiss me into madness.
(I. ii. 8-14)

비록 Prospero의 분노가 타당성 있다고 하더라도 Caliban에 대한 Prospero의 징벌은 그가 옛날에 Caliban에게 친절했던 것만큼이나 사악하다. 결국 Caliban은 Prospero의 이중적 심리상태에 따라 좌우된다.

그런데 어조에 있어서 Prospero가 Ferdinand를 취급할 때는 Caliban의 그것처럼 잔인하지 않다. Prospero의 친절한 주선[38]으로 Miranda와 Ferdinand가 만날 때에 그의 신중성과 변덕성이 교차한다. Miranda와 Ferdinand는 처음 만날 때 서로를 'thing divine'(1막 2장 428)과 'Goddess'(1막 2장 421행)라 칭하며 서로에게 매료된다.

Prospero는 그들 상호간의 애정에 내심 기뻐한다. 왜냐하면 그들의 만남은 그의 계획의 일부분이기 때문이다. 그는 딸의 결혼을 조심스럽게 주선하는 아버지의 모습을 보여준다. 그러나 Miranda와 Ferdinand가 서로 사랑하는 것을 발견하고는 기뻐하는 동시에 오히려 화를 내는 양면성을 표출한다.

Mir. Sir, have pity;
I'll ve his surety.
Pro. Silence! one word more
Shall make me chide thee, if not hate thee. What!
An advocate for an imposter!
(I. ii. 475)

"쉽게 얻은 것의 가치를 소홀히 하지 않게 하기 위하여"라고 언

38 Foakes points out that, "After the shipwreck of the opening scene, Prospero's first exercise of his art is to use Ariel to lure Ferdinand to the presence of Miranda" in the *Shakespeare*, p. 148

급하지만, 우리 독자들이 주시해야 할 것은 Prospero의 난폭한 언어라 할 수 있겠다. 극 상황의 맥락 속에서 보면 이 말은 아주 극단적인 표현에 해당한다.(1막 2장 475행) Miranda와 Ariel, Caliban과 Ferdinand를 각자 만날 때마다 Prospero는 동정심과 잔인성이 순간 순간 교차함에 따라 동요한다. 3막이 시작할 때 질서와 무질서로의 반복되는 전환 운동은 climax 시점에 접근할 수록 더욱 신속해진다.

비언어적 미학 요소들이 *The Tempest*의 극 구조에 침투되어 있다는 것은 일반적으로 알려져 있었다.[39] 그러나 폭풍 장면과 Ariel의 노래를 제외하면 비언어적 요소들의 대다수가 극의 후반부에서 발생한다는 것은 거의 주지되지 않고 있다. 균형과 불균형간의 전환 운동들이 강화됨에 따라 Prospero의 상태는 비언어적 요소들 속에서 체현된다. 노래, 무용, 스펙터클과 메커니즘의 고안품들이 나오는 장면은 조화적 해결로 직행한다. 그러므로 만약 우리들이 극의 액션을 연구하지 않는다면 이 극의 액션은 설정할 수 없다.

3막 1장은 Miranda와 Ferdinand의 사랑의 고백에서 시작한다. 여기에서 Prospero는 그의 딸과 Ferdinand의 결합을 위해 마력을 행사한다. 그리고 그들은 사랑의 성실성에 깊은 감명을 받게 된다:

> Fair encounter
> Of two most affections! Heavens rain grace
> On that which breeds between 'em!
>
> (Ⅲ. i. 74-6)

---

[39] Northrop Frye, *Romance as Masque*, quoted in *Shakespeare's Romances Reconsidered*, edited by Carol McGinnis Kay and Henry E. Jacobs, pp. 11～39.

3막 1장은 연인들의 결합과 조화이며 반면에 3막 2장은 Caliban의 음모가 계획됨으로써 조화를 파괴하며 무질서로 향한다.

'this a custom with him,
I' th' afternoon to sleep: there thou mayst brain him,
Having first seized his books, or with a log
Batter his skull, or paunch him with a stake,
Or cut his wezand with thy knife. Remember
First to possess his books; for without them
He's but a sot, as I am, nor has not
One spirit to command: they all do hate him
As rootedly as I, Burn but his books.

(Ⅲ. ii. 85-95)

여기에서 Prospero를 살해하고자 하는 Caliban의 잔인성이 노출된다. 그리고 극 액션은 전장(3막 1장)의 Miranda와 Ferdinand의 결합에서 상징된 질서로부터 무질서(3막 2장)로 전환되었다. Caliban의 음모는 파괴적일 뿐만 아니라, Prospero를 살해하고 주인의 권능의 근원을 뿌리째 뽑아버리려는 시도에서 보면 인습(因習) 타파주의자에 해당한다. 결국 Caliban이 열거하는 무기가 문명사회의 그것과 비교하면 정교하지는 못하지만 이 원시적 무기들이 침략의 도구로 사용될 때는 치명적일 수밖에 없다.

다음의 3막 3장은 조난자들의 처지가 악화됨에 따라서 침울한 분위기에서부터 시작된다. Ferdinand의 수색을 위하여 섬을 배회함으로써 기진맥진한 Alonso는 실망하며, 궁신 Gonzalo는 휴식을 왕에게 권하지만 그들 일행의 약점을 찾고 있는 Sebastian과 Antonio는 Alonso의 시해를 음모한다. 이 장면의 어둡고 절망적인 분위기는 장중하고 불가사의한 음악에 의해 즉시 전환된다.

> Alon. What harmony is this? My good friends, hark!
> Gon. Marvellous sweet music!
>
> Prospero *on the top, invisible. Enter several strange Shapes, bringing in a banquet; they dance about it with gentle actions of salutations; and, invisiting the King, &c., to eat, they depart.*
>
> Alon. Give us kind keepers, heavens! What were these?
> Seb. A living drollery.
>
> (Ⅲ. iii. 18-21)

정령들이 궁중 일행들에게 환대의 무용을 하며 그들에게 먹을 음식을 제공한다. 이 무도자들의 친절한 행동들은 Gonzalo가 'Marvellous Sweet'라고 표명하는 음악에 의해 강조된다. 그리고 Alonso는 무도자들이 추는 춤의 특성을 곰곰이 생각한다 :

> I cannot too much muse
> Such shapes, such gesture and such sound, expressing,
> Although they want the use of tongue, a kind
> Of excellent dumb discourse, (Ⅲ. iii. 37-40)

이 '무언의 대화(dumb discourse)'에 의해 셰익스피어는 이 궁중인들에게 그들의 공포를 버리고 마술의 음식을 먹도록 권유하는 환경을 만들어 낸다. *The Magic Flute* (Mozart의 Opera임)에 등장하는 공포에 질린 Tamino가 그의 악기 소리에 매료된 유순한 동물들에 의해 마음이 진정될 때 이와 유사한 장면이 발생한다.[40] 극 구조의 액션에서 등장 인물뿐만 아니라 청중들에게 평화의 환경을 제시하는 경이감(驚異感)을 만드는 극적 요소(Alonso가 언급한 the 'shapes,' 'gesture'와 'sound')를 이용해야 한다.

음식(마술의 음식)이 사라질 때 환희에서 충격으로 분위기(*Thunder and lightning. Enter Ariel, like a harpy; claps his wings upon the table; and, with a quaint device, the banquet vanishes*(53).)가 전환된다.[41]

이 3막 3장은 유순한 정령들의 무도에서 Harpy새로 변장한 Ariel의 등장으로 인하여 공포의 분위기로 극 환경이 신속히 전환된다. 사라진 연회와 음악에서 천둥으로의 전환은 질서에서 무질서로 전환하는 매체들이다. 이 시점에서 Ariel이 Harpy새로 등장하는 것은 가장 적합한 인물임에 틀림없다. Ariel이 가면극 속에서 Alonso와 Sebastian, Antonio에게 'Three men of sin'(III. iii. 53)이라고 언급할 때 Ariel과 그의 동료(가면극에 등장한 인물들)들은 'minister of fate'(III. iii. 61), 'servants of destiny,' 'the powers'(III. iii. 73)라고 주장한다. 동시에 그는 Harpy새뿐만 아니라 Prospero의 대행자 Ariel로서 말하며

---

40 Northrop Frye, pp. 37-8.

41 J. R. Sutherland interpretes that, "The harpy was a fabulous monster, with a woman's face and the wings and claws of a bird, often sent by the gods to torment mortals. In Virgil's Book iii, Aeneas describes how he and his followers are driven by storms to the islands where the harpies dwell. Every time that they sit down to eat, the harpies come beating their wings and snatching at the food" in Notes to *The Tempest* (Oxford: The Clarendon Press, 1971), p. 139.

주인의 명령을 수행한다. 가면극 속의 괴상한 모양의 사람들은 무도를 하면서 등장했던 것처럼 이제는 무도를 하면서 식탁을 치우고 퇴장한다. 그리고 Ariel은 천둥 속에 사라진다. 그들을 질책한 불가사의한 환상에 의해 양심의 고통을 받은 죄인들은 절망적인 태도(3막 3장 104행)로 고통을 표출한다. 그들은 Ariel이 Harpy새로 등장했을 때, 그들의 칼을 뽑아들었으나 마력에 걸려 칼을 사용하지 못하게 된다. 그리고 그 환상이 사라진 후 괴상한 모습으로 무대를 퇴장한다. 이들의 모습은 Gonzalo의 'All three of them are desperate'(III. iii. 104)의 장면에서 알 수 있는 것처럼 결국 무질서로 종료된다.[42] 극의 외형적 구조에 주안점을 두고 있는 비평가들은 이 극의 climax를 3막 3장의 Ariel의 'three men of sin'(58-82)에 설정하였다.

그러나 만약 *The Tempest*가 대다수의 비평가들이 동의하는 것처럼 조화적 해결로 종결하려면, 3막 3장에 극의 climax를 설정할 수 없다. Prospero가 복수를 시도했거나 혹은 하지 않거나 간에 Ariel의 말의 결과는 무질서를 초래한다. Derek Traversi가 *The Last Phase*의 서문에서, "A study of such plays as *The Winter's Tale* and *The Tempest* reveals the full meaning of the commonplace assertion that poetry and drama are in Shakespeare intimately fused into the unity of 'poetic drama'."[43]라고 시어와 극의 액션의 통일에 관하여 언급한 후, *The Tempest* 구조의 climax 설정에서("Needless to say, it was not part of the artist's purpose to substantiate this objective conception of Destiny by argument; but it was his aim, inevitable and necessary, to place it in the center of his play, to allow

---

[42] Foakes, p. 157.

[43] Traversi, p. 18.

the symbolic structure elaborated through the converging action of images, plot, and character to from around it, to see if it would, in the last analysis, fit."[44] 3막 3장에 조화적 목적을 발견해야 한다는 것은 아이러니하다고 생각된다.

이 극, *The Tempest*를 형성하는 비언어적 요소들은 이와는 정반대의 결론을 초래하는 사례로, Ariel이 말을 끝낸(*He vanishes in thunder; then to soft music, enter the Shapes again, and dance, with mocks and mows, and carrying out the table*(83).) 후, 극의 분위기가 완전히 전환되었다. 이상한 모습의 인물들이 얼굴을 찡그리고 괴상한 몸짓으로 그들의 이동을 강조한다. 그들의 몸짓에 맞춰진 부드러운 음악이 유순하다면 그 불평스런 몸짓의 결과는 그와 상반된 분위기를 강조하게 된다. 음악은 교대로 액션을 보완할 수 있다. 아마 청중들은 Ariel의 퇴장 때 수반되는 폭풍의 마지막 메아리 소리를 들을 것이다. 어느 경우든 그 효과는 조화적이 될 수 없다.

공포에 사로잡힌 Alonso는 음악적 용어들로서 Ariel의 말을 설명한다:

> O, it is monstrous, monstrous !
> Methought the billows spoke and told me of it;
> The winds did sing it to me, and the thunder,
> That deep and dreadful organ - pipe, pronounc'd
> The name of Prospero: it did bass my trespass.
> Therefore my son i'th'ooze is bedded, and
> I'll seek him deeper than e'er plummet sounded
> And with him there lie mudded.

---

[44] Traversi, p. 250.

(Ⅲ. iii. 95-102)

자연의 신은 Alonso 왕을 심하게 꾸짖어 죄의 고통을 체험하게 한 것 같다. 왜냐하면 그 결과로 Alonso 왕은 공포에 떨면서 도망치고 자살을 기도한다. 비록 Prospero가 Ariel을 통해서 마음의 고통('heart's sorrow / And a clear life ensuing'(III. iii. 81-2))을 주려고 시도한다고 해도 그 결과는 분명히 정반대로 악화되었다. Ariel의 말은 폭풍과 같은 공포를 유발한다. 부언하면 Robert Egan이 성공적으로 설명한 것처럼 죄지은 세 사람들 중 유일하게 Alonso 왕만이 Ariel의 말에 의해 감동받고 회개한다. 그리고 그는 이미 깊이 뉘우치고 있었다. 비록 놀라기는 했지만 Antonio와 Sebastian은 거칠게 허풍을 떨면서 퇴장하기 때문에 근본적으로 회개한 것이 아니라고 생각한다:

Seb : But one fiend at a time
I'll fight their legion o'er
Ant : I will be thy second.
(Exeunt Sebastian and Antonio) (Ⅲ. iii. 103-4)

이 극의 Climax를 3막 3장에 설정할 수 없는 두 번째의 이유는 마력의 연회가 갑자기 전개되었다가 사라지는 것은 극 구조를 형성하는 질서로부터 무질서로의 일련의 운동일 뿐이다. 만약 Ariel의 말이 Climax에 설정된다면 특별히 다음의 가면극 장면들은 극적 활성(活性)을 상실할 것이다. 이러한 비평적 오류는 가면극이 종종 불필요한 것으로 취급되어 온 이유를 설명한다고 생각한다.

4막 1장에서 Prospero는 동정심의 순간들로부터 잔혹한 순간들로 급히 전환된다. 4막은 Miranda와 Ferdinand의 조화적 결합으로 시작한다. Ferdinand에게 그의 딸을 제공하는 Prospero는 그들 사이에 결합의 증인이 되어 달라고 하늘의 신들에게 호소한다:

> All thy vexations
> Were but my trials of thy love, and thou
> Hast strangely stood the test: here afore Heaven,
> I rafty this my rich gift. (Ⅳ. i. 5-8)

그러나 우주의 힘을 인식하는 순간에도 Prospero의 심리 상태는 변하기 시작한다.

> If thou dost break her virgin knot before
> All sanctimonious ceremonies may
> With full and holy rite be ministered,
> No sweet aspersion shall the heavens let fall
> To make this contract grow; but barren hate,
> Sour-ey'd disdain and discord shall bestrew
> The Union of your bed with weeds so loathly
> That you shall hate it both… (Ⅳ. i. 15-22)

여기서 Prospero가 Ferdinand에게 당부하는 'virginity'에 대한 강조를 G. Wilson Knight는 다음과 같이 설명한다:

> … and lastly, his kindly purpose revealed, is nevertheless careful to warn Ferdinand of the consequences of breaking Miranda's 'virginity' before the 'holy rite' of marriage, with stern hints of matrimonial discord and infertility (IV. i. 13-23) that serve

to relate our present incident to the long story of Shakespearean jealousy. Prospero is a puritanical father, warning Ferdinand, … Ferdinand answers with many assertions of his honour and almost crudely emphatic definition of true love's purity:

> The white-cold virgin snow upon my heart
> Abates the ardour of my liver. (Ⅳ. i. 55)[45]

만약 Ferdinand와 Miranda가 'all sanctimonious ceremonies'를 준수하지 아니하면 Prospero는 딸과 사위의 결혼 신방에 '불모(不毛)의 증오(憎惡)'와 '잡초(雜草)들'이 무성하기를 기원할 것이다. 그의 말이 지닌 극단성은 Leontes와 Polixenes가 화가 났을 때 했던 말들이 연상되게 한다. 그러나 Ferdinand의 "The white virgin snow upon my heart / Abates the ardour of my liver"라는 재치있는 대답에 의해 노여움이 누그러진다. Prospero는 이 연인들의 여흥을 위한 가면극을 만들었다.

Prospero는 질서의 표출을 만들기 위하여 우주의 질서와 조화의 반영으로서 가면극의 상징적, 극적 도구들을 사용한다. 풍요의 여신 Ceres는 젊은 연인들을 축복할 때 그녀의 언니 Juno가 참석하도록 청한다.

> Juno. Honour, riches, marriage-blessing
> Long continuance, and increasing,
> Hourly joys be still upon you !
> Juno sings her blessings on you.

---

[45] Knight, *The Crown of Life: Essayns in Interpretation of Shakespeare's Final Plays* (London: Methuen & Co, Ltd., 1982), p. 244.

Cer. Earth's increase, foison plenty,
Barns and garners never empty,
Vines with clust'ring bunches growing,
Plants with goodly burthen bowing;

Spring come to you at the farthest
In the very end of harvest!
Scarcity and want shall shun you;
Ceres' blessing so is on you. (IV. i. 160-72)

Ferdinand는 그들이 부르는 노래의 '조화적(調和的)' 효과에 대해서 논평한다. 이 노래는 가면극의 조화적 기능성을 달성한다. 거기다가, 만약 여신들이 듀엣으로 노래한다면 결합의 심상(心象)은 조화를 달성하는 강조점이 될 것이다.

Iris는 전원의 무도(in the country footing－138)에 추수자들과 합류함으로써 진정한 사랑의 결혼을 축하하기 위하여("to help celebrate / a contract of true love"－132 - 33) Nymphs를 초대한다. 다시 한 번 무도는 결합의 상징으로 사용된다. 결혼을 축하하는 Jacobean 가면극이 영광스러운 신혼부부가 참석한 무도에서 절정을 이룬다는 사실을 부여함으로써 셰익스피어는 Nymphs와 추수자들로 하여금 그들의 무도회에 Miranda와 Ferdinand를 끌어넣으려고 시도한 것이라 생각된다.

무도극의 전막은 언제라도 파괴의 위협을 가하는 잠재적 난폭성을 나타낸다. 무대지시(극 액션)(*Enter certain Reapers, properly habited: they join with Nymphs in a graceful dance; towards the end whereof Prospero starts suddenly, and speaks; after which to a strange, hollow, and confused noise, they heavily vanish*(138))는 무질서의 신속한 전환을 나타낸다. Prospero는

"갑자기 놀란다." — 그는 수성 같은 Caliban과 그의 공모자들의 사악한 음모를 깜박 잊었다(139-40). 음악을 덮치는 이상스러운, 공허한 소음처럼 그들의 무도가 절정에 달하였을 때 무도인들을 Prospero가 철수시키는 것은 가면극 세계의 조화에 대한 침략이다. 무도와 음악의 르네상스적 견해의 맥락에서 볼 때, Prospero의 가면극에 대한 간섭은 난폭한 행위로서 설명되어야 한다. 다음의 Ferdinand와 Miranda의 대화 속에서 우리들은 Prospero의 분노의 정도를 알 수 있겠다.

Fer. This is strange: your father's agitation:
That works him strongly.
Mir. Never till this day.
Saw I him touch'd with anger so distemper'd.
(Ⅳ. iv. 43-4)

대부분의 비평에서 Miranda와 Ferdinand의 이러한 관찰들이 충분히 고찰되지 못하고 있다. 다음의 Prospero의 유명한 대사는 예술의 특성에 대한 존경으로써 경건한 어조로 언급되고 있다. 그리고 극 구조의 증거는 이 대사가 그 인물의 분노의 맥락에서 언급되어야 한다는 것을 암시하고 있다:

You do look, my son, in a mov'd sort,
As if you were dismay'd: be careful, sir.
Our revels now are ended. These our actors,
As I foretold you, were all spirits and
Are melted into air, into thin air:

And, like the baseless fabric of this vision,
The cloud - capp'd tow'rs, the gorgeous palaces,
The solemn temples, the great globe itself,
Yea, all which it inherit, shall dissolve
And, like this insubstantial pageant faded,
Leave not a rack behaind. We are such stuff
As drams are made on, and our little life / Is rounded with a sleep.

(IV. i. 146-58)

예술의 형식을 창안하는 능력은 선과 악의 잠재력을 가진 신과 같은 지위에 Prospero를 격상시키는 것이다.[46] 그의 마술에 의해 Prospero는 자연 질서를 반영할 뿐만 아니라, 스스로 자연 질서에 역행도 할 수 있다. 또한 마술의 이원성은 그의 심리적인 성격의 극단을 설명한다. 그의 마술이 자연 질서를 반영할 때, 그것은 우주의 조화를 가진 자연 질서가 된다. *Pericles*에 등장하는 Cerimon의 마술은 그것이 자연의 힘 속에 근간을 두고 있기 때문에 인자하다. Prospero가 자기 의지의 질서를 강행할 때 우주의 자연 질서를 왜곡하는 결과를 초래한다.

이 대사에서 Prospero는 쓰라린 고통 속에서 그의 마술에 의해 질서를 강행하려는 시도들이 헛되이 끝났다는 것을 깨닫고 반응한다. 아무리 아름답고 정교하다고 해도 모든 형식은 궁극에 가서는 쇠퇴해야 되는 것이다. 가면극 속에는 James 왕의 본질적인 신앙이

---

46 Foakes insists that "Instead of an oracles, miracles, or appearances of gods, this play in Prospero a contrlooer who exercises through his magic a power like that of heaven" in *Shakespeare*, p. 145, and *The Crown of Life*, pp. 233-4.

내재되어 있기 때문에 이 장면을 정치적인 도전으로 설명하지 않을 수 없을 것이다. "The cloud-capp'd two'rs, the grogeous palaces, / The solemn temples"는 Willam Alexander의 *The Tragedy of Darious*에 나오는 구절로 생각된다.[47] 셰익스피어는 진리를 충분히 포용할 수 있는 마술의 능력을 의심한다. Prospero의 심리 상태의 악화는 자연질서에 자기 의지의 형식을 부여하려는 권좌에 앉아 있는 사람들에 대한 경고이다.

Prospero는 그의 설레는 마음("to still" his "beating mind" (163))을 달래기 위하여 심약("in weakness"(158))한 마음으로 동굴로 돌아간다. 그러나 그의 강력한 분노는 그의 정령들(*A noise of hunters heard. Enter divers Spirits, in shape of dogs and hounds, hunting them about,* Prosepro *and* Ariel *setting them on*)을 Caliban과 Stephane, Trinculo에 보낼 때 다시 환원된다.

인간이 짐승에 의해 사냥되는 자연 질서의 역행은 이 극본의 가장 난폭한 순간들 중의 하나이다. 위험스럽게 극본을 유지하고 있는 이 극본은 혼돈 상태로 들어가려고 한다. Egan이 언급했던 것처럼 Prospero는 세계를 개혁하는 수단으로써 그의 마력을 사용하는 것을 포기하고, 대신 복수의 사탄적인 체현을 하려고 위협한다.[48]

극 구조에서 체현된 질서에서 무질서로의 동요는 Prospero의 성격

---

47 Sutherland insists that, "These famous lines appear to owe something to a passage in *The Tragedy of* Darius, by William Alexander, Carl Stering, which was published in 1603 in Note to *The Tempest*, p. 144."

48 *Drama Within Drama: Shakespeare's Sense of His Art in "King Lear", "The Winter's Tale," and "The Tempest"* (New York: Columbia Unversity Press, 1975), p. 110.

속에 인격화되어 있었다. 그가 Miranda, Ariel, Caliban과 Ferdindan를 처음 만날 때 동정심과 잔인성이 교차되는 것을 볼 수 있다. 3막, 4막에서도 이러한 동요들이 점점 고조되어 드디어 Ariel이 그 주인의 인간적인 성품에 호소하기 위하여 Prospero와 대좌하는 5막의 시점까지 그 강도가 고조된다. 이때 5막 1장에서 Ariel이 Alonso 왕과 그의 일행에 대해서 보고하며, Prospero에게 자비를 촉구한다.

> Ariel. Your charm so strongly works'em
> That if you know beheld them, your affections
> Would become tender.
> Pro. Dost thou think so, spirit ?
> Ariel. Mine would, sir, were I human.
> Pros. And mine shall.
> (V. i. 17-20)

극 구조의 분석에 나타낸 것처럼 Prospero가 그의 '분노(fury)'와 그의 '고매한 이성(nobler reason)' 간의 대위적 동기들 중의 하나를 선택해야 하는 순간 이 시점에 이 극 구조의 전환점이 형성된다. 다음의 대사가 이 극의 climax이다:

> Hast thou, which art but air, a touch, a feeling
> Of their afflications, and shall not myself,
> One of their kind, that relish all as sharply,
> Passion as they, be kindler mov'ed than thou art ?
> Though with their high wrongs I am struck to th'quick,
> Yet with my nobler reason 'gainst my fury
> Do I take part: the rarer action is

In virtue than in vengeance: they being penitent,
The sole drift of my purpose doth extent
Not a frown further. (V. i. 20-9)

복수보다는 덕을 택함으로써[49] Prospero는 극의 조화적 해결로 향해 이 극의 액션을 진행시킨다.

Go release them, Ariel:
My charms I'll break, their sense I'll restore,
And they shall be themselves. (V. i. 30-2)

Prospero는 약속 이행을 위하여 그의 마력의 대행자들을 호출(呼出)해야 한다.

"Ye elves of hills"로부터 시작하는 Prospero의 대사는 폭풍을 만들어낸 마술의 최후 주문이다.

I have bedimm'd
The nontide sun, call'd forth the mutinous winds,
And 'twixt the green sea and the azur'd vault
Set roaring war: to the dread rattling thunder
Have I given fire and rifted Jove's stout oak
With his own bolt; the strong-bas'd promontory
Have I made shake and by the spurs pluck'd up
The pine and cedar; gaves at my command

---

49 Kermode points out that "Here 'pardon' would be the obvious word, rather than 'virtue' in his notes to *The Tempest*" ed: *The Arden Shakespeare* (London: Methuen and Co. Ltd., 1977), p. 144.

> Have wak'd their sleepers, op'd, and let 'em forth
> By my so potent art, But this rough magic
> I here abjure… (Ⅵ. i. 41-51)

이 시점에서 하늘의 장중한 음악이 조화적으로 이 극을 해결한다. 그런데 여기의 "Ye elves of hills, brook, standing lakes, and groves… By my so potent art"(5막 1장 33-55행)은 *Ovid's Metamorphoses*, vii. 197-206에 나오는 구절을 Arthur Golding이 번역한 것인데 이를 셰익스피어가 인용한 것으로 J. R. Sutherland가 *The Tempest*의 주(註)에서 지적하고 있다.[50] Prospero는 이제 그의 마술(*Solemn music.*(장중한 음악) *Here enters Ariel before: then* Alonso, *with a fantastic gesture, attended by* Adrian *and* Francisco*: they all enter the circle which* Prospero *had made, and there stand chamed; which* Prospero *observing, speaks :*)을 버린다. 장중한 음악이 연주될 때 광적인 Alonso 왕과 그의 궁신 일행들이 'magic circle'로 이끌리어 들어와서 마술에 걸린 채로 서 있다. 음악이 연주되는 동안 Prospero는 Alonso와 궁신 일행들에게 명쾌한 이성이 되돌아올 때, 그들의 이성의 회복 과정을 언급한다.

이러한 조화적 형식의 효과는 무시되어서는 안 된다. '마력의 원' 속으로의 운동은 우주 질서의 상징적 회귀일 뿐만 아니라 실제적인 회귀이다. 극의 조화적 해결은 이제 가능하다.

이 극 *The Tempest*의 climax 설정에 대한 비평적 논쟁은, 어떤 비평가들은 극본의 시어에 그들의 결론을 두었기 때문에 발생하였다. 극 액션의 맥락에서는 Ariels의 '죄지은 세 사람'이란 대사에 이 극

---

[50] Sutherland, p. 147.

의 전환점을 설정할 수 없다. 마지막으로 Prospero가 '복수(復讐)'보다는 '덕(德)'을 택하는 순간까지는 액션은 질서에서 무질서로 반복하여 전진, 후퇴의 운동을 계속한다. 복수보다는 덕을 선택하는(The rarer action is / In vertue than in vengeance :(5막 1장 1-3행)) Prospero의 의지에 의하여 이 극을 조화적 해결(resolution)로 향하게 하다. 이와 같이 극 액션의 분석은 극 의미를 명확하게 밝혀준다 할 수 있겠다.

결국 셰익스피어 후기 극들의 올바른 극 구조의 이해는 이 로만스 극본들 속에 내재하고 있는 미학 요소들, 즉 언어 요소와 비언어 요소들(무도와 음악)과 대사와 액션의 통합적 확대된 심상의 표출과 무대미학이 시사하는 상징을 통하여 가능함을 필자는 발견하였다.

제 4 장 결 론

제임스 왕 치세 초기는 영국 미학 예술의 대륙화의 유입 시기라 할 수 있다. 이때 새로운 불란서 예술 양식과 이태리 예술 양식이 영국에 유입됨으로써 스튜어트 왕가의 사치와 낭비 풍조를 조장하였다. 제임스 왕조의 풍부한 국고는 왕이 궁신들에게 많은 작위의 하사를 할 수 있게 하였으며, 그래서 궁신들의 경제적 안정을 도모하는데 기여함이 있었다. 따라서 스튜어트 왕가의 궁신들은 영국 최초의 궁중 예술형식, 즉 가면극을 관람하기 위하여 궁중 대연회장에 운집하게 되었다. 셰익스피어 역시 그 궁중 극예술 공연과 연회행사에 참석함으로써 그의 극작 환경(후기극들)에 지대한 영향을 받은 것으로 사료된다. 따라서 셰익스피어 후기 극본들에는 미학적 요소들이 명시적으로 내재되어 있었다. 특히 미학의 비언어적 요소들(무도와 음악)이 가면극 형식으로 그의 후기 극본들 속에 산재되어 있음을 발견하였다.

필자가 연구한 셰익스피어 후기 극 속에 나타난 미학, 특히 극 구조의 미학적 분석은 제2장, 제3장의 각 장에서 소결 처리하였음으로 여기에서는 총괄적으로 언급하고자 한다.

의미로서의 구조에서는 죤슨의 가면극 『오베런』의 상호관련된 구조적 의미, 즉 비언어적 요소들은 극 의미를 전달 가능하게 할 뿐만 아니라 시적 상징의 확대된 심상으로서 극 액션을 가능하게 하였다. 또, 극 구조의 총체성은 극의 시공 속에 시적 의도의 사실적 실현으로 해석될 수 있는 가능성이 시사되었다. 『태풍』에 나오는 장중한 음악은 프로스페로가 설정한 마술의 원 속으로 광란한 알론소 왕과 그의 일행들을 인도하는 극적 기능을 하였다. 즉 마력의 원 속으로 이동은 우주질서의 상징적 회귀일 뿐만 아니라 사실적 회귀의 의미로서 극의 조화적 대단원을 가능하게 함이 시사되었다.

필자의 시각은 셰익스피어 후기 극들을 이해하기 위하여 가면극 형식의 연구가 선행되어야 한다는 것이다. 가면극은 무도, 음악, 스펙터클의 사용을 위한 모형이 필요하다. 특히 가면극은 미학・철학적 환경의 소산이다. 따라서 셰익스피어 후기 극에 있어서 미학적 요소들의 소홀은 극 해석의 오류를 유발할 수 있다고 필자는 생각한다.

제 2 부

『템페스트』의 원문주해

『템페스트』 해설

1623년 John Heminge와 Henry Condell이 셰익스피어의 동료 배우들의 희곡들을 수집하여 『작품집』을 발행하였을 때, 그들은 *The Tempest*를 이 책의 맨 첫 자리에 배치하였다. 그러나 이 극본을 그의 최초의 극본이었다고 믿는 사람은 없다. 그 극본은 맨 마지막에 쓰여진 극들 중의 한 작품이다. 그것을 Folio판의 첫 순서에 배열한 이유는 그 작품이 대중의 기억에 아직도 생생하였다는 이유였다. 그것은 1611년에 후기 극들이 지닌 문체의 모든 흔적을 지녔을 뿐만 아니라 그의 후기 극본들 즉, *Pericles*, *Cymbeline*, 그리고 *The Winter's Tale*과 공통점이 너무 많다는 사실을 두고라도 1611년에 출간 날짜를 확실히 고정하는 보다 특별한 몇 가지 이유들이 있다.

첫째, 이 극본에 대한 최초기의 언급은 *The Account Books of Revels Office*에서 찾아볼 수 있다. '폭풍'이라고 부르는 이 극본은 1611년 만성제날 밤에 James 1세 어전에서 공연되었다. 그것은 James 1세의 딸 Elizabeth 공주와 Palatine Elector 왕자 Frederick과의 약혼식을 기념하기 위하여 궁정 축하연의 일부로서 1612~13년 사이의 겨울 동안 다시 공연되었다.

둘째, 1609년 여름에 Virginia로 출항한 함대가 서인도제도 먼 바다에서 태풍을 만났다. The Sea-Venture호의 Sir George Somers의 기함이 폭풍을 만나 Bermuda 해안으로 떠밀려 순식간에 두 개의 바위 사이에 갇혀 난파되었다. 그러나 승무원들은 운좋게도 탈출하였다. *The Tempest*에서처럼 나머지 함대들은 파선을 면했다. 다음해 5월(1610년)까지 난파선의 수부들은 그 섬에 자라는 삼목들을 이용하여 두 척의 배를 건조하였다. 그들은 이 배들을 타고 Virginia에 가까스로 도착하였다. 그곳으로부터 그들 수부들의 모험의 뉴스가 영국으로 전달되었다. 이 난파에 대한 여러 가지 설명들이 1610년경에 인쇄물로 출간되었다. 그래서 셰익스피어는 그의 극본을 집필할 때 이 조난의 이야기들에 분명히 도움을 받았다고 생각된다. 그러므로 *The Tempest*는 이 기사들을 사용한 어떤 초기의 책이 없었다면 1610년보다 더 일찍 출간될 수 없었을 것이다.

셋째, 상류사회 생활의 어떤 특정한 결혼을 위하여 쓰여졌던 것으로 널리 수용되고 있는 4막 1장의 가면극이 만약 독자들이 그것이 원래 그 결혼을 목적으로 집필되었다는 것을 확신할 수 있으면 이 극본의 출간 날짜를 정하는 데 매우 중요한 도움이 될 것이다. 이 극본이 1611년 황실 결혼식의 축제의 일부로서 궁중에서 공연된 사실에 비추어 볼 때 이 가면극은 Elizabeth 공주와 그녀의 신랑을 위하여 특별히 집필되었다는 강력한 근거가 있다 할 수 있다. 그러나 설혹 그 가면극이 왕의 딸을 위하여 집필되었다는 증거가 있다 하더라도, 또 그것이 전기 공연으로부터 그녀를 위하여 되풀이하여 공연되지 않았다고 해도, 이 가면극을 집필한 날짜를 추정할 수 있었지만 이 극본 자체의 집필 날짜는 추정할 수 없었을 것이다. 사실 *The Tempest*는 궁정에서의 공연을 위하여 개정되었을 가능성이 있다. 만약 그러하다면 우리가 가지고 있는 이 극본은 확실히 개정판이거나, 또는 원본이 아닐 가능성이 있다고 하겠다.

그러나 이 극본이 50세에 달하는 극작가(인생과 극본집필의 경험에 있어서 원숙한)에 의하여, 셰익스피어의 생애 말기에 쓰여졌다는 것은 틀림없다고 할 수 있다.

극의 플롯

1막 1장 : 배의 갑판 위에서의 소란스런 장면과 더불어 *The Tempest*의 막이 열린다. 배를 바다로 향하게 하려는 수부들의 필사적 노력에도 불구하고 폭풍우가 그 배를 육지 쪽으로 몰고 간다. Alonso, Sebastian, Antonio, Ferdinand, Gonzalo는 모두 갑판 위로 나온다. 이 장은 그 배의 침몰로 끝난다.

1막 2장 : 이 장(전체 극 길이의 4분의 1에 달하는)은 4부분으로 나누어진다. 1행부터 186행까지는 Prospero와 Miranda 두 사람만이 무대에 등장하며, Prospero는 그의 딸 Miranda에게

Milan에서의 그의 과거 인생에 대해 설명해 준다. 그때 Miranda는 아버지의 마술의 주문에 의해 잠에 빠져든다(189). Prospero는 이제 친근한 정령 Ariel을 불러내고, Ariel은 어떻게 그가 Prospero의 명령에 의해 모든 사람들을 배의 갑판에서 괴롭혔으며 수부들을 갑판 아래에 잠재운 채 그 배를 안전하게 정박시켜 놓았는지를 보고한다. 그는 Alonso와 나머지 사람들은 안전하게 해안가로 데려왔으며 '그 섬 주변에' 그들을 흩어 두었다. 이제 Ariel은 주인을 위해 할 일을 충분히 했다고 생각하지만, Prospero는 자신이 Ariel에게 어떻게 자유를 주었는지를 상기시키고서 만약 반항하면 자유를 박탈하겠다고 위협한다. Ariel은 Prospero의 명령을 수행하기 위해 신속히 퇴장한다(187-304). Prospero는 Miranda를 깨워서 그가 그곳에 상륙했을 때 그 섬에 살고 있는 것을 발견한 마녀 Sycorax의 아들인 Caliban을 만나러 간다. Caliban은 그의 동굴에서 나와서, 장작을 운반하라고 시키며 만약 거절하면 육체적 고통으로 그를 위협한 Prospero에게 저주를 퍼붓는다. Caliban은 투덜대며 퇴장한다(305-74). Ariel은 연주하고 노래하며 재등장한다. 그 난파선에서 유일한 생존자라고 스스로 확신하고 있는 왕자 Ferdinand가 그의 뒤를 따라 등장한다. Miranda는 최초로 만난 젊은이를 보고 감탄한다. 그 둘은 열렬히 대화를 나눈다. 이는 그 둘이 사랑에 빠지기를 희망하면서 그들을 함께 데려온 Prospero를 기쁘게 하지만 그는 당분간 그 감정을 숨기고 Ferdinand에게 엄격하게 말한다. Ferdinand는 칼을 뽑으려 하지만 Prospero의 마법에 의해 제지당하고 한 죄수로 전락한다(375-497).

2막 1장 : 그 섬의 또 다른 부분에서는 Alonso가 아들을 잃고 애통해하고 있다. Gonzalo는 그를 위로하려고 애쓰지만 Antonio와 Sebastian은 무정하게도 농담을 하고 있다. Ariel이 나타나 Alonso, Gonzalo 및 다른 영주들에게 마법을 걸어 잠들게 한다. Antonio와 Sebastian만이 깨어 있다. Antonio는 잠자고 있는 왕을 죽이자는 잔인한 음모를 제안한다. Antonio는 자신이 Alonso를 살해할 때, Sebastian에게 잠자는 왕을 공격하라고 설득했다. 그때 Ariel은 '보이지 않게' 다시 나타나 잠든 사람들을 깨운다. 적어도 당분간 Alonso는 안전하다.

2막 2장 : 장작을 나르는 Caliban은 Trinculo를 만나게 되고, 그에게 고통을 가하기 위해 Prospero가 보낸 정령(精靈)이라고 믿고서, 앞으로 푹 꼬꾸라진다. 폭풍우가 불어닥치자 Trinculo는 Caliban의 망토 밑으로 피신한다. Stephano가 만취해서 노래하며 흐느적거릴 때 그 둘은 함께 땅에 누워 있다. Stephano는 Caliban에게 병에서 술을 한 모금 건넨다. 그를 신이라고 여기며 Caliban은 그에게 기꺼이 봉사한다.

3막 1장 : Miranda와 Ferdinand(이제 Prospero를 위해 장작을 쌓고 있는) 간의 사랑의 장면. 그는 Miranda에게 그의 사랑을 고백한다. 그녀는 솔직하게 '당신이 나와 결혼하면 나는 당신의 아내예요' 라고 그에게 말한다. Prospero는 뒤에서 만족스럽게 지켜본다.

3막 2장 : Caliban, Stephano, Trinculo는 여전히 술을 마시고 있다. Caliban은 이제 그의 주인에게 복수할 기회를 엿보고, Stephano에게 Prospero가 잠든 사이에 그의 골통을 깨부수어서 그 섬의 왕이 되어 Miranda와 결혼할 수 있도록 Prospero의 오두막으로 안내해 줄 수 있다고 말한다. 이번에는 이 모든 이야기를 다 듣고 있었던 Ariel이 그의 북과 피리 소리로 그 음모자들을 쫓아버린다.

3막 3장 : Ferdinand를 찾아 헤매느라 지친 Alonso와 그의 무리들은 장엄한 음악을 들으며, 연회장에서의 이상한 형상들을 보게 된다. 그들이 그 음식에 손을 대기도 전에 그 연회(Prospero의 또 다른 마법 속임수)는 사라진다. Ariel은 그 '세 사람에게 그들의 죄'를 입증한다. Alonso는 혼비백산하여 달아나고, Antonio와 Sebastian이 그 뒤를 따른다. 그 세 사람 모두는 Prospero의 마법에 걸려 있다.

4막 1장 : 이제 Prospero는 공식적으로 딸을 Ferdinand에게 인도하고 또 한번 Ariel과 그의 동료 정령들의 작품인 가면무도회를 열어 그들을 기쁘게 한다. 갑자기 그는, 그가 알고 있듯이, 그를 살해하려고 계획을 진행중인 Caliban과 공모자들을 기억하게 된다. Ariel은 잠시 그들이 가시밭길에서 춤추도록

하고 나서 마침내 더러운 웅덩이에 던져 넣었다. 이제 그들이 옷이 젖은 채 등장한다. Caliban은 Prospero가 살해되기를 조바심내지만, Stephano와 Trinculo는 Prospero가 Ariel로 하여금 오두막 바깥의 줄에 매달아 놓으라고 시킨 트라이플을 훔치려고 시간을 허비하고 있다. 마침내 사냥개의 모습으로 바뀐 Prospero의 정령들은 Prospero와 Ariel의 부추김에 의해 그들을 무대 주변으로 몰아댄다.

5막 1장 : 지팡이를 가지고 Prospero는 땅에다 마법의 원을 그린다. Alonso와 그의 무리들은 그 원 안으로 들어와서 마법에 걸린 채 서있다. Prospero는 이제 그들에게 한가하게 이야기를 걸 여유가 생긴다. 그는 자신이 누구인지를 밝히고, 지난 몇 시간 동안 무슨 일이 일어난 것인지를 설명한다. 드디어 그는 그의 오두막을 가리고 있는 장막을 당기자 Ferdinand와 Miranda가 함께 장기를 두고 있는 것이 발견된다. Alonso와 Prospero는 자식들의 사랑으로 인해 화해한다. Antonio와 Sebastian은 엄히 용서받거나, 혹은 더 이상의 처벌이 가해지지 않는다. Prospero의 정령들에 의해 철저히 고문당한 Caliban과 그의 동료들은 치욕스럽게 내쫓기고, 마침내 Ariel은 해방된다. 다음날 모든 사람들은 Prospero와 함께 나폴리로 향해 항해할 것이며, 거기서 Ferdinand와 Miranda의 결혼식이 마땅히 엄숙하게 치러질 것이다.

DRAMATIS PERSONAE

ALONSO, King of Naples.

SEBASTIAN, his Brother.

PROSPERO, the right Duke of Milan.

ANTONIO, his Brother, the usurping Duke of Milan.

FERDINAND, Son to the King of Naples.

GONZALO, and honest old Counsellor.

ADRIAN,
FRANCISCO, } Lords.

CALIBAN, a savage and deformed Slave.

TRINCULO, a Jester.

STEPHANO, a drunken Butler

Master of s Ship, Boatswain, Mariners.

MIRANDA, Daughter to Prospero.

ARIEL, an airy Spirit.

IRIS,
CERES,
JUNO,
Nymphs,
Reapers, } presented by Spirits.

Other Spirits attending on Prospero.

SCENE—*The Sea, with a Ship; afterwards an Island.*

Act One

Scene One

ON A SHIP AT SEA. A TEMPESTUOUS NOISE OF THUNDER AND LIGHTNING HEARD.

Enter a Shipmaster *and a* Boatswain *severally.*

Master. Boatswain!

Boatswain. Here, master: what cheer?

Master. Good, speak to the mariners: fall to't, yarely, or we run ourselves aground: bestir, bestir. [*Exit.*

Enter Mariners.

Boatswain. Heigh, my hearts! cheerly, cheerly, my hearts! yare, yare! Take in the topsail. Tend to the master's whistle. Blow, till thou burst thy wind, if room enough!

Enter ALOSO, SEBASTIAN, ANTONIO, FERDINAND, GONZALO, *and others.*

Alonso. Good boatswain, have care. Where's the master? Play the men.

---

3 **Good** : good sir (vocative) *[N]*. **yarely** : briskly. 5 **cheerly** : be cheerful, do your work heartily. **my hearts** : cf. my hearties. 6 **yare!** : quick! **Tend** : attent to. 7 **if room enough** : so long as we have sea-room. *[N]*. 9 **Play the men** : act like (brave) men. *[N]*.

Boatswain. I pray now, keep below.

Antonio. Where is the master, boatswain?

Boatswain. Do you not hear him? You mar our labour: keep your cabins: you do assist the storm.

Gonzalo. Nay, good, be patient.

Boatswain. When the sea is. Hence! What cares these roarers for the name of king? To cabin: silence! trouble us not.

Gonzalo. Good, yet remember whom thou hast aboard.

Boatswain. None that I more love than myself. You are a counsellor; if you can command these elements to silence, and work the peace of the present, we will not hand a rope more; use your authority: if you can—not, give thanks you have lived so long, and make your—self ready in your cabin for the mischance of the hour, if it so hap. Cheerly, good hearts! Out of our way, I say. [*Exit.*

Gonzalo. I have great comfort from this fellow: me—thinks he hath no drowning mark upon him; his complexion is perfect gallows. Stand fast, good Fate, to his hanging: make the rope of his destiny our cable, for our own doth little advantage. If he be not born to be hanged, our case is miserable. [*Exeunt.*

Re-enter Boatswain.

Boatswain. Down with the topmast! yare! lower, lower! Bring her to try with main-course. [*A cry within.*] A plague upon this howling! they are louder than the weather or our office.

Re-enter SEBASTIAN, ANTONIO, *and* GONZALO.

Yet again! what do you here? Shall we give o'er and drown?

---

18 **Good** : cf. I . 3. 22 **hand** : handle. 28 **complexion** : aspect. *[N].* 31 **advantage** : (verb) prove beneficial. 34 **Bring her to try with main-course** : bring the ship clase into the wind with only the mainsail set ('try' = 'lie to', asil close to the wind). 35 **they** : the passengers below. 36 **office** : function, job. *[N].*

Have you a mind to sink?
Sebastian. A pox o' your throat, you bawling, blasphemous, incharitable dog!
Boatswain. Work you then.
Antonio. Hang, cur! hang, you whoreson, insolent noisemaker! We are less afraid to be drowned than thou art.
Gonzalo. I'll warrant him for drowning; though the ship were no stronger than a nutshell.
Boatswain. Lay her a-hold, a-hold! set her two courses off to sea again; lay her off.

Enter Mariners, *wet.*

Mariners. All lost! to prayers, to prayers! all lost! [*Exeunt.*
Boatswain. What, must our mouths be cold?
Gonzalo. The king and prince at prayers! let's assist them,
For our case is as theirs.
Sebastian. I'm out of patience.
Antonio. We are merely cheated of our lives by drunkards:
This wide-chapp'd rascal—would thou mightst lie drowning,
The washing of ten tides!
Gonzalo. He'll be hang'd yet,
Though every drop of water swear against it,
And gape at widest to glut him.
[*A confused noise within*:—'Mercy on us!'—
'We split, we split!'—'Farewell, my wife and children!'—
'Farewell, brother!'—'We split, we split, we split!']

---

44 **I'll warrant . . . drowning** : I'll guarantee he won't drown. 46 **Lay her a-hold** : bring her into the wind. **her two courses** : i.e. the foresail and the mainsail. *[N].* 47 **lay her off** : steer her away from the shore. 49 **must our mouths be cold?** : must we be drowned? *[N].* 52 **merely** : absolutely. 53 **wide-chapped** : wide-jawed. *[N].* 54 **The washing . . . tides** : till ten tides have washed over you. *[N].* 56 **glut** : swallow greedily.

Antonio. Let's all sink with the king. [*Exit.*

Sebastian. Let's take leave of him. [*Exit.*

Gonzalo. Now would I give a thousand furlongs of sea for an acre of barren ground, long heath, brown furze, any thing. The wills above be done! but I would faindie a dry death. [*Exit.*

---

62 **long heath** : heather. *[N]*. 62–3 **any thing** : i.e. however barren. *[N]*.

Scene Two

THE ISLAND: BEFORE THE CELL OF PROSPERO.

Enter PROSPERO *and* MIRANDA

Miranda. If by your art, my dearest father, you have
put the wild waters in this roar, allay them.
The sky, it seems, would pour down stinking pitch,
But that the sea, mounting to the welkin's cheek,
Dashes the fire out. O, I have suffered
With those that I saw suffer: a brave vessel,
Who had, no doubt, some noble creature in her,
Dash'd all to pieces. O, the cry did knock
Against my very heart. Poor souls, they perish'd.
Had I been any god of power, I would
Have sunk the sea within the earth or ere
It should the good ship so have swallow'd and
The fraughting souls within her.
Prospero. Be collected:
No more amazement: tell your piteous heart
There's no harm done.
Miranda. O, woe the day!
Prospero. No harm.
I have done nothing but in care of thee,
Of thee, my dear one, thee, my daughter, who
Art ignorant of what thou art, nought knowing
Of whence I am, nor that I am more better
Than Prospero, master of a full poor cell,

---

4 **welkin's** : siy's. 6 **brave** : gallant. 11 **or e'er** : before. 13 **fraughting** : forming a freight, or cargo. **Be collected** : compose yourself. 14 **piteous** : pitiful *[N]*. 19 **nor that** : and not knowing that. *[N]*. 20 **full** : very.

And thy no greater father.
Miranda. More to know
Did never meddle with my thoughts.
Prospero. 'Tis time
I should inform thee farther. Lend thy hand,
And pluck my magic garment from me.—So:
[*Lays down his mantle.*
Lie there, my art.—Wipe thou thine eyes; have comfort.
The direful spectacle of the wreck, which touch'd
The very virtue of compassion in thee,
I have with such provision in mine art
So safely ordered that there is no soul—
No, not so much perdition as an hair
Betid to any creature in the vessel
Which thou heard'st cry, which thou saw'st sink. Sit down;
For thou must now know further.
Miranda. You have often
Begun to tell me what I am, but stopp'd
And left me to a bootless inquisition,
Concluding 'Stay: not yet.'
Prospero. The hour's now come;
The very minute bids thee ope thine ear;
Obey and be attentive. Canst thou remember
A time before we came unto this cell?
I do not think thou canst, for then thou wast not
Out three years old.
Miranda. Certainly, sir, I can.
Prospero. By what? by any other house or person?

---

21 **thy no greater father** : nothing grander than your father, i.e. not a Duke. 22 **meddle with** : ningle with, engage. 27 **virtue** : soul, essence. 28 **provision** : preparation beforehand. 29 **no soul** : no one (hurt). *[N].* 30 **perdition** : loss. *[N].* 31 **Betid** : happened. 35 **bootless inquisition** : unavailing inquiry. 41 **Out** : fully.

Of any thing the image tell me that
Hath kept with thy remembrance.
Miranda. 'Tis far off
And rather like a dream than an assurance
That my remembrance warrants. Had I not
Four or five women once that tended me?
Prospero. Thou hadst, and more, Miranda. But how is it
That this lives in thy mind? What seest thou else
In the dark backward and abysm of time?
If thou remember'st aught ere thou camest here,
How thou camest here thou mayst.
Miranda. But that I do not.
Prospero. Twelve year since, Miranda, twelve year since,
Thy father was the Duke of Milan and a prince of power.
Miranda. Sir, are not you my father?
Prospero. Thy mother was a piece of virtue, and
She said thou wast my daughter; and thy father
Was Duke of Milan; and thou his only heir
And princess no worse issued.
Miranda. O the heavens!
What foul play had we, that we came from thence?
Or blessed was't we did?
Prospero. Both, both, my girl:
By foul play, as thou say'st, were we heaved thence,
But blessedly holp hither.
Miranda. O, my heart bleeds
To think o' the teen that I have turn'd you to,

---

46 **remembrance warrants** : memory can vouch for. 47 **tended** : looked after (or, perhaps, 'attended', i.e. waited upon as servants). 56 **piece** : example. 59 **issued** : born. 61 **Or blessed . . . did?** : was it a blessing (in disguise) that we did? 62 **heav'd** : removed, carried away. 63 **holp** : helped. 64 **teen** : sorrow.

Which is from my remembrance! Please you, farther.
Prospero. My brother and thy uncle, call'd Antonio—
I pray thee, mark me—that a brother should
Be so perfidious!—he whom next thyself
Of all the world I loved and to him put
The manage of my state; as at that time
Through all the signories it was the first
And Prospero the prime duke, being so reputed
In dignity, and for the liberal arts
without a parallel; those being all my study,
The government I cast upon my brother
And to my state grew stranger, being transported
And rapt in secret studies. Thy false uncle—
Dost thou attent me?
Miranda. Sir, most heedfully.
Prospero. Being once perfected how to grant suits,
How to deny them, who to advance and who
To trash for over-topping, new created
The creatures that were mine, I say, or changed 'em,
Or else new form'd 'em; having both the key
Of officer and office, set all hearts i' the state
To what tune pleased his ear; that now he was
The ivy which had hid my princely trunk,
And suck'd my verdure out on't. Thou attend'st not.
Miranda. O, good sir, I do.

---

65 **from my remembrance** : beyond my recollection. **Please you further** : tell me more, please. 70 **manage** : control (of a horse), administration. 71 **signiories** : domains. **it** : my state, i.e. Milan was the first (chief) of all states (in Italy) and Prospero first among dukes. *[N].* 76 **transported** : carried away. 79 **Being once perfected** : having once thoroughly learnt.

81 **To trash for over-topping** : to check if he was going ahead of the rest. *[N].* 82 **creatures** : dependants. 85 **that** : so that. 87 **verdure** : sap, vigour. **on't** : of it.

Prospero. I pray thee, mark me.
I, thus neglecting worldly ends, all dedicated
To closeness and the bettering of my mind
With that which, but by being so retired,
O'er-prized all popular rate, in my false brother
Awaked an evil nature; and my trust,
Like a good parent, did beget of him
A falsehood in its contrary as great
As my trust was; which had indeed no limit,
A confidence sans bound. He being thus lorded,
Not only with what my revenue yielded,
But what my power might else exact, like one
Who having into truth, by telling of it,
Made such a sinner of his memory,
To credit his own lie, he did believe
He was indeed the duke; out o' the substitution
And executing the outward face of royalty,
With all prerogative: hence his ambition growing—
Dost thou hear?
Miranda. Your tale, sir, would cure deafness.
Prospero. To have no screen between this part he play'd
And him he play'd it for, he needs will be
Absolute Milan. Me, poor man, my library
Was dukedom large enough: of temporal royalties
He thinks me now incapable; confederates—

---

90 **closeness** : retirement, solitude. 91 **that** : i.e. study. **but by . . . retir'd** : but for the fact that it involves so much withdrawal from public affairs. 92 **O'erpriz'd all popular rate** : was worth more than the esteem of the people(i.e. popularity). 94 **of him** : in him. *[N].* 97 **sans** : without. **lorded** : ennobled. 99 **what . . . else** : (with) whatever else my power might. 102 **To** : as to. *[N].* 103 **out o' the substitution** : in consequence of having taken my place.

109 **Absolute Milan** : the actual Duke of Milan (but in I. 110 **temporal royalties** : worldly kingdom. 111 **confederates** : makes a bargain.

So dry he was for sway—wi' the King of Naples
To give him annual tribute, do him homage,
Subject his coronet to his crown and bend
The dukedom yet unbow'd—alas, poor Milan!—
To most ignoble stooping.
Miranda. O the heavens!
Prospero. Mark his condition and the event; then tell me
If this might be a brother.
Miranda. I should sin
To think but nobly of my grandmother:
Good wombs have borne bad sons.
Prospero. Now the condition.
The King of Naples, being an enemy
To me inveterate, hearkens my brother's suit;
Which was, that he, in lieu o' the premises
Of homage and I know not how much tribute,
Should presently extirpate me and mine
Out of the dukedom and confer fair Milan
With all the honours on my brother: whereon,
A treacherous army levied, one midnight
Fated to the purpose did Antonio open
The gates of Milan, and, i' the dead of darkness,
The ministers for the purpose hurried thence
Me and thy crying self.
Miranda. Alack, for pity!
I, not remembering how I cried out then,
Will cry it o'er again: it is a hint
That wrings mine eyes to't.

---

112 **dry . . . for sway** : thirsting for sovereign power. 117 **his condition and the event** : the terms he made and what happened. 118 **If this . . . brother** : i.e. if this is the sort of conduct you would expect of a brother. 119 **but** : except, other than. 125 **presently** : immediately. 128 **levied** : (having been) levied.

Prospero. Hear a little further
And then I'll bring thee to the present business
Which now's upon's; without the which this story
Were most impertinent.
Miranda. Wherefore did they not
That hour destroy us?
Prospero. Well demanded, wench:
My tale provokes that question. Dear, they durst not,
So dear the love my people bore me, nor set
A mark so bloody on the business, but
With colours fairer painted their foul ends.
In few, they hurried us aboard a bark,
Bore us some leagues to sea; where they prepared
A rotten carcass of a boat, not rigg'd,
Nor tackle, sail, nor mast; the very rats
Instinctively had quit it: there they hoist us,
To cry to the sea that roar'd to us, to sigh
To the winds whose pity, sighing back again,
Did us but loving wrong.
Miranda. Alack, what trouble
Was I then to you!
Prospero. O, a cherubin
Thou wast that did preserve me. Thou didst smile.
Infused with a fortitude from heaven,
When I have deck'd the sea with drops full salt,
Under my burthen groan'd; which raised in me
An undergoing stomach, to bear up
Against what should ensue.

141—2 **nor set . . . business** : nor (did they dare to) stain themselves with a deed of blood. 144 **In few** : in short. 146 **butt** : tub. *[N]*. 147 **Nor tackle** : i.e. not having tackle. 148 **have** : vivid ofr 'had' (historic present). 152 **cherubin** : cherub, angel *[N]*. 155 **deck'd** : adorned. *[N]*. 156 **Under** : i.e. (and) under. **which** : i.e. your smile. 157 **undergoing stomach** : a resolution to endure.

Miranda. How came we ashore?
Prospero. By Providence divine.
Some food we had and some fresh water that
A noble Neapolitan, Gonzalo,
Out of his charity, being then appointed
Master of this design, did give us, with
Rich garments, linens, stuffs and necessaries,
Which since have steaded much; so, of his gentleness,
Knowing I loved my books, he furnish'd me
From mine own library with volumes that
I prize above my dukedom.
Miranda. Would I might
But ever see that man!
Prospero. Now I arise: [*Resumes his mantle.*
Sit still, and hear the last of our sea-sorrow.
Here in this island we arrived; and here
Have I, thy schoolmaster, made thee more profit
Than other princesses can that have more time
For vainer hours and tutors not so careful.
Miranda. Heavens thank you for't! And now, I pray you, sir,
For still 'tis beating in my mind, your reason
For raising this sea-storm?
Prospero. Know thus far forth.
By accident most strange, bountiful Fortune,
Now my dear lady, hath mine enemies
Brought to this shore; and by my prescience
I find my zenith doth depend upon

---

165 **steaded** : been of use. **of his gentleness** : in the kindness of his heart. 172 **made thee more profit** : made you benefit more. 179 **Now my dear lady** : (who is) now my auspicious mistress (in contrast with what she was formerly). 181 **zenith** : the highest point (of my fortune). *[N]*.

A most auspicious star, whose influence
If now I court not but omit, my fortunes
Will ever after droop. Here cease more questions:
Thou art inclined to sleep; 'tis a good dulness,
And give it way: I know thou canst not choose.
[*Miranda sleeps.*
Come away, servant, come. I am ready now.
Approach, my Ariel, come.

Enter ARIEL.

Ariel. All hail, great master! grave sir, hail! I come
To answer thy best pleasure; be't to fly,
To swim, to dive into the fire, to ride
On the curl'd clouds, to thy strong bidding task
Ariel and all his quality.
Prospero. Hast thou, spirit,
Perform'd to point the tempest that I bade thee?
Ariel. To every article.
I boarded the king's ship; now on the beak,
Now in the waist, the deck, in every cabin,
I flamed amazement: sometime I'ld divide,
And burn in many places; on the topmast,
The yards and boresprit, would I flame distinctly,
Then meet and join. Jove's lightnings, the precursors
O' the dreadful thunder-claps, more momentary
And sight-outrunning were not; the fire and cracks
Of sulphurous roaring the most mighty Neptune

---

186 **give it way** : let it have its course. *[N].* 192 **to thy strong bidding** : (in obedience) to thy powerful commands. **task** : set to work. 193 **quality** : profession (i.e. Ariel's companion spirits). 194 **to point** : precisely. 195 **To every article** : in every detail. 196 **beak** : prow. 197 **waist** : the middle part of the upper deck. 198 **sometime** : sometimes. *[N].* 200 **boresprit** : bowsprit. **distinctly** : separately. 204 **Neptune** : god of the sea.

Seem to besiege and make his bold waves tremble,
Yea, his dread trident shake.
Prospero. My brave spirit!
Who was so firm, so constant, that this coil
Would not infect his reason?
Ariel. Not a soul
But felt a fever of the mad and play'd
Some tricks of desperation. All but mariners
Plunged in the foaming brine and quit the vessel,
Then all afire with me: the king's son, Ferdinand,
hair up-staring,—then like reeds, not hair,—
Was the first man that leap'd; cried, 'Hell is empty
And all the devils are here.'
Prospero. Why that's my spirit!
But was not this nigh shore?
Ariel. Close by, my master.
Prospero. But are they, Ariel, safe?
Ariel. Not a hair perish'd;
On their sustaining garments not a blemish,
But fresher than before: and, as thou badest me,
In troops I have dispersed them 'bout the isle.
The king's son have I landed by himself;
Whom I left cooling of the air with sighs
In an odd angle of the isle and sitting,
His arms in this sad knot.
Prospero. Of the king's ship
The mariners say how thou hast disposed
And all the rest o' the fleet.
Ariel. Safely in harbour
Is the king's ship; in the deep nook, where once

---

206 **brave** : fine. 207 **coil** : tumult, confusion. 208 **infect** : affect injuriously. 209 **of the mad** : such as mad men feel. 213 **up-staring** : standing on end. 218 **sustaining** : supporting. *[N].* 223 **angle** : corner. 227 **nook** : creek.

Thou call'dst me up at midnight to fetch dew
From the still-vex'd Bermoothes, there she's hid:
The mariners all under hatches stow'd;
Who, with a charm join'd to their suffer'd labour,
I have left asleep; and for the rest o' the fleet
Which I dispersed, they all have met again
And are upon the Mediterranean flote,
Bound sadly home for Naples,
Supposing that they saw the king's ship wreck'd
And his great person perish.
Prospero. Ariel, thy charge
Exactly is perform'd: but there's more work.
What is the time o' the day?
Ariel. Past the mid season.
Prospero. At least two glasses. The time 'twixt six and now
Must by us both be spent most preciously.
Ariel. Is there more toil? Since thou dost give me pains,
Let me remember thee what thou hast promised,
Which is not yet perform'd me.
Prospero. How now? moody?
What is't thou canst demand?
Ariel. My liberty.
Prospero. Before the time be out? no more!
Ariel. I prithee,
Remember I have done thee worthy service;
Told thee no lies, made thee no mistakings, served
Without or grudge or grumblings: thou didst promise
To bate me a full year.

---

229 **still-vex'd Bermoothes** : constantly disturbed Bermudas. *[N]*. 234 **flote** : sea. *[N]*. 239 **the mid season** : noon. 240 **glasses** : hours. *[N]*. 242 **pains** : trouble, tasks. 243 **remember** : remind. 244 **me** : for me. 249 **grudge** : complaint.

Prospero. Dost thou forget
From what a torment I did free thee?
Ariel. No.
Prospero. Thou dost, and think'st it much to tread the ooze
Of the salt deep,
To run upon the sharp wind of the north,
To do me business in the veins o' the earth
When it is baked with frost.
Ariel. I do not, sir.
Prospero. Thou liest, malignant thing! Hast thou forgot
The foul witch Sycorax, who with age and envy
Was grown into a hoop? hast thou forgot her?
Ariel. No, sir.
Prospero. Thou hast. Where was she born? speak; tell me.
Ariel. Sir, in Arigier.
Prospero. O, was she so? I must
Once in a month recount what thou hast been,
Which thou forget'st. This damn'd witch Sycorax,
For mischiefs manifold and sorceries terrible
To enter human hearing, from Argier,
Thou know'st, was banish'd: for one thing she did
They would not take her life. Is not this true?
Ariel. Ay, sir.
Prospero. This blue-eyed hag was hither brought with child
And here was left by the sailors. Thou, my slave,
As thou report'st thyself, wast then her servant;
And, for thou wast a spirit too delicate
To act her earthy and abhorr'd commands,
Refusing her grand hests, she did confine thee,
By help of her more potent ministers

---

250 **bate** : remit. *[N]*. 252 **much** : a hard task. 258 **envy** : malice. 261 **Argier** : Algiers. *[N]*. 272 **for** : because. 274 **grand hests** : great commands.

And in her most unmitigable rage,
Into a cloven pine; within which rift
Imprison'd thou didst painfully remain
A dozen years; within which space she died
And left thee there; where thou didst vent thy groans
As fast as mill-wheels strike. Then was this island—
Save for the son that she did litter here,
A freckled whelp hag-born—not honour'd with
A human shape.

Ariel. Yes, Caliban her son.

Prospero. Dull thing, I say so; he, that Caliban
Whom now I keep in service. Thou best know'st
What torment I did find thee in; thy groans
Did make wolves howl and penetrate the breasts
Of ever angry bears: it was a torment
To lay upon the damn'd, which Sycorax
Could not again undo: it was mine art,
When I arrived and heard thee, that made gape
The pine and let thee out.

Ariel. I thank thee, master.

Prospero. If thou more murmur'st, I will rend an oak
And peg thee in his knotty entrails till
Thou hast howl'd away twelve winters.

Ariel. Pardon, master;
I will be correspondent to command
And do my spiriting gently.

Prospero. Do so, and after two days
I will discharge thee.

Ariel. That's my noble master!
What shall I do? say what; what shall I do?

Prospero. Go make thyself like a nymph o' the sea: be subject

---

275 **ministers** : cf. I. 131, above. 297 **correspondent** : submissive. 298 **spiriting** : work of spirit. **gently** : courteously. *[N].*

To no sight but thine and mine, invisible
To every eyeball else. Go take this shape
And hither come in't: go, hence with diligence! [*Exit Ariel.*
Awake, dear heart, awake! thou hast slept well; awake!

Miranda. The stangeness of your story put Heaviness in me.

Prospero. Shake it off. Come on;
We'll visit Caliban my slave, who never
Yields us kind answer.

Miranda. 'Tis a villain, sir, I do not love to look on.

Prospero. But, as 'tis,
We cannot miss him: he does make our fire,
Fetch in our wood and serves in offices
That profit us. What, ho! slave! Caliban!
Thou earth, thou! speak.

Caliban. [*Within.*] There's wood enough within.

Prospero. Come forth, I say! there's other business for thee:
Come, thou tortoise! when?

Re-enter Ariel like a water-nymph.

Fine apparition! My quaint Ariel,
Hark in thine ear.

Ariel. My lord it shall be done. [*Exit.*

Prospero. Thou poisonous slave, got by the devil himself
Upon thy wicke dam, come forth!

Enter Caliban.

Caliban. As wicked dew as e'er my mother brush'd
With raven's feather from unwholesome fen
Drop on you both! a south-west blow on ye

---

306 **Heaviness** : drowsiness.

311 **miss** : do without. 314 **Thou earth** : i.e. you lump of earth. *[N].* 316 **when?** : an exclamation of impatience- 'How long am I to wait ofr you?' 317 **quaint** : dainty. 319 **got** : begotten.

And blister you all o'er!
Prospero. For this, be sure, to-night thou shalt have cramps,
Side-stitches that shall pen thy breath up; urchins
Shall, for that vast of night that they may work, [72]
All exercise on thee; thou shalt be pinch'd
As thick as honeycomb, each pinch more stinging
Than bees that made 'em.
Caliban. I must eat my dinner.
This island's mine, by Sycorax my mother,
Which thou takest from me. When thou camest first,
Thou strokedst me and madest much of me, wouldst give me
Water with berries in't, and teach me how
To name the bigger light, and how the less,
That burn by day and night: and then I loved thee
And show'd thee all the qualities o' the isle,
The fresh springs, brine-pits, barren place and fertile:
Cursed be I that did so! All the charms
Of Sycorax, toads, beetles, bats, light on you!
For I am all the subjects that you have,
Which first was mine own king: and here you sty me
In this hard rock, whiles you do keep from me
The rest o' the island.
Prospero. Thou most lying slave,
Whom stripes may move, not kindness! I have used thee,
Filth as thou art, with human care, and lodged thee
In mine own cell, till thou didst seek to violate
The honour of my child.
Caliban. O ho, O ho! would't had been done!

---

325 **cramps** : rheumatic pains. 326 **urchins** : hedgehogs. *[N]*. 327 **for that vast of night** : during that empty part in the meddle of the night when men are asleep. **that they** : when they. *[N]*. 328 **exercise on** : practise on, torment. 330 **'em** : the cells of the honeycomb. *[N]*. 331 **by** : by right of inheritance from. 342 **sty** : confine like a pig in a sty, pen up.

Thou didst prevent me; I had peopled else
This isle with Calibans.
Prospero. Abhorred slave,
Which any print of goodness wilt not take,
Being capable of all ill! I pitied thee,
Took pains to make thee speak, taught thee each hour
One thing or other: when thou didst not, savage,
Know thine own meaning, but wouldst gabble like
A thing most brutish, I endow'd thy purposes
With words that made them known. But thy vile race,
Though thou didst learn, had that in't which good natures
Could not abide to be with; therefore wast thou
Deservedly confined into this rock,
Who hadst deserved more than a prison.
Caliban. You taught me language; and my profit on't
Is, I know how to curse. The red plague rid you
For learning me your language!
Prospero. Hag-seed, hence!
Fetch us in fuel; and be quick, thou'rt best,
To answer other business. Shrug'st thou, malice?
If thou neglect'st or dost unwillingly
What I command, I'll rack thee with old cramps,
Fill all thy bones with aches, make thee roar
That beasts shall tremble at thy din.
Caliban. No, pray thee.
[*Aside.*] I must obey: his art is of such power,
It would control my dam's god, Setebos,
And make a vassal of him.
Prospero. So, slave; hence! [*Exit Caliban.*

---

363 **on't** : of, from it. 364 **rid** : destroy. *[N]*. 364 **learning** : teaching (as still in colloquial usage). **Hag-seed** : witch's offspring. 366 **thou'rt best** : thou wert best, i.e. 'or it will be the worse for you'. 369 **old** : of old age (cf. Ⅳ. ⅰ. 258). *[N]*.

Re-enter Ariel, invisible, playing and singing; Ferdinand following.

ARIEL'S song.

Come unto these yellow sands,
  And then take hands:
Courtsied when you have and kiss'd,—
  The wild waves whist,—
Foot it featly here and there;
And, sweet sprites, the burthen bear.
  Hark, hark!
        [*Burthen:* Bow, wow, *dispersedly.*
The watch-dogs bark!
        [*Burthen Bow, wow, dispersedly.*
  Hark, hark! I hear
The strain of strutting chanticleer
        Cry, Cock-a-diddle-dow.

Ferdinand. Where should this music be? i' the air or the earth?
It sounds no more: and sure, it waits upon
Some god o' the island. Sitting on a bank,
Weeping again the king my father's wreck,
This music crept by me upon the waters,
Allaying both their fury and my passion
With its sweet air: thence I have follow'd it,
Or it hath drawn me rather. But 'tis gone.
No, it begins again.

---

378 **whist** : being hushed, silent. *[N].* 379 **Foot it featly** : dance nimbly. 380 **the burden bear** : join in the chorus. 388 **again** : over and over again. 390 **passion** : grief.

ARIEL *sings*:

Full fathom five thy father lies;
Of his bones are coral made;
Those are pearls that were his eyes:
Nothing of him that doth fade,
But doth suffer a sea-change
Into something rich and strange.
Sea-nymphs hourly ring his knell :
[*Burthen Ding-dong.*
Hark! now I hear them,—Ding-dong, bell.

Ferdinand. The ditty does remember my drown'd father.
This is no motal business, nor no sound
That the earth owes. I hear it now above me.
Prospero. The fringed curtains of thine eye advance
And say what thou seest yond.
Miranda. What is't? a spirit?
Lord, how it looks about! Believe me, sir,
It carries a brave form. But 'tis a spirit.
Prospero. No, wench; it eats and sleeps and hath such senses
As we have, such. This gallant which thou seest
Was in the wreck; and, but he's something stain'd
With grief that's beauty's canker, thou mightst call him
A goodly person: he hath lost his fellows
And strays about to find 'em.
Miranda. I might call him
A thing divine, for nothing natural

402 **remember** : commemorate. 403 **no mortal business** : not the work of mortals. 404 **owes** : owns, possesses. 406 **yond** : yonder. 408 **brave** : noble (cf. I. ii. 6, &c.). *[N].* **form** : outward appearance. 411 **but** : except (for the fact that). **something** : somewhat. 412 **that's beauty's canker** : that destroys beauty. *[N].*

I ever saw so noble.
Prospero. [*Aside.*] It goes on, I see,
As my soul prompts it. Spirit, fine spirit! I'll free thee
Within two days for this.
Ferdinand. Most sure, the goddess
On whom these airs attend! Vouchsafe my prayer
May know if you remain upon this island;
And that you will some good instruction give
How I may bear me here: my prime request,
Which I do last pronounce, is, O you wonder!
If you be maid or no?
Miranda. No wonder, sir; but certainly a maid.
Ferdinand. My language! heavens!
I am the best of them that speak this speech,
Were I but where 'tis spoken.
Prospero. How? the best?
What wert thou, if the King of Naples heard thee?
Ferdinand. A single thing, as I am now, that wonders
To hear thee speak of Naples. He does hear me;
And that he does I weep: myself am Naples,
Who with mine eyes, never since at ebb, beheld
The king my father wreck'd.
Miranda. Alack, for mercy!
Ferdinand. Yes, faith, and all his lords; the Duke of Milan
And his brave son being twain.
Prospero. [Aside.]The Duke of Milan
And his more braver daughter could control thee,

---

415 **natural** : in nature (not in the world of spirits). 416 **It** : i.e. my plan. 420 **remain** : dwell. 422 **bear me** : conduct myself. **prime** : chief. 429 **single** : solitary. *[N]*. 430 **Naples** : i.e. the King of Naples. **He does herar me** : He (the King of Naples) hears me (i.e. I, Ferdinand, who am now King, hear the King speak when I hear myself speak). 432 **at ebb** : free from tears. 434 **twain** : two (of them). *[N]*.

If now 'twere fit to do't. At the first sight
They have changed eyes. Delicate Ariel,
I'll set thee free for this.[*To Ferdinand.*] A word, good sir;
I fear you have done yourself some wrong: a word.
Miranda. Why speaks my father so ungently? This
Is the third man that e'er I saw, the first
That e'er I sigh'd for: pity move my father
To be inclined my way!
Ferdinand. O, if a virgin,
And your affection not gone forth, I'll make you
The queen of Naples.
Prospero. Soft, sir! one word more.
[*Aside.*] They are both in either's powers; but this swift business
I must uneasy make, lest too light winning
Make the prize light. [*To Ferdinand.*] One word more; I charge thee
That thou attend me: thou dost here usurp
The name thou owest not; and hast put thyself
Upon this island as a spy, to win it
From me, the lord on't.
Ferdinand. No, as I am a man.
Miranda. There's nothing ill can dwell in such a temple:
If the ill spirit have so fair a house,
Good things will strive to dwell with't.
Prospero. [*To Ferdinand.*] Follow me.
[*To Miranda.*] Speak not you for him; he's a traitor.

---

436 **control** : challenge, confute. 438 **changed eyes** : fallen in love (because lovers see with one another's eyes ; not 'exchanged glances'). 440 **you have . . . wrong** : you are mistaken. 445 **gone forth** : engaged. 447 **either's** : one another's. 448 **light** : easy. 449 **light** : of little value. 450 **attend** : pay attention to, listen to. 451 **ow'st** : own, possess. 453 **on't** : of it (cf. I. ii. 87, &c.).

[*To Ferdinand.*] Come; I'll manacle thy neck and feet together:
Sea-water shalt thou drink; thy food shall be
The fresh-brook muscles, wither'd roots and husks
Wherein the acorn cradled. Follow.

Ferdinand. No; I will resist such entertainment till
Mine enemy has more power
[*Draws, and is charmed from moving.*

Miranda. O dear father!
Make not too rash a trial of him, for
He's gentle and not fearful.

Prospero. What? I say,
My foot my tutor? Put thy sword up, traitor;
Who makest a show but darest not strike, thy conscience
Is so prossess'd with guilt: come from thy ward,
For I can here disarm thee with this stick
And make thy weapon drop.

Miranda. Beseech you, father.

Prospero. Hence! hang not on my garments.

Miranda. Sir, have pity; I'll be his surety.

Prospero. Silence! one word more
Shall make me chide thee, if not hate thee. What!
An advocate for an imposter! hush!
Thou think'st there is no more such shapes as he,
Having seen but him and Caliban: foolish wench!
To the most of men this is a Caliban
And they to him are angels.

Miranda. My affections are then most humble; I have no
Ambition to see a goodlier man.

Prospero. [*To Ferdinand.*] Come on; obey:

---

464 **He's gentle . . . fearful** : either (a) He is of gentle birth, and not a coward, or (b) He is not violent, and not terrifying. 466 **My foot my tutor?** : Am I to take lessons from my inferior? (The foot is lower than, 'inferior to', the head.) 468 **ward** : posture of defence (in fencing).

Thy nerves are in their infancy again
And have no vigour in them.
Ferdinand. So they are;
My spirits, as in a dream, are all bound up.
My father's loss, the weakness which I feel,
The wreck of all my friends, nor this man's threats,
To whom I am subdued, are but light to me,
Might I but through my prison once a day
Behold this maid: all corners else o' the earth
Let liberty make use of; space enough
Have I in such a prison.
Prospero. [Aside.] It works. [*To Ferdinand.*] Come on.
Thou hast done well, fine Ariel! [*To Ferdinand.*] Follow me.
[*To Ariel.*] Hark what thou else shalt do me.
Miranda. Be of comfort;
My father's of a better nature, sir,
Than he appears by speech: this is unwonted
Which now came from him.
Prospero. Thou shalt be free
As mountain winds: but then exactly do
All points of my command.
Ariel. To the syllable.
Prospero. [*To Ferdinand.*] Come, follow. Speak not for him.
[*Exeunt*

---

481 **nerves** : sinews. 488 **else** : other. 489 **liberty** : i.e. men who are free. 492 **what thou elase &c** : what other (service) thou &c. 497 **To the syllable** : in exact detail.

Act Two

Scene One

ANOTHER PART OF THE ISLAND.

Enter ALONSO, SEBASTIAN, ANTONIO, GONZALO, ADRIAN, FRANCISCO, *and others.*

Gonzalo. Beseech you, sir, be merry; you have cause,
So have we all, of joy; for our escape
Is much beyond our loss. Our hint of woe
Is common; every day some sailor's wife,
The masters of some merchant and the merchant
Have just our theme of woe; but for the miracle,
I mean our preservation, few in millions
Can speak like us: then wisely, good sir, weigh
Our sorrow with our comfort.
Alonso. Prithee, peace.
Sebastian. He receives comfort like cold porridge.
Antonio. The visitor will not give him o'er so.
Sebastian. Look he's winding up the watch of his wit; by and

---

3 **hint** : occasion (cf. I. ii. 134). 5 **some merchant** : some merchant vessel. 6 **theme of woe** : subject for grief.

by it will strike.
Gonzalo. Sir,—
Sebastian. One: tell.
Gonzalo. When every grief is entertain'd that's offer'd,
Comes to the entertainer—
Sebastian. A dollar.
Gonzalo. Dolour comes to him, indeed: you have spoken truer than you purposed.
Sebastian. You have taken it wiselier than I meant you should.
Gonzalo. Therefore, my lord,—
Antonio. Fie, what a spendthrift is he of his tongue!
Alonso. I prithee, spare.
Gonzalo. Well, I have done: but yet,—
Sebastian. He will be talking.
Antonio. Which, of he or Adrian, for a good wager, first begins to crow?
Sebastian. The old cock.
Antonio. The cockerel.
Sebastian. Done. The wager?
Antonio. A laughter.
Sebastian. A match!
Adrian. Though this island seem to be desert,—
Sebastinan. Ha, ha, ha! So, you're paid.
Adrian. Uninhabitable and almost inaccessible,—
Sebastian. Yet,—
Adrian. Yet,—

---

15 **tell** : count. *[N]*. 16 **When . . . offer'd** : when a man takes every opportunity of grieving that presents itself. 25 **spare** : i.e. spare your words, desist. 30 **The old cock** : i.e. Gonzalo. 31 **The cockrel** : i.e. Adrian. 33 **laughter** : (1) a laugh, (2) the whole number of eggs laid by a hen before she is ready to 'sit'. 34 **A match!** : It's a bot! 36 **you're paid** : you've won.

Antonio. He could not miss't.

Adrian. It must needs be of subtle, tender and delicate temperance.

Antonio. Temperance was a delicate wench.

Sebastian. Ay, and a subtle; as he most learnedly delivered.

Adrian. The air breathes upon us here most sweetly.

Sebastian. As if it had lungs and rotten ones.

Antonio. Or as 'twere perfumed by a fen.

Gonzalo. Here is everything advantageous to life.

Antonio. True; save means to live.

Sebastian. Of that there's none, or little.

Gonzalo. How lush and lusty the grass looks! how green!

Antonio. The ground indeed is tawny.

Sebastian. With an eye of green in't.

Antonio. He misses not much.

Sebastian. No; he doth but mistake the truth totally.

Gonzalo. But the rarity of it is,—which is indeed almost beyond credit,—

Sebastian. As many vouched rarities are.

Gonzalo. That our garments, being, as they were, drenched in the sea, hold notwithstanding their freshness and glosses; being rather new-dyed than stained with salt water.

Antonio. If but one of his pockets could speak, would it not say he lies?

Sebastian. Ay, or very falsely pocket up his report.

Gonzalo. Methinks our garments are now as fresh as when we put them on first in Afric, at the marriage of the king's fair daughter Claribel to the King of Tunis.

---

42 **temperance** : temperature. 54 **indeed** : in actual fact (Antonio is contradicting, not agreeing with Gonzalo). 55 **eye** : spot. 56 **He misses not much** : he is not far wrong (ironical). 66 **pocket up** : conceal.

Sebastian. 'Twas a sweet marriage, and we prosper well in our return.

Adrian. Tunis was never graced before with such a paragon to their queen.

Gonzalo. Not since widow Dido's time.

Antonio. Widow! a pox o' that! How came that widow in? Widow Dido!

Sebastian. What if he had said 'widower Æneas' too?
Good Lord, how you take it!

Adrian. 'Widow Dido' said you? you make me study of that: she was of Carthage, not of Tunis.

Gonzalo. This Tunis, sir, was Carthage.

Adrian. Carthage?

Gonzalo. I assure you, Carthage.

Antonio. His word is more than the miraculous harp.

Sebastian. He hath raised the wall and houses too.

Antonio. What impossible matter will he make easy next?

Sebastian. I think he will carry this island home in his pocket and give it his son for an apple.

Antonio. And, sowing the kernels of it in the sea, bring forth more islands.

Gonzalo. Ay.

Antonio. Why, in good time.

Gonzalo. [*To Alonso.*] Sir, we were talking that our garments seem now as fresh as when we were at Tunis at the marriage of your daughter, who is now queen.

Antonio. And the rarest that e'er came there.

Sebastian. Bate, I beseech you, widow Dido.

Antonio. widow Dido! ay, widow Dido.

---

72 **to** : for, as. 79 **study of** : think intently about, reflect about. 91 **Ay?** : what is that you say? *[N]*. 97 **Bate** : except.

Gonzalo. Is not, sir, my doublet as fresh as the first day
I wore it? I mean, in a sort.
Antonio. That sort was well fished for.
Gonzalo. When I wore it at your daughter's marriage?
Alonso. You cram these words into mine ears against
The stomach of my sense. Would I had never
Married my daughter there! for, coming thence,
My son is lost and, in my rate, she too,
Who is so far from Italy removed
I ne'er again shall see her. O thou mine heir
Of Naples and of Milan, what strange fish
Hath made his meal on thee?
Francisco. Sir, he may live:
I saw him beat the surges under him,
And ride upon their backs; he trod the water,
Whose enmity he flung aside, and breasted
The surge most swoln that met him; his bold head
'Bove the contentious waves he kept, and oar'd
Himself with his good arms in lusty stroke
To the shore, that o'er his wave-worn basis bow'd,
As stooping to relieve him: I not doubt
He came alive to land.
Alonso. No, no, he's gone.
Sebastian. Sir, you may thank yourself for this great loss,
That would not bless our Europe with your daughter,
But rather loose her to an African;
Where she at least is banish'd from your eye,

---

104 **The stomach of my sense** : the inclination of my sense (of hearing). 106 **rate** : opinion. 117 **his** : its (referring to the shore) *[N]*. basis : base, dege. 122 **loose her** : mate her with. *[N]*.

Who hath cause to wet the grief on't.
Alonso. Prithee, peace.
Sebastian. You were kneel'd to and importuned otherwise
By all of us, and the fair soul herself
Weigh'd between loathness and obedience, at
Which end o' the beam should bow. We have lost your son,
I fear, for ever: Milan and Naples have
More widows in them of this business' making
Than we bring men to comfort them: The fault's your own.
Alonso. So is the dear'st o' the loss.
Gonzalo. My lord Sebastian,
The truth you speak doth lack some gentleness
And time to speak it in: you rub the sore,
When you should bring the plaster.
Sebastian. Very well.
Antonio. And most chirurgeonly.
Gonzalo. It is foul weather in us all, good sir,
When you are cloudy.
Sebastian. Foul weather?
Antonio. Very foul.
Gonzalo. Had I plantation of this isle, my lord,—
Antonio. He'ld sow't with nettle-seed.
Sebastian. Or docks, or mallows.
Gonzalo. And were the king on't, what would I do?
Sebastian. 'Scape being drunk for want of wine.

---

123 **she . . . banish'd** : at any rate she is banished (if not lost altogether). 124 **Who hath . . . on't** : who has reason to weep for it. *[N].* 127 **Weigh'd between loathness** : balanced between unwillingness. *[N].* 130 **widows** : i.e. widows who will not receive their husbands again on account of this voyage and its results. *[N].* 132 **dearest** : hardest, severest. *[N].* 135 **time** : i.e. a fitting time. 136 **Very well** : i.e. very well said.(Sebastian speaks ironically.) 137 **chirurgeonly** : like a surgeon. 139 **cloudy** : gloomy. *[N].* 140 **plantation** : colonization. *[N].*

Gonzalo. I' the commonwealth I would by contraries
Execute all things; for no kind of traffic
Would I admit; no name of magistrate;
Letters should not be known; riches, poverty,
And use of service, none; contract, succession,
Bourn, bound of land, tilth, vineyard, none;
No use of metal, corn, or wine, or oil;
No occupation; all men idle, all;
And women too, but innocent and pure;
No sovereignty;—
Sebastian. Yet he would be king on't.
Antonio. The latter end of his commonwealth forgets the beginning.
Gonzalo. All things in common nature should produce
Without sweat or endeavour: treason, felony,
Sword, pike, knife, gun, or need of any engine,
Would I not have; but nature should bring forth,
Of it own kind, all foison, all abundance,
To feed my innocent people.
Sebastian. No marrying 'mong his subjects?
Antonio. None, man; all idle: whores and knaves.
Gonzalo. I would with such perfection govern, sir,
To excel the golden age.
Sebastian. 'Save his majesty!
Antonio. Long live Gonzalo!

---

144 **by contraries** : in the opposite manner to what is usual. 145 **traffic** : trade. *[N]*. 147 **Letters** : learning. 149 **Bourn** : boundary. **bound of land** : landmark. **tilth** : land under cultivation. 152 **but innocent &c.** : i.e. although idle. See I . 163 and *[N]*. 158 **engine** : engine of war (or, possibly, of torture). 160 **it own** : its own. **foison** : plenty. 163 **idle** : vain, worthless *[N]*. 165 **To** : as to. **'Save** : God save. *[N]*.

Gonzalo. And,—do you mark me, sir?

Alonso. Prithee, no more: thou dost talk nothing to me.

Gonzalo. I do well believe your highness; and did it to minister occasion to these gentlemen, who are of such sensible and nimble lungs that they always use to laugh at nothing.

Antonio. 'Twas you we laughed at.

Gonzalo. Who in this kind of merry fooling am nothing to you: so you may continue and laugh at nothing still.

Antonio. What a blow was there given!

Sebastian. And it had not fallen flat-long.

Gonzalo. You are gentlemen of brave metal; you would lift the moon out of her sphere, if she would continue in it five weeks without changing.

Enter ARIEL, *invisible, playing solemn music.*

Sebastian. We would so, and then go a bat-fowling.

Antonio. Nay, good my lord, be not angry.

Gonzalo. No, I warrant you; I will not adventure my discretion so weakly. Will you laugh me asleep, for I am very heavy?

Antonio. Go sleep, and hear us.

[*All sleep but* ALONSO, SEBASTIAN, *and* ANTONIO.

Alonso. What, all so soon asleep! I wish mine eyes
Would, with themselves, shut up my thoughts: I find
They are inclined to do so.

Sebastian. Please you, sir,

---

168 **nothing** : nonsense, trifles. 169 **sensible** : sensitive. **use to** : are accustoned to. 176 **And** : if. **flat-long** : with the flat of the sword (i.e. harmlessly). 177–9 **You are . . . changing** : i.e. you are such lively gentlemen that you can endure nothing serious or regular. *[N]*. 180 **a bat-fowling** : catching birds at night. *[N]*. 182–3 **adventure my discretion** : risk losing my reputation for good sense. 184 **heavy** : sleepy.

Do not omit the heavy offer of it:
It seldom visits sorrow; when it doth,
It is a comforter.
Antonio. We two, my lord,
Will guard your person while you take your rest,
And watch your safety.
Alonso. Thank you. Wondrous heavy.
[ALONSO *sleeps. Exit* ARIEL.
Sebastian. What a strange drowsiness possesses them!
Antonio. It is the quality o' the climate.
Sebastian. Why
Doth it not then our eyelids sink? I find not
Myself disposed to sleep.
Antonio. Nor I; my spirits are nimble.
They fell together all, as by consent;
They dropp'd, as by a thunder-stroke. What might,
Worthy Sebastian? O, what might?—No more:—
And yet me thinks I see it in thy face,
What thou shouldst be: the occasion speaks thee, and
My strong imagination sees a crown
Dropping upon thy head.
Sebastian. What, art thou waking?
Antonio. Do you not hear me speak?
Sebastian. I do; and surely
It is a sleepy language and thou speak'st
Out of thy sleep. What is it thou didst say?
This is a strange repose, to be asleep
With eyes wide open ; standing, speaking, moving,

---

188 **do so** : viz. shut themselves. 189 **it** : i.e. sleep. 196 **sink** : (trans.) cause to sink. 198 **They fell . . . consent** : i.e. Alonso, Gonzalo, &c., fell asleep as if by agreemen 202 **speaks** : calls.

And yet so fast asleep.
Antonio. Noble Sebastian,
Thou let'st thy fortune sleep—die, rather; wink'st
Whiles thou art waking.
Sebastian. Thou dost snore distinctly;
There's meaning in thy snores.
Antonio. I am more serious than my custom: you
Must be so too, if heed me; which to do
Trebles thee o'er.
Sebastian. Well; I am standing water.
Antonio. I'll teach you how to flow.
Sebastian. Do so: to ebb
Hereditary sloth instructs me.
Antonio. O!
If you but knew how you the purpose cherish
Whiles thus you mock it! how, in stripping it,
You more invest it! Ebbing men, indeed,
Most often do so near the bottom run
By their own fear or sloth.
Sebastian. Prithee, say on:
The setting of thine eye and cheek proclaim
A matter from thee, and a birth indeed
Which throes thee much to yield.

Antonio. Thus, sir:

---

211 **wink'st** : sleep'st. 212 **distinctly** : articulately. *[N]*. 215 **if heed me** : if you mean to heed me. 216 **Trebles thee o'er** : makes you three times as great/ *[N]*. **standing** : not flowing. *[N]*. 219–21 **If you . . . invest it!** : If you only knew how by jesting in this way you make the design (which Antonio has in mind) seem more disirable ; and how by stripping it of its seriousness you clothe it in greater seriousness. *[N]*. 224 **setting** : fixity. 225 **A matter** : a matter of importance. 226 **throes . . . yield** : agonizes, causes you much pain to utter. *[N]*.

Although this lord of weak remembrance, this,
Who shall be of as little memory
When he is earth'd, hath here almost persuade,—
For he's a spirit of persuasion, only
Professes to persuade,—the king his son's alive,
'Tis as impossible that he's undrown'd
As he that sleeps here swims.

Sebastian. I have no hope
That he's undrown'd. 90

Antonio. O! out of that 'no hope'
What great hope have you! no hope that way is
Another way so high a hope that even
Ambition cannot pierce a wink beyond,
But doubt discovery there. Will you grant with me
That Ferdinand is drown'd?

Sebastian. He's gone.

Antonio. Then, tell me
Who's the next heir of Naples?

Sebastian. Claribel.

Antonio. She that is queen of Tunis; she that dwells
Ten leagues beyond man's life; she that from Naples
Can have no note, unless the sun were post—
The man i' the moon's too slow—till new-born chins

---

227 **remembrance** : memory, i.e. faculty of remembering. *[N]*. 228 **as little memory** : as little remembered (as he remembers things). 229 **earth'd** : buried. 233 **As he** : i.e. as it is that he. 235–7 **no hope ... beyond** : no hope that Ferdinand is alive means so high a hope in another direction(i.e. for your prospects), that ambition cannot see the slightest degree further ahead. 238 **But doubts ... there** : but is doubtful of being able to discover anything there(i.e. beyond). *[N]*. **grant** : admit, acknowledge. 242 **Ten leagues ... life** : ten leagues farther (from Naples) than a man could travel in a life-time. 243 **note** : information. **post** : messenger. *[N]*.

Be rough and razorable; she that—from whom?
We all were sea-swallow'd, though some cast again,
And by that destiny to perform an act
Whereof what's past is prologue, what to come
In yours and my discharge.

Sebastian. What stuff is this! how say you?
'Tis true, my brother's daughter's queen of Tunis;
So is she heir of Naples; 'twixt which regions
There is some space.

Antonio. A space whose every cubit
Seems to cry out, 'How shall that Claribel
Measure us back to Naples? Keep in Tunis,
And let Sebastian wake.' Say, this were death
That now hath seized them; why, they were no worse
Than now they are. There be that can rule Naples
As well as he that sleeps; lords that can prate
As amply and unnecessarily
As this Gonzalo; I myself could make
A chough of as deep chat. O, that you bore
The mind that I do! what a sleep were this
For your advancement! Do you understand me?

Sebastian. Methinks I do.

Antonio. And how does your content
Tender your own good fortune?

244−5 **till new-born ... razorable** : till infants have grown to mangood and are fit to be shaved. 245 **she that from whom** : she, in coming from whon. *[N]*. 246 **though . . . again** : though some (of us were) cast (up) again. **cast** : vomited. *[N]*. 247 **by that destiny ot** : destined by that fortune to. 248−9 **what to come . . . discharge** : what is to come depends upon what you and I perform. 249 **discharge** : performance (a theatrical term). 252 **cubit** : a measure of about one and a half feet. 254 **us** : i.e. the cubits. **Keep** : remain. 255 **Say, this were death** : i.e. suppose this sleep (of Alonso, &c.) were death. 260−1 **make . . . chat** : prove myself a crow that prates as profoundly.

Sebastian. I remember
You did supplant your brother Prospero.
Antonio. True:
And look how well my garments sit upon me;
Much feater than before: my brother's servants
Were then my fellows; now they are my men.
Sebastian. But, for your conscience?
Antonio. Ay, sir; where lies that? if 't were a kide,
'Twould put me to my slipper: but I feel not
This deity in my bosom: twenty consciences,
That stand 'twixt me and Milan, candied be they
And melt ere they molest! Here lies your brother,
No better than the earth he lies upon,
If he were that which now he's like, that's dead;
Whom I, with this obedient steel, three inches of it,
Can lay to bed for ever; whiles you, doing thus,
To the perpetual wink for aye might put
This ancient morsel, this Sir Prudence, who
Should not upbraid our course. For all the rest,
They'll take suggestion as a cat laps milk;
They'll tell the clock to any business that
We say befits the hour.
Sebastian. Thy case, dear friend,
Shall be my precedent; as thou got'st Milan,
I'll come by Naples. Draw thy sword: one stroke

264–5 **And how . . . fortune?** : and how does your happiness cherish your own good fortune? *[N]*. 268 **feater** : better-fitting. 269 **fellows** : companions. **men** : sevants. 271–2 **if it were . . . slipper** : if it were a chilblain on the heel it would force me to wear a slipper. 274 **candied** : (probably) coated with sugar. *[N]*. 280 **eprpetual wink** : everlasting sleep, ie.e. death. 281–2 **who . . . upbraid** : so that he should not (then) reprove. *[N]*. 284 **They'll tell the clock** : they'll chime in with, acquiesce in.

Shall free thee from the tribute which thou payest;
And I the king shall love thee.
Antonio. Draw together;
And when I rear my hand, do you the like,
To fall it on Gonzalo.
Sebastian. O, but one word. [*They talk apart.*

Music. Re-enter Ariel, invisible.

Ariel. My master through his art foresees the danger
That you, his friend, are in; and sends me forth—
For else his prohect dies—to keep them living.
[*Sings in Gonzalo's ear.*

While you here do snoring lie,
Open-eyed conspiracy
His time doth take.
If of life you keep a care,
Shake off slumber, and beware:
Awake, awake!

Antonio. Then let us both be sudden.
Gonzalo. Now, good angels
Preserve the king. [*They wake.*
Alonso. Why, how now? ho, awake! Why are you drawn?
Wherefore this ghastly looking?
Gonzalo. What's the matter?
Sebastian. Whiles we stood here securing your repose,
Even now, we heard a hollow burst of bellowing
Like bulls, or rather lions: did't not wake you?

---

291 **fall** : let fall. 297 **time** : opportunity. 298 **keep** : have. 301 **sudden** : swift. 303 **drawn** : with drawn swords. 304 **looking** : expression.

It struck mine ear most terribly.
Alonso. I heard nothing.
Antonio. O, 'twas a din to fright a monster's ear,
To make an earthquake! sure, it was the roar
Of a whole herd of lions.
Alonso. Heard you this, Gonzalo?
Gonzalo. Upon mine honour, sir, I heard a humming,
And that a strange one too, which did awake me:
I shaked you, sir, and cried: as mine eyes open'd,
I saw their weapons drawn: there was a noise,
That's verily. 'Tis best we stand upon our guaed,
Or that we quit this place; let's draw our weapons.
Alonso. Lead off this ground; and let's make further search
For my poor son.
Gonzalo. Heavens keep him from these beasts!
For he is, sure, i' the island.
Alonso. Lead away. [*Exit with the others.*
Ariel. Prospero my lord shall know what I have done:
So, king, go safely on to seek thy son. [*Exeunt.*

---

317 **That's verily** : that's a fact.

Scene Two

ANOTHER PART OF THE ISLAND

Enter CALIBAN, *With a burden of wood. A noise of thunder heard.*

Caliban. All the infections that the sun sucks up
From bogs, fens, flats, on Prosper fall and make him
By inch-meal a disease! His spirits hear me
And yet I needs must curse. But they'll nor pinch,
Fright me with urchin—shows, pitch me i' the mire,
Nor lead me, like a firebrand, in the dark
Out of my way, unless he bid 'em; but
For every trifle are they set upon me;
Sometime like apes that mow and chatter at me
And after bite me, then like hedgehogs which
Lie tumbling in my barefoot way and mount
Their pricks at my footfall; sometime am I
All wound with adders who with cloven tongues
Do hiss me into madness.

Enter TRINCULO.

Lo, now, lo!
Here comes a spirit of his, and to torment me
For bringing wood in slowly. I'll fall flat;
Perchance he will not mind me.

---

3 **By inch-meal** : inch by inch. 4 **nor** : neither. 5 **urchin-shows** : apparitions of hobgoblins. **pitch** : both (1) toss, and (2) smear as with pitch. 9 **mow** : make mouths. 11−2 **mount Their pricks** : erect their prickles. 13 **wound** : twined about with (from the verb 'wind'). 17 **mind** : notice.

Trinculo. Here's neither bush nor shrub, to bear off any weather at all, and another storm brewing; I hear it sing i' the wind: yond same black cloud, yond huge one, looks like a foul bombard that would shed his liquor. If it should thunder as it did before, I know not where to hide my head: yond same cloud cannot choose but fall by pailfuls. What have we here? a man or a fish? Dead or alive? A fish: he smells like a fish; a very ancient and fish-like smell; a kind of not of the newest Poor-John. A strange fish! Were I in England now, as once I was, and had but this fish painted, not a holiday fool there but would give a piece of silver: there would this monster make a man; any strange beast there makes a man: when they will not give a doit to relieve a lame beggar, they will lazy out ten to see a dead Indian. Legged like a man and his fins like arms! Warm o' my troth! I do now let loose my opinion; hold it no longer: this is no fish, but an islander, that hath lately suffered by a thunderbolt. [*Thunder.*] Alas, the storm is come again! my best way is to creep under his gaberdine; there is no other shelter hereabouts: misery acquaints a man with strange bed-fellows. I will here shroud till the dregs of the storm be past.

18–9 **to bear off any weather** : to afford any shelter. 20 **yond** : cf. I. ii. 406. 21 **bombard** : a large leather evssel for holding wine. 27 **Poor-John** : salted hake. 28 **painted** : i.e. made into a picture. *[N]*. 29 **holiday fool** : fool on holiday. 30 **make** : make te fortune of. 31 **doit** : a small Dutch coin, worth half a farthing. 32 **Legg'd** : with legs. (Trinculo refers to Caliban.) 34 **o' my troth!** : upon my word! 38 **gaberdine** : a loose upper garment, a cloak. 40 **shroud** : shelter. *[N]*.

Enter STEPHANO, *singing: a bottle in his hand.*

Stephano. I shall no more to sea, to sea,
Here shall I die ashore—
This is a very scurvy tune to sing at a man's funeral:
Well, here's my comfort. [*Drinks.*
The master, the swabber, the boatswain and I,
The gunner and his mate
Loved Mall, Meg and Marian and Margery,
But none of us cared for Kate;
For she had a tongue with a tang,
Would cry to a sailor, Go hang!
She loved not the savour of tar nor of pitch,
Yet a tailor might scratch her where'er she did itch:
Then to sea, boys, and let her go hang!
This is a scurvy tune too: but here's my comfort. [*Drinks.*

Caliban. Do not torment me: Oh!

Stephano. What's the matter? Have we devils here? Do you puttricks upon's with savlages and men of Ind, ha? I have not scaped drowning to be afeard now of your four legs; for it hath been said, As proper a man as ever went on four legs cannot make him give ground; and it shall be said so again while Stephano breathes at's nostrils.

Caliban. The spirit torments me; Oh!

---

45 **swabber** : a sailor who cleans the decks. 57 **salvages** : savages. 58 **Ind** : India. *[N].* 59–60 **As proper a man** : as fine a fellow. *[N].* 62 **at 'nostrils** : at the nostrils, by the nose.

Stephano. This is some monster of the isle with four legs, who hath got, as I take it, an ague. Where the devil should he learn our language? I will give him some relief, if it be but for that. if I can recover him and keep him tame and get to Naples with him, he's a present for any emperor that ever trod on neat's leather.

Caliban. Do not torment me, prithee; I'll bring my wood home faster.

Stephano. He's in his fit now and does not talk after the wisest. He shall taste of my bottle: if he have never drunk wine afore will go near to remove his fit. If I can recover him and keep him tame, I will not take too much for him; he shall pay for him that hath him, and that soundly.

Caliban. Thou dost me yet but littlehurt; thou wilt anon,
I know it by thy trembling: now Prosper works upon thee.

Stephano. Come on your ways; open your mouth; here is that which will give language to you, cat: open your mouth; this will shake your shaking, I can tell you, and that soundly: you cannot tell who's your friend: open your chaps again.

Trinculo. I should know that voice: it should be—but he is drowned; and these are devils: O defend me!

---

66 **should he learn** : can he have learnt. 67 **recover** : bring about his recovery. 69 **neat's leather** : ox or cow hide. 74 **afore** : before. 75–6 **I will not . . . him** : no price will be too high for him, i.e. he's worth any money. 79 **anon** : presently. 84–5 **you cannot . . . friend** : you don't know your own friends. 85 **chaps** : jaws.

Stephano. Four legs and two voices: a most delicate monster! His forward voice now is to speak well of his friend; his backward voice is to utter foul speeches and to detract. If all the wine in my bottle will recover him, I will help his ague. Come. Amen! I will pour some in thy other mouth.

Trinculo. Stephano!

Stephano. Doth thy other mouth call me? Mercy, mercy! This is a devil, and no monster: I will leave him; I have no long spoon.

Trinculo. Stephano! If thou beest Stephano, touch me and speak to me: for I am Trinculo be not afeard thy good friend Trinculo.

Stephano. If thou beest Trinculo, come forth: I'll pull thee by the lesser legs: if any be Trinculo's legs, these are they. Thou art very Trinculo indeed! How camest thou to be the siege of this moon-calf? can he vent Trinculos?

Trinculo. I took him to be killed with a thunder-stroke. But art thou not drowned, Stephano? I hope now thou art not drowned. Is the storm overblown? I hid me under the dead moon-calf's gaberdine for fear of the storm. And art thou living, Stephano? O Stephano, two Neapolitans 'scaped!

Stephano. Prithee, do not turn me about; my stomach is not constant.

Caliban. [*Aside.*] These be fine things, an if they be not sprites.
That's a brave god and bears celestial liquor.
I will kneel to him.

Stephano. How didst thou 'scape? How camest thou hither?

---

104 **siege** : excrement. 105 **him** : i.e. Stephano. 108 **moon-calf** : mis-shapen birth, monster. 112 **constant** : firm, steady. 113 **an if** : if.

swear by this bottle how thou camest hither. I escaped upon a butt of sack which the sailors heaved o'er-board, by this bottle; which I made of the bark of a tree with mine own hands since I was cast ashore.

Caliban. I'll swear upon that bottle to be thy true subject; for the liquor is not earthly.

Stephano. Here; swear then how thou escapedst.

Trinculo. Swum ashore. man, like a duck: I can swim like a duck, I'll be sworn.

Stephano. Here, kiss the book [*gives Trinculo drink*]. Though thou canst swim like a duck, thou art made like a goose.

Trinculo. O Stephano. hast any more of this?

Stephano. The whole butt, man: my cellar is in a rock by the sea-side where my wine is hid. How now, moon-calf! how does thine ague?

Caliban. Hast thou not dropp'd from heaven?

Stephano. Out o' the moon, I do assure thee: I was the man i' the moon when time was.

Caliban. I have seen thee in her and I do adore thee: my mistress show'd me thee and thy dog and thy bush.

Stephano. Come, swear to that; kiss the book: I will furnish it anon with new contents swear.

Trinculo. By this good light, this is a very shallow monster! I afeard of him! A very weak monster! The man i' the moon! A most poor credulous monster! Well drawn, monster, in good sooth!

Caliban. I'll show thee every fertile inch o' th' island; And I will kiss thy foot: I prithee, be my god.

---

118 **sack** : Spanish white wine. 135 **when time was** : once upon a time. 142–3 **Well drawn** : you have taken a fine pull (draw) at the bottle.

Trinculo. By this light, a most perfidious and drunken monster! when 's god's asleep, he'll rob his bottle.

Caliban. I'll kiss thy foot; I'll swear myself thy subject.

Stephano. Come on then; down, and swear.

Trinculo. I shall laugh myself to death at this puppy-headed monster. A most scurvy monster! I could find in my heart to beat him,—

Stephano. Come, kiss.

Trinculo. But that the poor monster's in drink: an abominable monster!

Caliban. I'll shew thee the best springs; I'll pluck thee berries;
I'll fish for thee and get thee wood enough.
A plague upon the tyrant that I serve!
I'll bear him no more sticks, but follow thee,
Thou wondrous man.

Trinculo. A most ridiculous monster, to make a wonder of a Poor drunkard!

Caliban. I prithee, let me bring thee where crabs grow;
And I with my long nails will dig thee pignuts;
Show thee a jay's nest and instruct thee how
To snare the nimble marmoset; I'll bring thee
To clustering filberts and sometimes I'll get thee
Young scamels from the rock. Wilt thou go with me?

Stephano. I prithee now, lead the way without any more talking. Trinculo, the king and all our company else being drowned, we will inherit here: here; bear my bottle: fellow Trinculo, we'll fill him by and by again.

---

163 **crabs** : crab-apples. 164 **pig-nuts** : earth-nuts, edible roots. 167 **filberts** : hazel nuts. 168 **scamels** : possibly 'sea-mews'. *[N]*. 170 **all our company else** : all the res of our party. 171 **inherit** : enter into possession, dwell. *[N]*.

Caliban. Farewell master; farewell, farewell.

[*Sings drunkenly.*

Trinculo. A howling monster: a drunken monster!

Caliban. No more dams I'll make for fish;
Nor fetch in firing
At requiring;
Nor scrape trenchering, nor wash dish
Ban, 'Ban, CaCaliban
Has a new master: get a new man.
Freedom, hey-day! hey-day, freedom! freedom, high-day, freedom!

Stephano. O brave monster! Lead the way. [*Exeunt.*

---

177 **trenchering** : Caliban's drunken rendering of trencher = a plate, or platter.

Act Three

Scene One

Before Prospero's Cell

Enter FERDINAND, *bearing a log*

Ferdinand. There be some sports are painful, and their labour
Delight in them sets off: some kinds of baseness
Are nobly undergone and most poor matters
Point to rich ends. This my mean task
Would be as heavy to me as odious, but
The mistress which I serve quickens what's dead
And makes my labours pleasures: O, she is
Ten times more gentle than her father's crabbed,
And he's composed of harshness. I must remove
Some thousands of these logs and pile them up,
Upon a sore injunction: my sweet mistress
Weeps when she sees me work, and says, such baseness
Had never like executor. I forget:

---

2 **sets off** : cancels. *[N]*. **most poor** : This is ambiguous. Either (1) very trivial, or (2) the majority of trivial (matters). 5 **but** : but that. 6 **which** : archaic for 'whom'. **quickens** : makes quick (i.e. alive), gives life to. 11 **sore injunction** : harsh order.

But these sweet thoughts do even refresh my labours,
Most busy lest, when I do it.

Enter MIRANDA; *and* PROSPERO *behind.*

Miranda. Alas, now, pray you
Work not so hard: I would the lightning had
Burnt up those logs that you are enjoin'd to pile!
Pray, set it down and rest you: when this burns,
'Twill weep for having wearied you. My father
Is hard at study; pray now, rest yourself;
He's safe for these three hours.

Ferdinand. O most dear mistress,
The sun will set before I shall discharge
What I must strive to do.

Miranda. If you'll sit down,
I'll bear your logs the while: pray, give me that;
I'll carry it to the pile.

Ferdinand. No, precious creature:
I had rather crack my sinews, break my back,
Than you should such dishonour undergo,
While I sit lazy by.

Miranda. It would become me
As well as it does you: and I should do it
With much more ease; for my good will is to it,
And yours it is against.

Prospero. [*Aside.*] Poor worm, thou art infected!
This visitation shows it.

Miranda. You look wearily.

---

12 **baseness** : humble task. 13 **like executor** : such a person performing (it). 15 **Most busy lest when I do it** : i.e. busiest when I am least busy. *[N]*.

Ferdinand. No, noble mistress; 'tis fresh morning with me
When you are by at night. I do beseech you—
Chiefly that I might set it in my prayers—
What is your name?
Miranda. Miranda.—O my father,
I have broke your hest to say so!
Ferdinand. Admired Miranda!
Indeed the top of admiration! worth
What's dearest to the world! Full many a lady
I have eyed with best regard and many a time
The harmony of their tongues hath into bondage
Brought my too diligent ear: for several virtues
Have I liked several women; never any
With so fun soul, but some defect in her
Did quarrel with the noblest grace she owed
And put it to the foil: but you, O you,
So perfect and so peerless, are created
Of every creature's best.
Miranda. I do not know
One of my sex; no woman's face remember,
Save, from my glass, mine own; nor have I seen
More that I may call men than you, good friend,
And my dear father: how features are abroad,
I am skilless of; but, by my modesty,
The jewel in my dower, I would not wish
Any companion in the world but you,
Nor can imagination form a shape,

---

37 **hest** : command. *[N]*. 40 **best regard** : closest attention. 42 **several** : different. 45 **ow'd** : possessed. 46 **put it to the foil** : defeated it. 48 **Of every creature's best** : out of the best features in all others. 53 **skill-less** : ignorant.

Besides yourself, to like of. But I prattle
Something too wildly and my father's precepts
I therein do forget.

Ferdinand. I am in my condition
A prince, Miranda; I do think, a king;
I would, not so!—and would no more endure
This wooden slavery than to suffer
The flesh-fly blow my mouth. Hear my soul speak:—
The very instant that I saw you, did
My heart fly to your service; there resides,
To make me slave to it; and for your sake
Am I this patient log—man.

Miranda. Do you love me?

Ferdinand. O heaven, O earth, bear witness to this sound,
And crown what I profess with kind event
If I speak true! if hollowly, invert
What best is boded me to mischief! I
Beyond all limit of what else i' the world
Do love, prize, honour you.

Miranda. I am a fool
To weep at what I am glad of.

Prospero. [*Aside.*] Fair encounter
Of two most rare affections! Heavens rain grace
On that which breeds between 'em!

Ferdinand. Wherefore weep you?

---

59 **condition** : worldly state. 61 **would no more endure** : i.e. if it were not for your sake. *[N]*. 62 **wooden slavery** : the slavery of bearing logs. 63 **blow** : literally, 'deposit its eggs in' (cf. 'fly-blown'). 69 **kind event** : prosperous result. 70 **hollowly** : falsely. 70—1 **invert . . . mischief!** : turn all the best fortune that is promised me into evil. 72 **what else** : whatever else may be. 76 **that which breeds** : i.e. their growing affection.

Miranda. At mine unworthiness that dare not offer
What I desire to give, and much less take
What I shall die to want. But this is trifling;
And all the more it seeks to hide itself,
The bigger bulk it shows. Hence, bashful cunning!
And prompt me, plain and holy innocence!
I am your wife, it you will marry me;
If not, I'll die your maid: to be your fellow
You may deny me; but I'll be your servant,
Whether you will or no.

Ferdinand. My mistress, dearest;
And I thus humble ever.

Miranda. My husband, then?

Ferdinand. Ay, with a heart as willing
As bondage e'er of freedom: here's my hand.

Miranda. And mine, with my heart in't; and now farewell
Till half an hour hence.

Ferdinand. A thousand thousand!

[*Exeunt* FERDINAND *and* MIRANDA *severally.*

Prospero. So glad of this as they I cannot be,
Who are surprised withal; but my rejoicing
At nothing can be more. I'll to my book,
For yet ere supper-time must I perform
Much business appertaining. [*Exit.*

---

79 **to want** : for wanting, i.e. for being without. 80 **it** : i.e. my love. 84 **maid** : unmarried girl. *[N]*. **fellow** : ef. Ⅱ. ⅰ. 269. 89 **As bondage e'er of freedom** : as the prisoner is to be free (of =for). *[N]*. 93 **withal** : Either (1) in addition, as well, or (2) with it, at it. *[N]*.

Scene Two

ANOTHER PART OF THE ISLAND

Enter CALIBAN, *with a bottle,* STEPHANO, *and* TRINCULO.

Stephano. Tell not me:—when the butt is out, we will drink water; not a drop before: therefore bear up, and board 'em.— Servant- monster, drink to me.

Trinculo. Servant-monster! the folly of this island! They say there's but five upon this isle: we are three of them; if th' other two be brained like us, the statetotters.

Stephano. Drink, servant-monster, when I bid thee: thy eyes are almost set in thy head.

Trinculo. Where should they be set else? he were a brave monster indeed, if they were set in his tail.

Stephano. My man-monster hath drown'd his tongue in sack: for my part, the sea cannot drown me; I swam, ere I could recover the shore, five and thirty leagues off and on. By this light, thou shalt be my lieutenant, monster, or my standard.

Trinculo. Your lieutenant, if you list; he's no standard.

Stephano. We'll not run, Monsieur Monster.

Trinculo. Nor go neither; but you'll lie like dogs and yet say nothing neither.

Stephano. Moon-calf, speak once in thy life, if thou beest a good moon-calf.

Caliban. How does thy honour? Let me lick thy shoe.
I'll not serve him; he's not valiant.

Trinculo. Thou liest, most ignorant monster: I am in case to

---

1 **out :** empty. 2 **bear up** : sail towards. *[N]*. 6 **be brained** : have brains. 9 **set** : fixed. *[N]*. 13 **recover** : reach. 15 **standard** : standard-bearer. *[N]*. 18 **go** : walk. **lie** : (1) lie down, (2) tell lies.

justle a constable.

Why, thou deboshed fish thou, was there ever man a coward that hath drunk so much sack as I to-day?

Wilt thou tell a monstrous lie, being but half a fish and half a monster?

Caliban. Lo, how he mocks me! wilt thou let him, my lord?

Trinculo. 'Lord' quoth he! That a monster should be such a natural!

Caliban. Lo, lo, again! bite him to death, I prithee.

Stephano. Trinculo, keep a good tongue in your head: if you prove a mutineer,—the next tree! The poor monster's my subject and he shall not suffer indignity.

Caliban. I thank my noble lord. Wilt thou be pleased to hearken once again to the suit I made to thee?

Stephano. Marry, will I kneel and repeat it; I will stand, and so shall Trinculo.

Enter ARIEL, *invisible.*

Caliban. As I told thee before, I am subject to a tyrant, a sorcerer, that by his cunning hath cheated me of the island.

Ariel. Thou liest.

Caliban. Thou liest, thou jesting monkey, thou: I would my valiant master would destroy thee! I do not lie.

Stephano. Trinculo, if you trouble him any more in his tale, by this hand, I will supplant some of your teeth.

Trinculo. Why, I said nothing.

Stephano. Mum, then, and no more. [*To Caliban.*] Pro-ceed.

24—5 **in case to** : in a condition to. 25 **deboshed** : besotted. 31 **natural** : simpleton. 35 **the next tree** : i.e. you will be hanged on the nearest tree. 39 **Marry** : a mild oath ('by Mary'), equivalent to 'By Jove!' 47 **supplant** : uproot. 49 **Mum** : silence!

Caliban. I say, by sorcery he got this isle;
From me he got it. if thy greatness will
Revenge it on him,—for I know thou darest,
But this thing dare not,—

Stephano. That's most certain.

Caliban. Thou shalt be lord of it and I'll serve thee.

Stephano. How now shall this be compassed? Canst thou bring me to the party?

Caliban. Yea, yea, my lord: I'll yield him thee asleep,
Where thou mayst knock a nail into his bead.

Ariel. Thou liest; thou canst not.

Caliban. What a pied ninny's this! Thou scurvy patch!
I do beseech thy greatness, give him blows
And take his bottle from him: when that's gone
He shall drink nought but brine; for I'll not show him
Where the quick freshes are.

Stephano. Trinculo, run into no further danger: interrupt the monster one word further, and, by this hand, I'll turn my mercy out o' doors and make a stock-fish of thee.

Trinculo. Why, what did I? I did nothing. I'll go farther off.

Stephano. Didst thou not say he lied?

Ariel. Thou liest.

Stephano. Do I so? take thou that. [*Strikes* TRINCULO.]
As you like this, give me the lie another time.

Trinculo. I did not give the lie. Out o' your wits and bearing too?—A pox o' your bottle! this can sack and drinking do.—

---

52 **thy greatness** : i.e. your lordship. 54 **this thing** : i.e. Trinculo. 58 **the party** : the person concerned. *[N]*. 59 **yield him thee** : give him up to you. 62 **pied ninny** : motley fool. *[N]*. **patch** : clown. 66 **quick freshes** : flowing springs, or streams. 69 **stock-fish** : dried and salted cod. *[N]*. 75 **give me the lie** : contradict me. 78 **murrain** : a (cattle) disease.

A murrain on your monster, and the devil take your fingers!
Caliban. Ha, ha, ha!
Stephano. Now, forward with your tale.—Prithee, stand further off.
Cnaliban. Beat him enough: after a little time
I'll beat him too.
Stephano. Stand farther. Come, proceed.
Caliban. Why, as I told thee, 'tis a custom with him,
I' th' afternoon to sleep: there thou mayst brain him,
Having first seized his books, or with a log
Batter his skull, or paunch him with a stake,
Or cut his wezand with thy knife. Remember
First to possess his books; for without them
He's but a sot, as I am, nor hath not
One spirit to command: they all do hate him
As rootedly as I. Burn but his books.
He has brave utensils,—for so he calls them,—
Which when he has a house, he'll deck withal:
And that most deeply to consider is
The beauty of his daughter; he himself
Calls her a nonpareil: I never saw a woman,
But only Sycorax my dam and she;
But she as far surpasseth Sycorax
As great'st does least.
Stephano. Is it so brave a lass?
Caliban. Ay, lord; she will become thy bed, I warrant.

---

88 **paunch** : stab in the stomach. 89 **wezand** : wind-pipe. 90 **possess** : get possession of. 91 **sot** : blockhead. 93 **but** : only. 94 **brave** : cf. I. ii. 6, &c. *[N].* 95 **Which . . . withal** : with which he will adorn his house when he has one. 96 **that most deeply to consider** : the thing most worth considering, the greatest attraction.

And bring thee forth brave brood.

Stephano. Monster, I will kill this man: his daughter and I will be king and queen—save our graces!—and Trinculo and thyself shall be viceroys. Dost thou like the plot, Trinculo?

Trinculo. Excellent.

Stephano. Give me thy hand: I am sorry I beat thee; but, while thou livest, keep a good tongue in thy head.

Caliban. Within this half hour will he be asleep;
Wilt thou destroy him then?

Stephano. Ay, on mine honour.

Ariel. This will I tell my master.

Caliban. Thou makest me merry; I am full of pleasure:
Let us be jocund: will you troll the catch
You taught me but while-ere?

Stephano. At thy request, monster, I will do reason, any reason. Come on, Trinculo, let us sing. [*Sings.*
Flout 'em and scout 'em ; and scout 'em and flout 'em ;
Thought is free.

Caliban. That's not the tune.

[ARIEL *plays the tune on a tabour and pipe.*

Stephano. What is this same?

Trinculo. This is the tune of our catch, played by the picture of Nobody.

Stephano. If thou beest a man, show thyself in thy likeness: if thou beest a devil, take't as thou list.

Trinculo. O, forgive me my sins!

Stephano. He that dies pays all debts: I defy thee.

---

105 **save** : cf. Ⅱ. ⅰ. 165. 115 **troll the catch** : sing the partsong. *[N].* 116 **but while-ere** : only a short time ago. 117 **do reason** : give you satisfaction. *[N].* ***(s.d.) tabor*** : a small drum carried at the side. 126 **as thou list** : as you like. *[N].*

—Mercy upon us!
Caliban. Art thou afeard?
Stephano. No, monster, not I.
Caliban. Be not afeard; the isle is full of noises,
Sounds and sweet airs, that give delight and hurt not.
Sometimes a thousand twangling instruments
Will hum about mine ears, and sometime voices
That, if I then had waked after long sleep,
Will make me sleep again: and then, in dreaming,
The clouds methought would open and show riches
Ready to drop upon me that, when I waked,
I cried to dream again.

Stephano. This will prove a brave kingdom to me, where I shall have my music for nothing.

Caliban. When Prospero is destroyed.

Stephano. That shall be by and by: I remember the story.

Trinculo. The sound is going away; let's follow it, and after do our work.

Stephano. Lead, monster; we'll follow.—I would I could see this tabourer; he lays it on.

Trinculo. Wilt come? I'll follow, Stephano. [*Exeunt.*

---

144 **by and by** : immediately (cf. 'presently'). *[N]*. 148 **he lays it on** : he thumps his drum vigorously.

Scene Three

ANOTHER PART OF THE ISLAND

Enter ALONSO, SEBASTIAN, ANTONIO, GONZALO, ADRIAN, FRANCISCO, *and others.*

Gonzalo. By'r lakin, I can go no further, sir;
My old bones ache: here's a maze trod indeed
Through forth-rights and meanders! By your patience,
I needs must rest me.

Alonso. Old lord, I cannot blame thee,
Who am myself attach'd with weariness,
To the dulling of my spirits: sit down, and rest.
Even here I will put off my hope and keep it
No longer for my flatterer: he is drown'd
Whom thus we stray to find, and the sea mocks
Our frustrate search on land. Well, let him go.

Antonio. [*Aside to* SEBASTINAN.]I am right glad that he's so out of hope.
Do not, for one repulse, forego the purpose
That you resolved to effect.

Sebastian. [*Aside to* ANTONIO.] The next advantage
Will we take throughly.

Antonio. [*Aside to Sebastian.*] Let it be to-night;
For, now they are oppress'd with travel, they
Will not, nor cannot, use such vigilance
As when they are fresh.

---

1 **By'r lakin** : by our ladykin (i.e. little Lady, viz. the Virgin Mary). 3 **forth-rights** : straight paths. **meanders** : wandering paths. **by your patience** : with your leave. 5 **attach'd** : seized. 6 **To the dulling . . . spirits** : to such an extent that my spirits are dulled. 8 **for my flatterer** : to be my flatterer, to flatter me. 10 **frustrate** : vain, unavailing. 13 **advantage** : opportynity. 13 **throughly** : thoroughly.

Sebastian. [*Aside to* ANTONIO.] I say, to-night: no more.

Solemn and strange music; and PROSPERO *on the top, invisible. Enter several strange Shapes, bringing in a banquet, and dance about it with gentle actions of salutation; and, inviting the King, &c., to eat, they depart.*

Alonso. What harmony is this? My good friends, hark!
Gonzalo. Marvellous sweet music!
Alonso. Give us kind keepers, heavens! What were these?
Sebastian. A living drollery. Now I will believe
That there are unicorns, that in Arabia
There is one tree, the phoenix' throne, one phoenix
At this hour reigning there.
Antonio. I'll believe both;
And what does else want credit, come to me,
And I'll be sworn 'tis true: travellers ne'er did lie,
Though fools at home condemn 'em.
Gonzalo. If in Naples
I should report this now, would they believe me?
If I should say, I saw such islanders—
For, certes, these are people of the island—
Who, though they are of monstrous shape, yet, note,
Their manners are more gentle-kind than of
Our human generation you shall find
Many, nay, almost any.
Prospero. [*Aside.*] Honest lord,
Thou hast said well; for some of you there present
Are worse than devils.

---

20 **keepers** : guardian angels. 21 **drollery** : puppet-show. 25 **want credit** : fail to gain belief. 25 **come to me** : come and ask me about it. 30 **certes** : truly. 32 **gentle-kind** : courteous. *[N]*. 33 **generation** : race. birth. 36 **muse** : marvel at.

Alonso. I cannot too much muse
Such shapes, such gesture and such sound, expressing,
Although they want the use of tongue, a kind
Of excellent dumb discourse.
Prospero. [*Aside.*] Praise in departing.
Francisco. They vanish'd strangely.
Sebastian. No matter, since
They have left their viands behind; for we have stomachs.
Will't please you taste of what is here?
Alonso. Not I.
Gonzalo. Faith, sir, you need not fear. When we were boys,
Who would believe that there were mountaineers
Dew-lapp'd like bulls, whose throats had hanging at 'em
Wallets of flesh? or that there were such men
Whose heads stood in their breasts? which now we find
Each putter-out of five for one will bring us
Good warrant of.
Alonso. I will stand to and feed,
Although my last: no matter, since I feel
The best is past. Brother, my lord the duke,
Stand to and do as we.

Thunder and lightning. Enter Ariel, like a harpy; claps his wings upon the table; and, with a quaint device, the banquet vanishes.

Ariel. You are three men of sin, whom Destiny,—

39 **Praise in departing** : Be careful how you praise! *[N]*. 48 **Each putter-out of five for one** : each traveller (who has taken out an insurance on his safe return). *[N]*. 49 **stand to** : fall to, i.e. begin to eat. *[N]*. 50 **Although my last** : i.e. although my last meal, if it is the last food I ever eat. 51 **The best** : i.e. the best part of my life.

That hath to instrument this lower world
And what is in't, the never-surfeited sea
Hath caused to belch up you; and on this island
Where man doth not inhabit; you 'mongst men
Being most unfit to live. I have made you mad;
[*Seeing Alonso, Sebastian, &c., draw their swords.*
And even with such-like valour men hang and drown
Their proper selves. You fools! I and my fellows
Are ministers of Fate: the elements,
Of whom your swords are temper'd, may as well
Wound the loud winds, or with bemock'd-at stabs
Kill the still-closing waters, as diminish
One dowle that's in my plume: my fellow-ministers
Are like invulnerable. If you could hurt,
Your swords are now too massy for your strengths,
And will not be uplifted. But remember—
For that's my business to you—that you three
From Milan did supplant good Prospero;
Exposed unto the sea, which hath requit it,
Him and his innocent child: for which foul deed
The powers, delaying, not forgetting, have
Incensed the seas and shores, yea, all the creatures,
Against your peace. Thee of thy son, Alonso,

---

54 **to instrument** : as its (i.e. Destiny) instrument. 55–6 **the never-surfeited . . . up you** : (whom Destiny) has caused the ever-hungry sea to vomit up. *[N]*. 57 **inhabit** : dwell. 57–8 **you . . . Being** : seeing that you are. 60 **Their proper selves** : their own essential selves, their true nature. 61 **ministers** : servants (cf. I. ii. 131). 62 **whom** : which. *[N]*. 64 **still-closing** : constantly closing (cf. 'still-vex'd', I. ii. 229). 65 **dowle** : down feather. 66 **like** : equally, in like manner. 67 **massy** : heavy. 71 **requit** : requited. 74 **all the creatures** : all creation.

They have bereft; and do pronounce by me:
Lingering perdition, worse than any death
Can be at once, shall step by step attend
You and your ways; whose wraths to guard you from—
Which here, in this most desolate isle, else falls
Upon your heads—is nothing but heart-sorrow
And a clear life ensuing.

He vanishes in thunder; then, to soft music enter the Shapes again, and dance, with mocks and mows, and carrying out the table.

Prospero. [*Aside.*] Bravely the figure of this harpy hast thou
Perform'd, my Ariel; a grace it had, devouring:
Of my instruction hast thou nothing bated
In what thou hadst to say: so, with good life
And observation strange, my meaner ministers
Their several kinds have done. My high charms work
And these mine enemies are all knit up
In their distractions; they now are in my power;
And in these fits I leave them, while I visit
Young Ferdinand, whom they suppose is drown'd,
And his and mine loved darling. [*Exit above.*
Gonzalo. I' the name of something holy, sir, why stand you
In this strange stare?

---

76 **pronounce** : pronounce (that). 79 **whose** : i.e. of the powers (I . 73). 81 **is nothing but** : i.e. there is nothing for it, no alternative, but. 82 **clear** : blameless. **(s.d.) mows** : grimaces. 84 **devouring** : absorbing. *[N]*. 85 **bated** : omitted. 86 **good life** : with great liveliness. *[N]*. 87 **observation** : observant care. **strange** : unusual, exceptional. 88 **Their several kinds** : according to their several natures. **high** : strong, powerful. 89 **knit up** : tied up, bound.

Alonso. O, it is monstrous, monstrous:
Methought the billows spoke and told me of it;
The winds did sing it to me, and the thunder,
That deep and dreadful organ-pipe, pronounced
The name of Prosper: it did bass my trespass.
Therefore my son i' the ooze is bedded, and
I'll seek him deeper than e'er plummet sounded
And with him there lie mudded. [*Exit.*

Sebastian. But one fiend at a time,
I'll fight their legions o'er.

Antonio. I'll be thy second.

[*Exeunt* SEBASTIAN, *and* ANTONIO.

Gonzalo. All three of them are desperate: their great guilt,
Like poison given to work a great time after,
Now 'gins to bite the spirits. I do beseech you
That are of suppler joints, follow them swiftly
And hinder them from what this ecstasy
May now provoke them to.

Adrian. Follow, I pray you. [*Exeunt.*

---

96 **it** : i.e. Alonso's fault. 99 **it did bass my trespass** : it told my fault in a deep voice. 102 **mudded** : buried in mud. 102–3 **But one . . . o'er** : provided I can take on the fiends one at a time, I'll fight them all. 105 **given . . . after** : administered with the intention that it should take effect much later (or, 'given to' = 'whose nature it is to'). 106 **'gins** : begins. 108 **ecstasy** : frenzy.

Act Four

Scene One

Before Prospero's Cell

Enter PROSPERO, FERDINAND, *and* MIRINDA.

Prospero. If I have too austerely punish'd you,
Your compensation makes amends, for I
Have given you here a third of mine own life,
Or that for which I live; who once again
I tender to thy hand: all thy vexations
Were but my trials of thy love and thou
Hast strangely stood the test here, afore Heaven,
I ratify this my rich gift. O Ferdinand,
Do not smile at me that I boast her off,
For thou shalt find she will outstrip all praise
And make it halt behind her.
Ferdinand. I do believe it
Against an oracle.
Prospero. Then, as my gift and thine own acquisition

---

7 **strangely** : wonderfully. **afore** : before. 9 **boast her off** : speak with pride of her. *[N]*. 11 **halt** : limp (verb). 12 **against an oracle** : i.e. if an oracle were to pronounce differently.

Worthily purchased take my daughter: but
If thou dost break her virgin-knot before
All sanctimonious ceremonies may
With full and holy rite be minister'd,
No sweet aspersion shall the heavens let fall
To make this contract grow: but barren hate,
Sour-eyed disdain and discord shall bestrew
The union of your bed with weeds so loathly
That you shall hate it both: therefore take heed,
As Hymen's lamps shall light you.

Ferdinand. As I hope
For quiet days, fair issue and long life,
With such love as 'tis now, the murkiest den,
The most opportune place, the strong'st suggestion.
Our worser genius can, shall never melt
Mine honour into lust, to take away [121]
The edge of that day's celebration
When I shall think: or Phoebus' steeds are founder'd,
Or Night kept chain'd below.

Prospero. Fairly spoke:
Sit then and talk with her; she is thine own.
What, Ariel! my industrious servant, Ariel!

Enter Ariel.

Ariel. What would my potent master? here I am.

---

14 **purchas'd** : acquired. 15 **break her virgin knot** : treat her as your wife. 16 **sanctimonious** : holy. 18 **aspersion** : that which is sprinkled, a shower. *[N]*. 22 **you . . . both** : both of you. 23 **As** : in such a way that. *[N]*. 24 **issue** : progeny, children. 25 **as 'tis now** : i.e. as my love now is. 26 **opportune** : convenient, fitting the circumstances (accent 'opportune'). **suggestion** : temptation. 27 **can** : i.e. can make. 28 **to take** : i.e. so as to take. *[N]*. 30 **founder'd** : gone lame. *[N]*. 33 **What, Ariel!** : Hullo there, Ariel! *[N]*.

Prospero. Thou and thy meaner fellows your last service
Did worthily perform; and I must use you
In such another trick. Go bring the rabble,
O'er whom I give thee power, here to this place:
Incite them to quick motion; for I must
Bestow upon the eyes of this young couple
Some vanity of mine art: it is my promise,
And they expect it from me.
Ariel. Presently?
Prospero. Ay, with a twink.
Ariel. Before you can say 'Come' and 'Go,'
And breathe twice and cry 'so, so,'
Each one, tripping on his toe,
Will be here with mop and mow.
Do you love me, master? no?
Prospero. Dearly my delicate Ariel. Do not approach
Till thou dost hear me call.
Ariel. Well, I conceive. [*Exit.*
Prospero. [*To* FERDINAND.] Look thou be true; do not give dalliance
Too much the rein: the strongest oaths are straw
To the fire i' the blood: be more abstemious,
Or else, good night your vow!
Ferdinand. I warrant you sir;
The white cold virgin snow upon my heart
Abates the ardour of my liver.
Prospero. Well.—

---

41 **vanity** : illusion (or, perhaps, 'trifle'). 42 **Presently** : at once. 43 **with a twink** : in a twinkle. 47 **mop and mow** : grimaces. 50 **Well** : it is well ; good! **conceive** : understand. 54 **good night your vow!** : it will be the end of your vow 55 **The white-cold . . . snow** : i.e. Miranda's pure breast. 55 **Well** : cf. I . 50. *[N]*.

Now come, my Ariel! bring a corollary,
Rather than want a spirit: appear and pertly!
No tongue! all eyes! be silent. [*Soft music.*

A Masque. Enter IRIS.

Iris. Ceres, most bounteous lady, thy rich leas
Of wheat, rye, barley, vetches, oats and pease;
Thy turfy mountains, where live nibbling sheep,
And flat meads thatch'd with stover, them to keep;
Thy banks with pioned and twilled brims,
Which spongy April at thy hest betrims,
To make cold nymphs chaste crowns; and thy broom groves,
Whose shadow the dismissed bachelor loves,
Being lass-lorn: thy pole-clipt vineyard;
And thy sea-marge, sterile and rocky-hard,
Where thou thyself dost air;—the queen o' the sky,
Whose watery arch and messenger am I,
Bids thee leave these, and with her sovereign grace,
Here on this grass-plot, in this very place,
To come and sport: her peacocks fly amain:
Approach, rich Ceres, her to entertain.

Enter CERES.

Ceres. Hail, many-colour'd messenger, that ne'er
Dost disobey the wife of Jupiter;

---

57 **corollary** : a surplus, too many. 58 **pertly** : promptly. 60 **leas** : arable land. *[N]*. 63 **stover** : cattle fodder. 64 **pioned and twilled** : trenched and ridged (?) *[N]*. 65 **spongy** : showery. 67 **dismissed** : rejected. 68 **pole-clipt** : with poles clasped (by vines). 70 **queen o'the sky** : Juno. 72 **her sovereign grace** : i.e. her Majesty. 74 **amain** : swiftly. *[N]*.

Who with thy saffron wings upon my flowers
Diffusest honey-drops, refreshing showers,
And with each end of thy blue bow dost crown
My bosky acres and my unshrubb'd down,
Rich scarf to my proud earth; why hath thy queen
Summon'd me hither, to this short-grass'd green?

Iris. A contract of true love to celebrate;
And some donation freely to estate
On the blest lovers.

Ceres. Tell me, heavenly bow,
If Venus or her son, as thou dost know,
Do now attend the queen? Since they did plot
The means that dusky Dis my daughter got,
Her and her blind boy's scandal'd company
I have forsworn.

Iris. Of her society
Be not afraid: I met her deity
Cutting the clouds towards Paphos and her son
Dove-drawn with her. Here thought they to have done
Some wanton charm upon this man and maid,
Whose vows are, that no bed-right shall be paid
Till Hymen's torch be lighted: but vain;
Mars's hot minion is returned again;
Her waspish-headed son has broke his arrows,
Swears he will shoot no more but play with sparrows

---

79 **honey-drops** : honey dew. *[N]*. 80 **blue bow** : i.e. the rainbow. 81 **bosky** : wooded. **unshrubb'd** : bare of shrubs. 82 **proud** : splendid, magnificent. *[N]*. 85 **estate** : give as an estate, bestow. *[N]*. 87 **her son** : i.e. Cupid. 89 **that** : by which. **Dis** : Pluto. *[N]*. 90 **scandal'd** : disgraced, shameful. 92 **her deity** : her godship, i.e. Venus. 93 **Cutting the clouds** : cleaving the sky. *[N]*. 98 **hot minion** : wonton darling (i.e. Venus).

And be a boy right out.
Ceres. High'st queen of state,
Great Juno, comes; I know her by her gait.

JUNO *descends.*

Juno. How does my bounteous sister? Go with me
To bless this twain, that they may Prosperous be,
And honour'd in their issue.

SONG

Juno. Honour, riches, marriage-blessing,
Long continuance, and increasing,
Hourly joys be still upon you!
Juno sings her blessings upon you.

Ceres. Earth's increase, foison plenty,
Barns and garners never empty,
Vines and clustering bunches growing,
Plants with goodly burthen bowing;
Spring come to you at the farthest
In the very end of harvest!
Scarcity and want shall shun you;
Ceres' blessing so is on you.

Ferdinand. This is a most majestic vision, and
Harmoniously charmingly. May I be bold
To think these spirits?
Prospero. Spirits, which by mine art

---

101 **a boy right out** : an out-and-out, real boy. 110 **foison** : abundance (cf. II. i. 160). 114 **farthest** : latest. *[N].* 117 **so** : to that end.

I have from their confines call'd to enact
My present fancies.

Ferdinand. Let me live here ever;
So rare a wonder'd father and a wife
Makes this place Paradise.

[JUNO *and* CERES *whisper, and send* IRIS *on employment.*

Prospero. Sweet, now, silence!
Juno and Ceres whisper seriously;
There's something else to do: hush, and be mute,
Or else our spell is marr'd.

Iris. You nymphs, call'd Naiads, of the windring brooks,
With your sedged crowns and ever-harmless looks,
Leave your crisp channels and on this green land
Answer your summons; Juno does command:
Come, temperate nymphs, and help to celebrate
A contract of true love; be not too late.

Enter certain Nymphs.

You sunburnt sicklemen, of August weary,
Come hither from the furrow and be merry:
Make holiday; your rye-straw hats put on
And these fresh nymphs encounter every one
In country footing.

Enter certain Reapers, *properly habited: they join with the* Nymphs *in a graceful dance; towards the end whereof* PROSPERO *starts suddenly, and speaks; after which, to a strange, hollow,*

---

121 **confines** : Either (1) places of confinement, or (2) territories. 123 **rare** : remarkable. **wonder'd** : performing wonders. 128 **windring** : winding. *[N]*. 129 **sedg'd** : reedy. 130 **crisp** : rippled. **land** : possibly a variant of 'laund' = glade. 135 **furrow** : here equivalent to 'cornfields'. 138 **footing** : dancing. **(s.d.) properly hatbited** : dressed as peapers would naturally be dressed.

and confused noise, they heavily vanish.

Prospero. [*Aside.*] I had forgot that foul conspiracy
Of the beast Caliban and his confederates
Against my life: the minute of their plot
Is almost come. [*To the Spirits.*] Well done! avoid ; no more!
Ferdinand. This is strange : your father's in some passion
That works him strongly.
Miranda. Never till this day
Saw I him touch 'd with anger so distemper'd.
Prospero. You do look, my son, in a moved sort,
As if you were dismay'd: be cheerful, sir.
Our revels now are ended. These our actors,
As I foretold you, were all spirits and
Are melted into air, into thin air:
And, like the baseless fabric of this vision,
The cloud-capp'd towers, the gorgeous palaces,
The solemn temples, the great globe itself,
Ye all which it inherit , shall dissolve
And, like this insubstantial pageant faded,
Leave not a rack behind. We are such stuff
As dreams are made on, and our little life
Is rounded with a sleep. Sir, I am vex'd;
Bear with my weakness; my, brain is troubled:
Be not disturb'd with my infirmity:
If you be pleased, retire into my cell
And there repose: a turn or two I'll walk,

---

142 **avoid** : begone. 143 **passion** : strong emotion. 144 **works** : agitates. 145 **distemper'd** : immoderate, violent. 146 **You do look . . . in a mov'd sort** : you seem to be deeply stirred. 154 **it inherit** :

To still my beating mind.
Ferdinand. Miranda. We wish your peace. [*Exeunt.*
Pro. Come with a thought—I thank thee, Ariel: come!

Enter ARIEL..

Ariel. Thy thoughts I cleave to. What's thy pleasure?
Prospero. Spirit,
We must prepare to meet with Caliban.
Ariel. Ay, my commander: when I presented Ceres,
I though to have told thee of it, but I fear'd
Lest I might anger thee.
Pro. Say again, where didst thou leave these varlets?
Ariel. I told you, sir, they were red-hot with drinking;
So fun of valour that they smote the air
For breathing in their faces; beat the ground
For kissing of their feet; yet always bending
Towards their project . Then I beat my tabour ;
At which, like unback'd colts, they prick'd their ears,
Advanced their eyelids, lifted up their noses
As they smelt music: so I charm'd their ears
That calf-like they my lowing follow'd through
Tooth'd briers, sharp furzes, pricking goss and thorns,
Which entered their frail shins: at last I left them
I' the filthy-mantled pool beyond your cell,
There dancing up to the chins, that the foul lake
O'erstunk their feet.

---

occupy, possess it. 156 **rack** : driving mist or fog. 157 **on** : of (cf. I . ii . 87).

163 **beating** : agitated. 166 **meet with** : encounter. 167 **presented** : represented, played the part of 170 **varlets** : rogues. 174 **bending** : proceeding. 176 **unback'd** : unbroken, never yet ridden. 178 **As** : as if. 180 **goss** : gorse. 182 **filthy-mantled** : covered with filthy scum. 184 **O'erstunk** : stank worse than. *[N]*.

Prospero. This was well done, my bird.
Thy shape invisible retain thou still:
The trumpery in my house, go bring it hither,
For stale to catch these thieves.
Ariel. I go, I go. [*Exit.*
Prospero. A devil, a born devil, on whose nature
Nurture can never stick; on whom my pains,
Humanely taken, all, all lost, quite lost;
And as with age his body uglier grows,
So his mind cankers. I will plague them all,
Even to roaring.

Re-enter ARIEL, *loaden with glistering apparel, &c.*
Come, hang them on this line.

PROSPERO *and* ARIEL *remain invisible. Enter* CALIBAN, STEPHANO, *and* TRINCULO, *all wet.*

Caliban. Pray you, tread softly , that the blind mole may not
Hear a foot fall: we now are near his cell.
Stephano. Monster, your fairy, which you say is a harmless fairy, has done little better than played the Jack with us.
Trinculo. Monster, I do smell all horse-piss; at which my nose is in great indignation.
Stephano. So is mine. Do you hear, monster? If I
should take a displeasure against you, look you,—
Trinculo. Thou wert but a lost monster.

---

187 **stale** : decoy, bait. *[N]*. 188 **A devil** : i.e. Caliban is a devil. 189 **Nurture** : education. 193 **to roaring** : till they roar. **line** : either 'lime-tree', 'clothes-line'. *[N]*. 196 **fairy** : i.e. ariel. 197 **played the Jack** : played the knave, tricked.

Caliban. Good my lord, give me thy favour still:
Be patient , for the prize I'll bring thee to
Shall hoodwink this mischance: therefore speak softly
All's hush'd as midnight yet.

Trinculo. Ay, but to lose our bottles in the pool,—

Stephano. There is not only disgrace and dishonour in that, monster, but an infinite loss.

Trinculo. That's more to me than my wetting: yet this is your harmless fairy, monster.

Stephano. I will fetch off my bottle, though I be o'er ears for my labour.

Caliban. Prithee, my king, be quiet. Seest thou here,
This is the mouth o' the cell: no noise, and enter.
Do that good mischief which may make this island
Thine own for ever, and I, thy Caliban,
For aye thy foot-licker.

Stephano. Give me thy hand. I do begin to have bloody thoughts.

Trinculo. O king Stephano! O peer ! O worthy Stephano! look what a wardrobe here is for thee!

Caliban. Let it alone, thou fool; it is but trash.

Trinculo. O, ho, monster! we know what belongs to a frippery O king Stephano!

Stephano. Put off that gown, Trinculo; by this hand, I'll have that gown.

Caliban. The dropsy drown this fool I what do you mean
To dote thus on such luggage? Let's along,
And do the murder first: if he awake,

---

205 **hoodwink this mischance** : hide this unfortunate event from our eyes, i.e. make it as if it had never happened. *[N]*. 225 **frippery** : old clothes shop.

From toe to crown he'll fill our skins with pinches,
Make us strange stuff.

Stephano. Be you quiet, monster. Mistress line, is not this my jerkin? Now is the jerkin under the line : now, jerkin, you are like to lose your hair and prove a bald jerkin.

Trinculo. Do, do: we steal by line and level, an't like your grace. 238

Stephano. I thank thee for that jest ; here's a garment
for't: wit shall not go unrewarded while I am king of
this country. 'Steal by line and level ' is an excellent pass
of pate; there's another garment for't.

Trinculo. Monster, come, put some lime upon your fingers, and away with the rest. 244

Caliban. I will have none on't: we shall lose our time,
And all be turn 'd to barnacles, or to apes
With foreheads villanous low.

Stephano. Monster, lay-to your fingers: help to bear this away where my hogshead of wine is, or I'll turn you out of my kingdom: go to, carry this. 250

Trinculo. And this.

Stephano. Ay, and this.

A noise of hunters heard. Enter divers Spirits, *in shape of dogs and hounds, and hunt them about,Prospero and* ARIEL *setting them on.*

Prospero. Hey, Mountain, hey!

Ariel. Silver I there it goes, Silver!

---

230 **luggage** : goods. 237 **by line and level** : methodically. **an't like** : if it please. 241–2 **pass of pate** : sally of wit. *[N]*. 243 **lime** : bird-lime. *[N]*.

Prospero. Fury, Fury! there, Tyrant, there! hark! hark!
[CALIBAN, STEPHANO, *and* TRINCULO, *are driven out.*
Go charge my goblins that they grind their joints
With dry convulsions, shorten up their sinews
With aged cramps, and more pinch-spotted make them
Than pard or cat o' mountain.
Ariel. Hark, they roar!
Prospero. Let them be hunted soundly. At this hour
Lie at my mercy all mine enemies:
Shortly shall all my labours end, and thou
Shalt have the air at freedom: for a little
Follow, and do me service. [*Exeunt.*

---

246 **barnacles** : wild geese. *[N].* 248 **lay-to** : bring to bear. 258 **aged cramps** : cramps such as attack the very old. 258–9 **more pinch-spotted . . . mountain** : give them more spots (from pinching) than there are on a leopard or wild cat. 263 **at freedom** : at liberty, as a free person.

Act Five

Scene One

Before the Cell of Prospero

Enter PROSPERO, *in his magic robes; and* ARIEL.

Prospero. Now does my project gather to a head:
My charms crack not; my spirits obey; and time
Goes upright with his carriage. How's the day?
Ariel. On the sixth hour; at which time, my lord,
You said our work should cease.
Prospero. I did say so,
When first I raised the tempest. Say, my spirit,
How fares the king and's followers?
Ariel. Confined together
In the same fashion as you gave in charge,
Just as you left them; all prisoners, sir,
In the line-grove which weather-fends your cell;
They cannot budge till your release. The king,

---

3 **carriage** : what he is carrying. *[N]*. 8 **gave in charge** : commanded. 10 **weather-fends** : shelters from the weather. 11 **till your release** : i.e. till you release them.

His brother and yours, abide all three distracted
And the remainder mourning over them,
Brimful of sorrow and dismay; but chiefly
Him that you term'd, sir, 'The good old lord Gonzalo;'
His tears run down his beard, like winter's drops
From eaves of reeds; your charm so strongly works them,
That if you now beheld them, your affections
Would become tender.

Prospero. Dost thou think so, spirit?

Ariel. Mine would, sir, were I human.

Prospero. And mine shall.
Hast thou, which art but air, a touch, a feeling
Of their afflictions, and shall not myself,
One of their kind, that relish all as sharply,
Passion as they, be kindlier moved than thou art?
Though with their high wrongs I am struck to the quick,
Yet with my nobler reason 'gaitist my fury
Do I take part: the rarer action is
In virtue than in vengeance: they being penitent,
The sole drift of my purpose doth extend
Not a frown further. Go release them, Ariel:
My charms I'll break, their senses I'll restore,
And they shall be themselves.

Ariel. I'll fetch them, sir. [*Exit.*

Prospero. Ye elves of hills, brooks, standing lakes and groves,

---

12 **abide** : continue to be. 17 **works** : moves, affects (cf. IV. i. 144). 21 **touch** : sensisbility. 23 **that relish all as sharply** : who feel (literally 'taste') just as keenly. 24 **Passion** : feel suffering. *[N]*. 25 **their high wrongs** : the deep wrongs done by them. 27 **rarer** : finer, nobler. *[N]*. 29 **The sole drift of my purpose** : my intentions which have been directed exclusively to one end. 30 **Not a frown further** : no further by way of hostility. 33 **standing** : stagnant (cf. II. i. 216).

And ye that on the sands with printless foot
Do chase the ebbing Neptune and do fly him
When he comes back; you demi-puppets that
By moonshine do the green sour ringlets make,
Whereof the ewe not bites, and you whose pastime
Is to make midnight mushrooms, that rejoice
To hear the solemn curfew; by whose aid,—
Weak masters though ye be,—I have bedimm'd
The noontide sun, call'd forth the mutinous winds,
And 'twixt the green sea and the azured vault
Set roaring war: to the dread rattling thunder
Have I given fire and rifted Jove's stout oak
With his own bolt; the strong-based promontory
Have I made shake and by the spurs pluck'd up
The pine and cedar: graves at my command
Have waked their sleepers, oped, and let 'em forth
By my so potent art. But this rough magic
I here abjure, and, when I have required
Some heavenly music, which even now I do,
To work mine end upon their senses that
This airy charm is for, I'll break my staff,
Bury it certain fathoms in the earth,
And deeper than did ever plummet sound
I'll drown my book. [*Solemn music.*

Re-enter ARIEL: *after him,* ALONSO, *with a frantic gesture, attended by* GONZALO; SEBASTIAN *and* ANTONIO *in like manner,*

---

36 **demi-puppets** : half-puppets (i.e. half the size of puppets)- fairies. 43 **azur'd** : blue. 45 **rifted** : split. *[N].* 47 **spurs** : roots. 49 **op'd** : opened. 51 **requir'd** : requested, called for. 53–4 **their senses . . . for** : the senses of those for whose benefit, &c. *[N].*

attended by ADRIAN *and* FRANCISCO: *they all enter the circle which* PROSPERO *had made, and there stand charmed; which* PROSPERO *observing, speaks:*

A solemn air and the best comforter
To an unsettled fancy cure thy brains,
Now useless, boil'd within thy skull! There stand,
For you are spell-stopp'd.
Holy Gonzalo, honourable man,
Mine eyes, even sociable to the show of thine,
Fall fellowly drops. The charm dissolves apace,
And as the morning steals upon the night,
Melting the darkness, so their rising senses
Begin to chase the ignorant fumes that mantle
Their clearer reason.—O good Gonzalo,
My true preserver, and a loyal sir
To him you follow'st! I will pay thy graces
Home both in word and deed.—Most cruelly
Didst thou, Alonso, use. me and my daughter:
Thy brother was a furtherer in the act;—
Thou art pinch'd fort now, Sebastian.—Flesh and blood,
You, brother mine, that entertain 'd ambition,
Expell'd remorse and nature; who, with Sebastian,—
Whose inward pinches therefore are most strong,—
Would here have kill'd your king; I do forgive thee,

---

57 **book** : i.e. fo magic (cf. III. ii. 90-3) 58 **A solemn air . . . best** : solemn music which is the best. *[N]*. 62 **Holy** : good, excellent. 63 **sociable to . . . thine** : companiable to (i.e. in sympathy with) the (tearful) appearance fo yours. 64 **Fall fellowly drops** : let fall drops in sympathy. 67 **mantle** : cover with scum. *[N]*. 69 **sir** : gentleman. 71 **Home** : thoroughly. 76 **remorse** : pity. **nature** : i.e. natural feeling.

Unnatural though thou art.—Their understanding
Begins to swell, and the approaching tide
Will shortly fill the reasonable shore
That now lies foul and muddy. Not one of them
That yet looks on me, or would know me Ariel,
Fetch me the hat and rapier in my cell:— [*Exit* ARIEL.
I will discase me, and myself present
As I was sometime Milan: quickly, spirit;
Thou shalt ere long be free.

[ARIEL *re-enters, singing, and helps to attire* PROSPERO.

Ariel. Where the bee sucks. there suck I:
In a cowslip's bell I lie;
There I couch when owls do cry.
On the bat's back I do fly
After summer merrily.
Merrily, merrily shall I live now
Under the blossom that hangs on the bough.

Prospero. Why, that's my dainty Ariel! I shall miss thee:
But yet thou shalt have freedom;—so, so, so.—
To the king's ship, invisible as thou art:
There shalt thou find the mariners asleep
Under the hatches; the master and the boatswain
Being awake, enforce them to this place,
And presently, I prithee.

---

81 **reasonable shores** : shores of the reason. 85 **discase me** : undress myself (i.e. throw off his magic robe, &c.). 86 **sometime Milan** : formerly Duke of Milan. 90 **couch** : lie. 92 **After** : in pursuit of. 99 **Under the hatches** : below deck. 100 **Being awake** : when they are awake. **enforce them** : compel them (to come). *[N]*. 101 **presently** : immediately.

Ariel. I drink the air before me, and return
Or ere your pulse twice beat. [*Exit.*
Gonzalo. All torment, trouble, wonder and amazement
Inhabits here: some heavenly power guide us
Out of this fearful country!
Prospero. Behold, sir king,
The wronged Duke of Milan, Prospero:
For more assurance that a living prince
Does now speak to thee, I embrace thy body;
And to thee and thy company I bid
A hearty welcome.
Alonso. Whe'r thou best he or no,
Or some enchanted trifle to abuse me,
As late I have been, I not know: thy pulse
Beats as of flesh and blood; and, since I saw thee,
The affliction of my mind amends, with which,
I fear, a madness held me: this must crave,—
An if this be at all, a most strange story.
Thy dukedom I resign and do entreat
Thou pardon me my wrongs.—But how should Prospero
Be living and be here?
Prospero. First, noble friend,
Let me embrace thine age, whose honour cannot
Be measured or confined.
Gonzalo. Whether this be
Or be not, I'll not swear.

---

103 **Or e'er** : before. 111 **Whe'r** : whether. 112 **enchanted trifle** : trick, deceptive appearance, due to magic. **abuse** : deceive. 113 **late** : lately. **have been** : i.e. have been deceived. 116 **crave** : demanc. 117 **And if . . . at all** : If this has any real existence, i.e. if I am not just dreaming. 119 **my wrongs** : the wrongs I have done (cf. I . 25). 121 **thine age** : you who are an old man.

Prospero. You do yet taste
Some subtilties o' the isle, that will not let you
Believe things certain. Welcome, my friends all:—
[*Aside to* SEBASTIAN *and* ANTONIO.] But you, my brace of lords, were I so minded,
I here could pluck his highness' frown upon you
And justify you traitors: at this time
I will tell no tales.
Sebastian. [*Aside.*] The devil speaks in him.
Prospero. No.
For you, most wicked sir, whom to call brother
Would even infect my mouth, I do forgive
Thy rankest fault; all of them; and require
My dukedom of thee, which perforce, I know,
Thou must restore.
Alonso. If thou be'st Prospero,
Give us particulars of thy preservation;
How thou hast met us here, who three hours since
Were wreck'd upon this shore; where I have lost,—
How sharp the point of this remembrance is!—
My dear son Ferdinand.
Prospero. I am woe for't, sir.
Alonso. Irreparable is the loss, and patience
Says it is past her cure.
Prospero. I rather think
You have not sought her help, of whose soft grace,
For the like loss I have her sovereign aid,

---

124 **subtlties** : delicacies. *[N]*. 125 **things certain** : things that are certain. 128 **justify** : prove. 132 **all of them** : all thy faults. require : call for, demand (cf. I . 51). 139 **woe** : sorry. 140−1 **patience . . . cure** : I cannot learn to bear it patiently. 142 **of whose soft grace** : by whose gentle favour.

And rest myself content.
Alonso. You the like loss!
Prospero. As great to me as late; and, supportable
To make the dear loss, have I means much weaker
Than you may call to comfort you, for I
Have lost my daughter.
Alonso. A daughter?
O heavens, that they were living both in Naples,
The king and queen there! that they were, I wish
Myself were mudded in that oozy bed
Where my son lies. When did you lose your daughter?
Prospero. In this last tempest. I perceive these lords
At this encounter do so much admire
That they devour their reason and scarce think
Their eyes do offices of truth, their words
Are natural breath: but, howsoe'er you have
Been justled from your senses, know for certain
That I am Prospero and that very duke
Which was thrust forth of Milan, who most strangely
Upon this shore, where you were wreck'd, was landed,
To be the lord on't. No more yet of this;
For 'tis a chronicle of day by day,
Not a relation for a breakfast nor
Befitting this first meeting. Welcome, sir;
This cell's my court: here have I few attendants

---

145 **late** : recent. 145–6 **supportable . . . loss** : to make the bitter loss supportable. *[N]*. 150 **that** : provided that. *[N]*. 151 **mudded** : embedded in mud (cf. III. iii. 102). 154 **admire** : wonder. 155 **devour their reason** : i.e. are open-mouthed with wonder. 156 **do offices of truth** : perform their functions truly, tell the truth. 156–7 **their words . . . breath** : that they hear and speak awake. *[N]*. 158 **justled** : jostled, hustled. 160 **of** : from. 162 **on't** : cf. I. ii. 87, &c. .

And subjects none abroad: pray you, look in.
My dukedom since you have given me again,
I will requite you with as good a thing;
At least bring forth a wonder, to content ye
As much as me my dukedom.

The entrance of the Cell opens, and discovers FERDINAND *and* MIRANDA *playing at chess.*

Miranda. Sweet lord, you play me false.
Ferdinand. No, my dear'st love,
I would not for the world.
Miranda. Yes, for a score of kingdoms you should wrangle,
And I would call it, fair play.
Alonso. If this prove
A vision of the Island, one dear son
Shall I twice lose.
Sebastian. A most high miracle!
Ferdinand. Though the seas threaten, they are merciful;
I have cursed them without cause.
[*Kneels to* ALONSO.
Alonso. Now all the blessings
Of a glad father compass thee about!
Arise, and say how thou camest here.
Miranda. O, wonder!
How many goodly creatures are there here!
How beauteous mankind is! O brave new world,
That has such people in't!
Prospero. 'Tis new to thee.

---

167 **abroad** : i.e. outside the island (or the cell). (s.d.) discovers : reveals 172 **play me false** : cheat (me). 174 **score** : twenty. *[N].* 183 **brave** : cf. I. ii. 6.

Alonso. What is this maid with whom thou wast at play?
Your eld'st acquaintance cannot be three hours:
Is she the goddess that hath sever'd us,
And brought us thus together?
Ferdinand. Sir, she is mortal;
But by immortal Providence she's mine:
I chose her when I could not ask my father
For his advice, nor thought I had one. She
Is daughter to this famous Duke of Milan,
Of whom so often I have heard renown,
But never saw before; of whom I have
Received a second life; and second father
This lady makes him to me.
Alonso. I am hers:
But, O, how oddly will it sound that I
Must ask my child forgiveness!
Prospero. There, sir, stop:
Let us not burthen our remembrance with
A heaviness that's gone.
Gonzalo. I have inly wept,
Or should have spoke ere this. Look down, you god,
And on this couple drop a blessed crown!
For it is you that have chalk'd forth the way
Which brought us hither!
Alonso. I say, Amen, Gonzalo!
Gonzalo. Was Milan thrust from Milan, that his issue

---

186 **eld'st** : at the longest. 193 **renown** : report. 194 **But never** : i.e. but (whom I) never.o is to Ferdinand). 196 **I am hers** : i.e. I am henceforward a second father to her (as Prosper is to Perdinand). 199 **remembrances** : memories. 200 **heaviness** : sorrow. 203 **chalk'd forth** : marked out. 204 **Amen** : so be it! 205 **Milan . . . Milan** : the Duke . . . the city.

Should become kings of Naples? O, rejoice
Beyond a common joy, and set it down
With gold on lasting pillars: In one voyage
Did Claribel her husband find at Tunis,
And Ferdinand, her brother, found a wife
Where he himself was lost, Prospero his dukedom
In a poor isle and all of us ourselves
When no man was his own.

Alonso. [*To* FERDINAND *and* MIRANDA.] Give me your hands:
Let grief and sorrow still embrace his heart
That doth not wish you joy!

Gonzalo. Be it so! Amen!

Re-enter ARIEL, *with the* Master *and* Boatswain *amazedly following.*

O, look, sir, look, sir! here is more of us:
I prophesied, if a gallows were on land,
This fellow could not drown. Now, blasphemy,
That swear'st grace o'erboard, not an oath on shore?
Hast thou no mouth by land? What is the news?

Boatswain. The best news is, that we have safely found
Our king and company; the next, our ship—
Which, but three glasses since, we gave out split—
Is tight and yare and bravely rigg'd as when
We first put out to sea.

Ariel. [*Aside to* PROSPERO.] Sir, all this service

---

213 **his own** : in his right senses. 214 **still** : for ever. 217 **if a gallows were** : if there existed a gallows (see Ⅰ. ⅰ. 29-31). 218 **blasphemy** : you blaspheming fellow. 219 **grace** : the grace of God. *[N]*. 223 **glasses** : cf. Ⅰ. ⅱ. 240. *[N]*. **gave out** : reported. 224 **yare** : in good trim (cf. Ⅰ. ⅰ. 6).

Have I done since I went.
Prospero. [*Aside to* ARIEL.] My ticksy spirit!
Alonso. These are not natural events; they strengthen
From strange to stranger.—Say, how came you hither?
Boatswain. If I did think, sir, I were well awake,
I'ld strive to tell you. We were dead of sleep,
And—how we know not—all clapp'd under hatches;
Where but even now with stange and several noises
Of roaring, shrieking, howling, jingling chains,
And momo diversity of sounds, all horrible,
We were awaked; straightway, at liberty;
Where we, in all her trim, freshly beheld
Our royal, good and gallant ship, our master
Capering to eye her: on a trice, so please you,
Even in a dream, were we divided from them
And were brought moping hither.
Ariel. [*Aside to* PROSPERO.] Was't well done?
Prospero. [*Aside to Ariel.*] Bravely, my diligence. Thou shalt be free.
Alonso. This is as strange a maze as e'er men trod;
And there is in this business more than nature
Was ever conduct of: some oracle
Must rectify our knowledge.
Prospero. Sir, my liege,
Do not infest your mind with beating on

---

226 **ticksy** : full of tricks, resouceful. 227–8 **strengthen . . . stranger** : increase more and more in strangeness. 230 **dead of sleep** : in a profound sleep. 232 **strange and several** : different strange. 234 **mo** : more. 236 **Where** : on which occasion, when. *[N]*. 238 **on a trice** : in a trice, moment. *[N]*. 239 **them** : i.e. the crew. 240 **moping** : moving in bewilderment. 241 **Bravely, my diligence** : excellently, my diligent (spirit). 244 **conduct of** : conductor of, instrumental in bringing about (cf. I . 227).

The strangeness of this business; at pick 'd leisure
Which shall be shortly, single I'll resovle you,—
Which to you shall seem probable,—of every
These happen'd accidents; till when, be cheerful
And think of each thing well.—[*Aside to* ARIEL.] Come hither, spirit:
Set Caliban and his companions free;
Untie the spell. [*Exit* ARIEL.] Howfare mygraciousir?
There are yet missing of your company
Some few odd lads that you remember not.

Re-enter ARIEL, *driving in* CALIBAN, STEPHANO *and* TRINCULO, *in their stolen apparel.*

Stephano. Every man shift for all the rest, and let no man take care for himself; for all is but fortune. Coragio, bully-monster, Coragio!

Trinculo. If these be true spies which I wear in my head, here's a goodly sight.

Caliban. O Setebos, these be brave spirits indeed!
How fine my master is! I am afraid
He will chastise me.

Sebastian. Ha, ha!
What things are these, my lord *Antonio*?

---

247 **pick'd** : chosen. 248 **single** : alone in private. *[N]*. **resolve you** : free you from perplexity. 249 **Which** : which (resolution), i.e. explanation. *[N]*. 249–50 **every These happen'd accidents** : every one of those events that have occurred. 251 **well** : as being for the best. 255 **odd** : not included among the others. 257 **Coragio!** : Courage! 258 **bully-monster** : gallant monster. *[N]*. 259 **If these . . . head** : if I can trust the eyes in my head. 261 **Setebos!** : cf. I. ii. 373. *[N]*. 246 **infest** : harass, trouble. **beating on** : hammering at, reasoning about (cf. I. ii. 176 ; IV. i. 163).

Will money buy 'em?
Antonio. Very like; one of them
Is a plain fish, and, no doubt, marketable.
Prospero. Mark but the badges of these men, my lords,
Then say if they be true.—This mis-shapen knave,—
His mother was a witch, and one so strong
That could control the moon, make flows and ebbs,
And deal in her command without her power.
These three have robb'd me; and this demi-devil—
For he's a bastard one—had plotted with them
To take my life. Two of these fellows you
Must know and own; this thing of darkness I
Acknowledge mine.
Caliban. I shall be pinch'd to death.
Alonso. Is not this Stephano, my drunken butler?
Sebastian. He is drunk now: where had he wine?
Alonso. And Trinculo is reeling ripe: where should they
Find this grand liquor that hath gilded 'em?
How camest thou in this pickle?
Trinculo. I have been in such a pickle since I saw you last that, I fear me, will never out of my bones: I shall not fear fly-blowing.
Sebastian. Why, how now, Stephano!
Stephano. O, touch me not; I am not Stephano, but a cramp.
Prospero. You'ld be king o' the isle, sirrah?
Stephano. I should have been a sore one then.

---

266 **a plain fish** : clearly a fish. 271 **deal in her command . . . power** : wield her (i.e. the moon's) authority without actually having the moon's power. 279 **reeling-ripe** : completely drunk. *[N]*. 279–80 **where should they Find** : where can they have found? 280 **gilded** : given a flush to (their faces). 281 **pickle** : sorry plight. 283 **that** : as. *[N]*. 288 **sore** : (1) aching, (2) severe.

Alonso. This is a strange thing as e'er I look'd on.
[*Pointing to* CALIBAN.
Prospero. He is as disproportion'd in his manners
As in his shape.—Go, sirrah, to my cell;
Take with you your companions: as you look
To have my pardon, trim it handsomely.
Caliban. Ay, that I will; and I'll be wise hereafter
And seek for grace. What a thrice-double ass
Was I, to take this drunkard for a god,
And worship this dull fool!
Prospero. Go to; away!
Alonso. Hence, and bestow your luggage where you found it.
Sebastian. Or stole it, rather.
[*Exeunt* CALIBAN, STEPHANO, *and* TRINCULO.
Prospero. Sir, I invite your highness and your train
To my poor cell, where you shall take your rest
For this one night; which, part of it, I'll waste
With such discourse as, I not doubt, shall make it
Go quick away; the story of my life
And the particular accidents gone by
Since I came to this isle: and in the morn
I'll bring you to your ship and so to Naples,
Where I have hope to see the nuptial
Of these our dear-beloved solemnized;
And thence retire me to my Milan, where
Every third though shall be my grave.
Alonso. I long

---

289 **a strange thing as e'er** : as strange a thing as ever. 290 **disproportion'd** : ill-conditioned. 292 **as you look** : in so far as you expect. 298 **luggage** : cf. Ⅳ. ⅰ. 230. 305 **particular** : in detail. **accidents** : incidents. 308 **nuptial** : marriage.

To hear the story of your life, which must
Take the ear strangely.

Prospero. I'll deliver all;
And promise you calm seas, auspicious gales
And sail so expeditious that shall catch
Your royal fieet far off. [*Aside to* ARIEL.] My Ariel, chick,
That is thy charge: then to the elements
Be free, and fare thou well! Please you, draw near.

[*Exeunt.*

---

313 **Take** : captivate. **deliver all** : tell (you) everything. 315 **sail** : sailing, voyage. **catch** : over-take. 316 **far off** : which has a long start.

EPILOGUE

Spoken bY PROSPERO

Now my charms are all o'erthrown,
And what strength I have's mine own ;
Which is most faint : now, 'tis true,
I must be here confin'd by you,
Or sent to Naples. Let me not,
Since I have my dukedom got
And pardon'd the deceiver, dwell
In this bare island by your spell ;
But release me from my bands
With the help of your good hands.
Gentle breath of yours my sails
Must fill, or else my project fails,
Which was to please. Now I want
Spirits to enforce, art to enchant ;
And my ending is despair,
Unless I be reliev'd by prayer,
Which pierces so that it assaults
Mercy itself and frees all faults.
As you from crimes would pardon'd be,
Let your indulgence set me free.

BIBLIOGRAPHY

하해성, 『셰익스피어 美學論』, 신아사, 1997.

______, 『맥베드의 미학적 읽기』, 신아사, 1998.

Adamson, Jane, *Othello as Tragedy: Some Problems of Judgement and Feeling,* Cambridge : Cambridge University Press, 1980.

Adamson, W. A., "Unpinned or Undone?: Desdemona's Critics and the Problem of Sexual Innocence", *Shakespeare Studies* 13(1980) : 169-86.

Aldus, P. J, Mousetrap, *Structure & Meaning in Hamlet,* Toronto Univ. Press, 1927.

Alexander, Niegel, Poison, Play and Duel : *A Study in Hamlet,* London: Kegan Paul, 1971.

Alexander, Peter, *Studies in Shakespeare,* New York : Oxford Univ. Press, 1964.

Antoninus, Marcus Aurelius, *The Meditations*, ed. and trans. A. S. L. Farquharson, 2vols. Oxford: The Clarendon Press, 1944.

Aristotle, Physics, trans. R. P. Hardie and R. K. Gaye, in vol. II of the *Works*, under the editorship of J. A. Smith and W. D. Ross, Oxford: the Clarendon Press, 1930.

Aronson, Alex, *Psyche and Symbol In Shakespeare*, Bloomington : Indiana University Press, 1972.

Auden, W. H., "Music in shakespeare", *Encounter* 9, No. 6(1957), 31~44.

B. Cawpbell, Lilly. *Shakespeare's Tragic Heroes,* London : Methuen, 1982.

B. E. Gent, *A New Dictionary of the Terms Ancient and Modern of the Canting Crew,* London : W. Hawes, 1699.

Badawi. M. M., *Background to Shakespeare*, London : MacMillan Press, 1981.

Barber, C. L., *Shakespeare's Festive Comedy*, Princeton University Press, 1959.

Bayley, John, *The Characters of Love*, 125-201, New York : Basic Books, 1960.

Bergson, Henry, *Time and Free Will*, trans. F. L. Pogson, London : S. Sonnenschein & Co., Ltd., 1910.

Berry, Ralph, *Shakespearean Structures*, London : Macmillan, 1981.

Betheel, S. L. "The Diabolic Images in Othello", *Shakespeare Survey* vol.V, 1952.

Bethell, S. L., *The Winter's Tale, a Study*, London : Staples Press, 1947.

Bonnard, G., "Are Othello and Desdemona Innocent or Guilty?", *English Studies* 30(1940) : 175~84.

Boose, Linda, "Othello's Handkerchief : 'The Recognizance and

Pledge of Love'", *English Literary Renaissance* 5(1975) : 360~74.

Booth Stephen, *King Lear. Macbeth Indefinition, Tragedy*, New Haven : Yale University Press, 1983.

Boswell-Stone, W. G., *Shakespeare's Holinshed*, London: Lawrence & Bullen, 1896.

Boyley, John, *Shakespeare and Tragedy*, London : Routledge & Kegan Paul, 1982.

Bradbrook, M. C., *Shakespeare the Poet in the World*, London : Weidenfeld and Nicolson, 1978.

Bradley, A. C., *Shakespearean Tragedy*, London : Macmillan & Co., Ltd., 1914(1904).

Bradley, A. C., *Shakespearean Tragedy* 2d(ed), London : Macmillan, 1924.

Bristo, Michael D., Big *Time Shakespeare*, London : Routledge, 1996.

Brown, Ivor, *Shakespeare*, London : Collins Clear-Press, 1955.

Brown, John Russell, *Shakespeare's Plays in Performance*, London : Edward Arnold Ltd., 1966.

______(Ed) : *Focus on Macbeth*, London : Routledge & Kegan Paul, 1982.

Bullough, Geoffrey, *Narrative and Dramatic Sources of Shakespeare*, London : Routledge & Kegan Paul, 1973.

______, *Narrative and Dramatic Sources* of *Shakespeare*, vol.Ⅶ, London : Routledge and Kegan Paul, 1975.

Bulman, James C., *The Heroic Idiom of Shakespearean Tragedy,*

Newark : University of Delaware Press, 1985.

Burke, Kenneth, "*Othello* : An Essay to Illustrate a Method", *The Hudson Review* 4(1951~52) : 165~203.

Burton, Robert, *The Anatomy of Melancholy*, 1621.

Bush, Geoffrey, *Shakespeare and The Natural Condition,* Cambridge : Harvard Uni. Press, 1956.

Camden, C., *The Elizabeth Woman*, New York : Paul, P., 1993.

Campbell, Lily B., *Shakespeare's Tragic Heroes, Slaves of Passion,* New York : Narnes and Noble, 1961.

Cecil, Lord David, *The Fine Art of Reading*. Indianapolis, New York : Bobbs-Merrill Co., 1957.

Chang, Vincent John, *Shakespeare and Joyce,* London : The Pennsylvania State Univ. Press, 1984.

Charlton, H. B., *Shakespearean Tragedy*, London : MacMillan, 1948.

________, *Shakespearian Comedy,* London : Methuen & Co. Ltd., 1956.

Cleman, W. H., *The Development of Shakespeare's Imagery*, London : Methuen, 1972.

_______, *Shakespeare's Dramatic Art*, Collected Essays, London : Methuen, 1972.

Clemen, Wolfgang H., *The Development of Shakespeare's Imagery*, London : Methuen & Co., 1951.

Coleridge, S. T., *Lecture's and Notes On Shakespeare and Other Dramatists,* London : Oxford University Press, 1931.

_____. *Shakespearean Criticism*, 2 vols., ed. Thomas Middetone Raysor, London: J. M. Dent & Sons, 1960.

_____. *Seven Lectures on Shakespeare and Milton*: transcript of notes by J.

Colie, Rosalie. *Shakespeare's Living Art*. Princeton, N.J.: Princeton University Press, 1974.

Collingwood, R. G., *The Idea of Nature*. Oxford: The Clarendon Press, 1945.

Cook, Ann Jennalie. "The Design of Desdemona: Doubt Raised and Resolved." *Shakespeare Studies* 13 (1980): 187~96.

Courson, H. R. *Shakespeare in Production*. Athens: Ohio Univ. Press, 1996.

Craig, W. J, Ed., *The Complete Works of William Shakespeare*, London: Oxford University Press, 1974.

Cutts, John. P., "Music and the Supernatural in *The Tempest* : A Study iterp Interpretation Music and Letters, 39 (October 1958), 347~58.

____________, *Rich and Strange: A Study of Shakespeare's Last plays*, Seattle : Washington University Press, 1968.

Danby, Johnson F., *Poets on Fortune's Hill: Study in Sidney*, Shakespeare, Beamount & Fletcher, London : Faber and Faber, 1953.

Davies, John, "Orchestra", Ed. E. M. W. Tillyard, London : Chatto and Windus, 1947.

Dean, Leonard F., Ed., *Shakespeare: Modern Essays in Criticism*, London : Oxford Press, 1977.

De Quincy, Thomas, "On The Knocking At The Gate in *Macbeth*", *Shakespeare Criticism*, 1623-1984, Ed., D. Nichol Smith,

London : Oxford University Press, 1961.

Dickes, Robert, "Desdemoan : An Innocent Victim?", *American Imago* 27(1970) : 279~97.

Doren, Mark Van., *Shakespeare,* New York : Holt, 1939.

Dowden, Edward, Shakespeare : *A Critical Study of His Mind and Art,* London : French, Trubner Co., 1892.

______, *Shakespeare : A Critical Study of His Mind and Art,* London : Kegan Paul, 1892.

Dusinberre, Juliet, *Shakespeare and The Nature of Women,* U.S.A. : ST. Martin's Press, 1996.

Duthie, G. F., "Antithesis in *Macbeth*", *Shakespeare Surveys,* Vol. 19Ed., Kenneth Muir, London : Cambridge University Press.

Egan, Robert, *Drama Within Drama : Shakespeare's Sense of His art in King Lear,* "The Winter's Tale," and "Tempest", New York : Columbia university, 1975.

Elan, Keir, *Shakespeare's Universe of Discourse,* London : Cambridge Univ. Press, 1984.

Eliot, T. S., "Shakespeare and the Stoicism of Seneca", *Selected Essays,* 110-11, New York: Harcourt, Brace, Jovanovich, 1950.

________, G. R. Flaming Minister : *A Study of Othello,* Durham, N. C. : Duke University Press, 1953.

________, *Collected Plays,* London : Faber & Faber, 1962.

________, *Four Quartets,* London : Faber & Faber, 1964(1944).

Elyot, Thomas, *The Boke Named the Governor,* Ed., Henry

Herbert Stephen Croft, 2 vols., London : K. Paul, Trench & Co., 1883.

Empson, William, *The Structure of Complex Words*, London : Chatto & Windus, 1951.

Evans, Gareth Lioyed, Ed., *The Upstart Crow : An Introduction To Shakespeare's Plays,* London : Jm Dent & Sons Ltd, 1982.

Ewbank, I. S., "Triumph of Time in The Winter's Tale", *Review of English Literature*, No. 5, 1964.

F. Dean, Leonard, Ed., *Shakespeare Modern Essays in Criticism,* New York : New York University Press, 1957.

Felperin, Howard, *Shakespearean Representation,* Princeton, N. J. : Princeton University Press, 1977.

Fiedler, Leslie, *The Stranger in Shakespeare,* New York : Stein & Day, 1972.

Flatter, Richard, *The Moor of Venice,* London : William Heinemann, 1950.

Florio, John, trans., *The Essays of Montaigne*, ed., J. I. M. Steward, 2 vols., London : The Nonesuch Press, 1931.

Fluchere, Henri, *Shakespeare,* Trans., Guy Hamilton, London : Longmans, 1953.

Fly, Richard, *Shakespeare's Mediated World,* Ambest : Univ. of Massachusetts Press, 1976.

Foakes, R. A., *Shakespeare the Dark Comedies to the Last Plays : From Satire to Celebration,* Charlottesville : The university Press of Vergina, 1971.

French, A. L., *Shakespeare And Critics,* Cambridge : Cambridge

Press, 1972.

Frey, Charles, *Shakespeare's Vast Romance : A Study of The Winter's Tale*, London : Universiity of Missouri Press, 1957.

Frye, Northrup, *A Natural persceptive : The Development of Shakespearean Comedy and Romance*, New York : Columbia University Press, 1965.

Furgusson, Francis, "Macbeth As The Imitation Of An Action", *English Institute Essays,* New York: Columbia University Press, 1952.

Gardner, Helen, "The Noble Moor", *Proceedings of the British Academy* 41(1955) : 189~205.

_______, "*Othello* : A Retrospect, 1900~67", *Shakespeare Survey* 21(1968) : 1-11.

Garner, S. N., "Shakespeare's Desdemona", *Shakespeare Studies* 9(1976) : 233~52.

Garrett, W. P., ed., *More Talking about shakespeare,* London : Longmans, Green & Co., 1959.

Gazowski, E., *The Art of Loving*, New York : University of Delaware Press, 1992.

Gesner, Carol, Shakespeare & The Greek Romance : A Study of origins, Lexington : The University Press of Kentucky, 1970.

Gohlke, Madelon, "'I wooed thee with my sword': Shakespeare's Tragic Paradigms", *The Women's Part : Feminist Criticism of Shakespeare*, ed., Carolyn Ruth Swift Lenz,

Gayle Greene and Carol Thomas Neely, Urbana : University of Illinois Press, 1980.

______________, "All that is spoke is marred': Language and Consciousness in *Othello*", *Women's Studies* 9 (1981~82) : 157~76.

Goldsmith, Robert Hills, *Wise Fools in Shakespeare*, Michigan : Michigan State Univ. Press, 1963.

Gottschalk, Paul, *The Meaning of Hamlet*, Albuquerque: University of New Mexico Press, 1972.

Granville-Barker, H., *Prefaces to Shakespeare,* London : Batsford, 1958.

Graig, W. J. ed., *The Complete Works of William Shakespeare*, London : Oxford Press, 1974.

Granville-Baker, H&G. B. Harrison, *A Companion to Shakespeare Studies,* Cambridge : Cambridge University Press, 1934.

Granville-Barker, Harley, *Prefaces to Shakespeare,* New York : Princeton Univ. Press, 1978.

______________________, *Prefaces to Shakespeare,* Second Series, London : Sidgwick & Jackson, Ltd., 1939.

Greene, Gayle, "This that you call love' : Sexual and Social Tragedy in *Othello*", *Journal of Women's Studies in Literature* 1(1979) : 16~32.

Gregson, J. M., *Public & Private Man in Shakespeare,* Toronto : Barnes & Noble Books, 1983.

Grenville, Fulke, Lord Brooke, *The Poems and Dramas*, ed., Geoffrey Bullough, Edinburgh : Oliver & Boyd, 1939.

Hankins, John Eerskine, *Background of Shakespeare's Thought,* U. S. A. : The Harvard Univ. Press, 1978.

Harbage, Alfred, ed., *Shakespeare The tragedies,* Englewood Cliffs : Prentice-Hall, Inc., 1970.

Harris, John, Stephen Orgel, and Roy Strong, *The king's Arcadia: Inigo Jones and the Stuart Court,* London : Lund Humphries for the Arts Council of Great Britain, 1973.

Harris, Laurie Lanzan, *Shakespearean Criticism,* Michigan : Gale Research Co., 1986.

______, Lanzan, *Shakespeare and The Reason,* London : Routledge & Kegan Paul, 1968.

Hawkes, T., *Twentieth Century Interpretations Of Macbeth,* Englewood Cliffs, N. J. : Prentice-Hall, 1977.

__________, *Shakespeare and The Reason,* London : Routledge & Kegan Paul, 1968.

Heilman, R, B., *Magic in the Web,* Lexington : University of Kentucky Press, 1956.

Hoeniger, F. D., "Irony and Romance *in cymbeline," Studies in English Literature,* 2(1962), 219~2.

____________, "Shakespeare's Romances Since 1958 : A Retrospect", *Shakespeare Survey 29*(1976), 1~10.

____________, ed., Pericles, The Arden Shakespeare. London : Methuen & Co. Ltd., 1963.

Holloway, John, *The Story of the Night,* London : Routledge & Kegan Paul, 1961.

Holtz, William, "Time's Chariot and *Tristram Shandy*", *Michigan*

Quarterly Review, vol.v., Summer 1966.

Hunter, G. K., "Othello and Colour Prejudice", *The Proceedings of the British Academy* 53(1967) : 139~63, Reprinted in *Dramatic Identities and Cultural Tradition,* New York : Barnes & Noble, 1978.

Hyman, Stanley Edgar, *Iago : Some Approaches to the Illusion of his Motivation,* New York : Atheneum, 1970.

Irring, Ribner, *Patterns in Shakespearean Tragedy,* London : Methuen, 1960.

Jacobs, Henry E. and Kay, Carol. M. ED., *Shakespeare's Romances Reconsidered,* Lincoln : The Univ. of Nebraska Press, 1976.

Jardine, Lisa, *Reading Shakespeare Historically,* London : Routledge, 1996.

Jeffrey, David L. and Patrick Grant, "Reputation in *Othello*", *Shakespeare Studies* 6(1970) : 197~208.

Johnson, Samuel, *Dictionary of the English Language*, London : C& J. Rivington, 1824(1755).

Kahn, Coppélia, *Man's Estate : Masculine Identity in Shakespeare.* Berkeley : University of California Press, 1981.

Kenner, Hugh, *The Counterfeiters*, Bloomington, Indian, and London : Indiana University Press, 1968.

Kermode, Frank, ed., *The Tempest*, The Arden Shakespeare, London : clarendon Press, 1954.

Kernoldle, George, *From Art to Theatre*, Chicago : University of

Chicago Press, 1944.

King James Authorized, *The Holy Bible*, Philadelphia : The National Bible Press, 1963.

Kirsch, Arthur, *Shakespeare and the Experience of Love*, 10~39, Cambridge : Cambridge University Press, 1981.

Kirschbaum, Leo, "The Modern Othello," *ELH* 11(1944) : 283~96.

Kittredge. G. L., *Witchcraft in Old and New England,* Cambridge, Massachusetts : Harvard University Press, 1929.

Knight, G. Wilson, *The Imperial Theme,* London : Methuen, 1931.

________, *The Shakeaspearean Tempest*, London : H. Milford, Oxford University Press, 1932.

________, *The Crown of Life : Essays in Interpretation of Shakespeare's Final Plays,* 1947, London : Methuen & Co., Ltd., 1948.

________, *The Wheel of Fire,* London : Methuen, 1949.

Knight, L. C., *Macbeth, Shakespeare, The Tragedy,* Ed., Alfred. Englewood Cliffs, N. J : Prentice-Hall Inc., 1964.

________, Ed., *Shakespeare Survey, Vol.XIX* Cambridge : Cambridge University Press, 1966. Volume Devoted To *Macbeth,* Murry, John Middelton, *Shakespeare,* London : Methuen, 1960.

________, *Explorations,* London, 1964, Edition Cited 1964.

________, *An Approach to Hamlet*, London : Chatto & Windus, 1960.

L. Styan, J., *The Shakespeare Revolution,* London : Cambridge Univ. Press, 1979.

Laing, R. D., *The Divided Self*, London : Tavistock Publications, 1960.

Laing, R. D., *The Politics of Experience*, London : Penguin Books, 1967.

Leach, E. R., *Rethinking Anthropology*, London : Athlone Press, 1961.

Leavis, F. R., *The Common Pursuit,* London : Chatto & Windus, 1952.

Lee, Sir Sidney, *Elizabethan and Other Essays*, selected and ed., F. S. Boas, Oxford : The Clarendon Press, 1929.

Leishman, J. B., *Themes and Variations in Shakespeare's Sonnets*, London : Hutchinson, 1961.

Lerner, Laurence, ed., *Shakespeare's Tragedies,* England : Penguin Book, 1968.

Leroy, Loys(Ludovicus Regius), *Of the Interchangeable Course, or Variety of Things in the Whole World*, trans., Robert Ashley, London : C. Yetsweirt, 1594.

Liebler, Naomi Conn, *Shakespeare's Festive Tragedy,* London : Routledge, 1995.

Long, John H., *Shakespeare's Use of Music*, 3vols., Gainsville : University of Florida Press, 1955~71.

Ludowyk, E. F. C., *Understanding Shakespeare*, London : Cambridge University Press, 1977.

Mahood, M. M., *Shakespeare's Wordplay*, London : Methuen, 1957.

Mann, Thomas, *The Magic Mountain*, trans., H. T. Lowe-Porter, New York : Alfred A. Knopf, 1939.

Mason, H. A., *Shakespeare's Tragedies of Love*, New York : Barnes & Noble, 1970.

Matteo, Gion J., *Shakespeare's Othello : The Study and the Stage, 1604~1904,* Salzburg, Austria : Institut für Englische Sprache and Literature, University Salzburg, 1974.

Mcelroy, Bernard, *Shakespeare's Nature Tragedy*, Princeton : Princeton University Press, 1973.

Mehl, Dieter, Tragedies : An Introduction. Cambridge : Harardu. P., 1978.

Mendl, R. W. S., *Revolution in Shakespeare,* London : Larke, Double and Brendon, 1964.

Milward, Peter, *Shakespeare's Religions Background,* London : Sidgwick & Jackson, 1973.

Money, John, 'Othello's "It is the cause", Shakespeare vol. 6, 1958.

Moulton, R. G., *Shakespeare The Ancient Drama*, London : Clarenden Press, 1890.

Mowat, Barabra A., *The Dramaturgy of Shakespeare's Romances,* Athens : The University of Georgia Press, 1976.

Muir, Kenneth, *William Shakespeare : the Great Tragedies,* London : Longman, Green & Co., 1961(Bibliographical Series of Supplements to British Book News, no. 133).

Murry, J. Middleton, *Shakespeare,* London : Jonathan Cape, 1965(1936).

Neill, Michael, "Changing Places in Othello", *Shakespeare Survey* 37(1984) : 115~31.

Nevo, Ruth, *Tragic Form in Shakespeare,* Princeton : Princeton

University Press, 1972.

Norden, John, *Vicissitudo Rerum*, 1600. *Shakespeare Association Facsimile*, no. 4, London : Oxford University Press, 1931.

Nosworthy, J. M. ed., *Cymbeline*, The Arden Shakespeare, London : Metheun andco Ltd., 1955.

Nowotty's Articles "Justice and love in *Othello*", *University of Toronto Quarterly*, vol. 21, 1951.

Onion, C. T., *A Shakespeare Glossary*, Oxford : The Clarendon Press, 1953.

P. Collier at Coleridge's lectures, 1811~12, London : Chapman & Hall, 1856.

P. Ker, William, ed., *Essays of John Dryden*, 2 vols., Oxford : Clarenden Press, 1900.

Partridge, Eric, *Shakespeare's Bawdy*, London : Routledge & Kegan Paul, 1955.

Paul H. N. *The Royal Paly of 'Mabeth'*, New York, 1950.

Pettet, E. C. *Shakespeare and the Romance Tradtion,* London : Staples Press, 1949.

Plato, *Timaeus*, trans., B. Jowett, New York : Liberal Arts Press, 1949(Also in *The Dialogues of Plato*, trans. B. Jowett, 5 vols. Oxford : The Clarendon Press, 1892(1868~71)).

Plotinus, *Enneads*, trans. S. Mac Kenna. London : Faber & Faber 1962(1917~30).

Poulet, Georges, *Etudes sur le temps humain*, Edinburgh University Press, 1949.

Quiller Coach, Arthur, *Shakespeare's Workmanship*, London :

Cambridge University Press, 1981.

Ray, Robert H. ed. *Approach to Teaching Shakespeare's King Lear*, New York : PMLA, 1986.

Rosenberg, Marvin, *The Masks of Othello*, Berkeley : University of California Press, 1961.

________________, *The Masks of Macbeth*, Berkley : University of California Press, 1978.

Rossiter, A. P., *Angel with Horns*, ed., Graham Storey, London : Longmans, Green, & Co., 1961.

____________, *Angel with Horns,* New York : Theatre Arts Books, 1961.

Schückling, *The Meaning of Hamlet*, London : Oxford Univ. Press, 1937.

Scofield, Martin, *The Ghosts of Hamlet*, London : Cambridge Univ. Press, 1980.

Seng, Peter J., *The Vocal Songs in the Plays of Shakespeare* : A Critical History, Cambridge : Harvard University Press, 1967.

Sewell, William Arthur, *Character and Society in Shakespeare*, Oxford : The Clarendon Press, 1951.

Shorey, Paul, *What Plato Said*, Chicago : University of Chicago Press, 1933.

Shuckin, *Character Problems in Shakespeare's Plays,* New York : Holt, 1922.

Siegel, Paul N., *Shakespearean Tragedy and The Elizbethan Compromise*. New York : New York University Press,

1957.

Smidt, Kristian, *Unconformities in Shakespeare History Plays,* London : Scarborough Typesetting Services, 1996.

Smith. D. Nichol, Ed., *Shakespeare Criticism: A Selection.* London: Oxford University Press, 1934.

Snow, Edward. "exual Anxiety and the Male Order of Things in *Othello." English Literary Renaissance* 10, no. 3 (1980): 385~411.

Sorell, Walter. "Shakespeare and the Dance." *Shakespeare's Quarterly*, 8 (1957), 367~84.

Spenser, Edmund, *Complete Works*, ed. T. C. Smith and E. De Selincourt, London : Oxford University Press, 1952(1909).

Spurgeon, Caroline F. E., *Shakespeare's Imagery and What It Tells Us*, Cambridge University Press, 1935.

St. Augustine of Hippo, *The Confessions*, trans., Sir Tobie Matthew, Kt., revised and emended by Dom Roger Hudleston, London : Orchard Books : Burns & Oates, 1954.

Sternfeld, F. W., *Music in Shakespearean Tragedy*, London : Routledge and Kegan Paul, 1967.

Stewart, J. I. M., *Character and Motive in Shakespeare*, London : Longmans, Green & Co., 1949.

Stoll, E. E., *Shakespeare and Other masters*, Cambridge, Mass.: Harvard University Press, 1940.

_________, "Source and Motive in *Macbeth* and *Othello*" *Review of English Studies*, xix (1943), 25.

Strong, Roy, *Splendour at Court : Renaissance Spectacle and the Thatre of Power,* Boston : Houghton Mifflin Company, 1973.

Taylor, Gary and Waren, Michael, *The Division of the Kingdoms,* Oxford : Clarendon Press, 1983.

Tillyard, E. M. W., *Shakespeare's Last Plays,* London : Chatto and Windus, 1964.

Todd, Loreto, Ed., *York Notes on The Winter's Tale,* London : York Press, 1980.

Tolkien, J. R. R., and Gordon, E. V., eds., *Sir Gawaine and the Green Knight,* Oxford : The Clarendon Press, 1955(1925).

Traversi, D. A., *An Approach to Shakespeare,* New York : New York, Double Day & Company, 1956.

____________, Shakespeare : *The Last Phase,* New York : Harcort, Brace & Company, 1955, Stanford University Press, 1965.

Turner, Frederick, *Shakespeare and The Nature of Time,* Oxford : At the Clarendon Press, 1971.

Turner, V. W., *The Forest of Symbols : Aspects of Ndembu Ritual,* Cornell University Press, 1967.

____________, *The Drums of Affliction.* Oxford : The Clarendon Press, 1968.

____________, *The Ritual Process : Structure and Anti-Structure,* Chicago University Press, 1969.

Uoyd Evans, Gareth, *The Upstart Crow : An Introduction to Shakespeare's Plays,* London : J. M. Dent & Sons Ltd.,

1982.

Walk Roy, *On The Design of Shakespearean Tragedy,* Toronto : University of Toronto Press, 1958.

Wells, Stanley, ed., *Shakespeare Survey 47,* London : Cambridge University Press, 1994.

Wheeler, Richard P., "'And my loud crying still': The Sonnets, *The Merchant of Venice, and Othello*", *Shakespeare's Rough Magic : Renaissance Essays for C. L. Barber,* Edited by Peter Erickson and Coppélia Kahn, Newark : University of Delaware Press, 1985.

William, Glaude C. H., *Reading on the Character of Hamlet*, New York : Gordian Press, 1972.

Wilson, J. Dover, *What Happens in Hamlet*, New York : Gordian Press, 1972.

Yates, Frances A., *The Theatre of the World*, Chicago : The University of Chicago Press. 1969.

________________, *Shakespeare's Last Plays :* A new Approach, London : Routledge Kegan Paul, 1975.

Zacha, Richard. "Iago and the *Commedia dell'arte*", *Arlington Quarterly* 2(1969) : 98~116.

『템페스트』의 미학적 읽기

인쇄 2001년 8월 20일
발행 2001년 8월 30일

지은이 • 하 해 성
펴낸이 • 한 봉 숙
편집인 • 김 현 정
펴낸곳 • 푸른사상사

등록 제2-2876호
서울시 중구 을지로2가 148-37 삼오B/D 302호
대표전화 02) 2268-8706－8707 팩시밀리 02) 2268-8708
메일 prun21c@yahoo.co.kr / prun21c@hanmail.net
홈페이지 //www.prun21c.com

값 10,000원

ISBN 89-89368-61-03840